W9-AAH-837

West of Penance

West of Penance

Thomas D. Clagett

FIVE STAR
A part of Gale, Cengage Learning

Farmington Hills, Mich • San Francisco • New York • Waterville, Maine
Meriden, Conn • Mason, Ohio • Chicago

Scripture quotes are from the "New American Bible."
Historical notes can be found at the back of the book.
Five Star™ Publishing, a part of Cengage Learning, Inc.

LIBRARY OF CONGRESS CATALOGING-IN-PUBLICATION DATA

Names: Clagett, Thomas D., 1956–
Title: West of penance / by Thomas D. Clagett.
Description: First edition. | Waterville, Maine : Five Star, A part of Gale, Cengage Learning, [2016]
Identifiers: LCCN 2015035878 | ISBN 9781432831417 (hardcover) | ISBN 1432831410 (hardcover) | ISBN 9781432831561 (ebook) | ISBN 1432831569 (ebook)
Subjects: LCSH: Clergy—Fiction. | GSAFD: Western stories.
Classification: LCC PS3603.L337 W47 2016 | DDC 813/.6—dc23
LC record available at http://lccn.loc.gov/2015035878

First Edition. First Printing: January 2016
Find us on Facebook– https://www.facebook.com/FiveStarCengage
Visit our website– http://www.gale.cengage.com/fivestar/
Contact Five Star™ Publishing at FiveStar@cengage.com

Printed in the United States of America
1 2 3 4 5 6 7 20 19 18 17 16

To my parents, Francis and Naomi Clagett

1861

★ ★ ★ ★ ★

CHAPTER ONE

MONTMARTRE DISTRICT, PARIS, FRANCE

"You have cheated me, *monsieur.*"

Clement Grantaire did not hear the accusation. He was lost in revelry about Marisene, whom he was planning to see as soon he left the *cercle* with his winnings from this long night. It was nearly five in the morning but no matter. He'd been a regular customer at *Le Artois* for the last three years. Madame Perot would bid him welcome. And then the raven-haired Marisene. Like a cat in heat, she'd rub and caress his body with her own, and whisper sweet promises of pleasure in his ear. He would lose himself in her violet-colored eyes, which gave new definition to invitation. She was as unforgettable as original sin.

"I owe you nothing."

Casting thoughts of Marisene away, Clement concentrated on the gentleman sitting across from him at the faro table. He was a young man, a few years younger than Clement's age of twenty-seven. Red wine had been this fellow's drink of choice upon arriving a few hours earlier. He finished off what remained in his glass and called for another. That would be his tenth. Clement had nursed only two glasses of wine all night. The life of a libertine, he believed, required limitations at times.

"Did you hear me? Or are you deaf, as well?"

Clement noted no frayed cuffs on the gentleman's frock coat and linen shirtsleeves, not unlike his own fashion. A gold watch fob hung from the gentleman's waistcoat pocket. His white cravat was tied in a loose knot. A gold stickpin that held it was encrusted with three diamonds that caught the light when he leaned back in his chair and raised his chin, an attempt, Clement thought, to appear bold in his resolve as well as his impudence.

The crack of billiards at the tables had ceased. The chatter of betting stopped. Tobacco smoke hung in the air. Clement felt the apprehensive looks from the others at the gaming tables. He smiled and said, "This is a gentleman's *cercle, monsieur.* Honorable men join it to enjoy the fraternity of company with like-minded men. There are no cheaters here. No cards are marked or shaved."

"I didn't say the cards were suspect. Only you," the young man said as another glass of wine was hastily set before him.

"I must differ with you there," Clement said calmly. "You said I cheated you. That is not suspicion, *monsieur.* That is an accusation."

"You say cheaters are not allowed. But you are here."

Clement saw his friend Antoine bolt up out of his chair at a neighboring table, the anger plain on his face. "See here," he began, and Clement raised his hand to stave him off.

"The game is faro," Clement said to the young man. "It's a simple game of chance. Choose a face card or number card, red suit or black. Place a wager on it." He indicated the dealer's card deck in front of him, a portrait of a fierce Bengal tiger printed on the back panel. "Twist the tiger's tale, as they say. Now, you have been at my table for most of the evening. You have won and lost. In the last few hours, you have had a streak of very poor luck."

"The poor luck is yours as you have been found out."

"No. The poor luck is yours in that your luck ran out and you didn't realize it. And as this is a gentleman's *cercle* and gentlemen are expected to pay their debts, you owe three hundred and fifty *francs.*"

The front door opened. A bearded man dressed in a dark coat and tall hat entered. Clement and his accuser did not take their eyes off each other. Removing his hat, the bearded man walked up to the young man. "Begging your pardon, *Monsieur* Rocheron. I have returned with the carriage as you requested."

"Wait by the door," Rocheron said, dismissing the coachman with a curt wave of his hand.

The coachman nodded and did as he was instructed.

As Clement watched Rocheron take a drink of wine, he noticed Antoine moving into his line of sight making a gesture with his hands. But Clement made no move to call him over.

"Let me make this quite clear," Rocheron said, setting down his glass. "You are the most long-winded bastard I have ever had the misfortune to encounter. Now, did you not hear me say I will not pay?"

"Yes, I did," Clement said, observing Rocheron's upper lip glistening with tiny beads of perspiration as he rubbed the stem of his wine glass with his thumb. This one was beginning to sweat out all that alcohol he'd consumed since coming in, Clement decided. The fool can't even drink properly. "Everyone here heard you. And I am willing to forget your lack of manners if you will pay what you owe."

"My lack of manners? Now you insult me as well as cheat me."

"And you cast aspersions on my birthright. So, we can call it even regarding insults. All that remains is that you pay me the three hundred and fifty *francs* and we can all go home."

"For the last time, I will pay nothing." He drained his glass and stood up.

"One is either fit to play in a society of gentlemen, or one is not," Clement said. "A man is either a good player, or he is not."

"Are you inferring that I am not a gentleman?"

"No. I am *saying* you are neither a gentleman nor a wise gambler. If you were a gentleman, you would pay your debts. If you were a wise gambler, you would know when to quit and cut your losses."

"You go too far."

"And you, *monsieur,* can go to hell. After you pay your debt."

"You all heard this scoundrel," Rocheron said, pointing his finger at Clement. "Satisfaction. I demand satisfaction."

"You are a fool."

The carriage driver coughed.

Rocheron's face flushed red, his fists clenched. "I will have satisfaction now! Or are you a coward as well as a cheat?"

"No!" Antoine shouted. "Duels are outlawed. I implore you, gentlemen—"

"The law be damned!" Rocheron cut him off.

"As you wish," Clement sighed and stood. "And even though I am the one challenged, I shall allow you the choice of weapons. What shall it be? Did you bring a pair of dueling pistols with you? No? Rapiers, then? Bare-knuckle fisticuffs? Perhaps we could break off a couple of table legs and club each other senseless. In any event, whatever you choose, I don't believe you have the stomach for any fight."

"We shall see who has the stomach for it."

Antoine stepped close to Clement. "Do you know who this man is?" he whispered.

"I don't care," Clement said, his anger rising. "He owes me three hundred and fifty *francs.*"

"Billiards," Rocheron said.

"Did you say billiards?"

"Yes. Or does that frighten you?"

Clement chuckled. "It's your choice. However silly."

The men in the *cercle* cleared a path. Clement saw some of them placing wagers on the outcome. He smiled. These were true gentlemen.

As Clement approached the closest billiard table, the two men who'd been playing stepped back out of the way, cue sticks still in their hands. Clement chose a cue from the rack and Rocheron laughed. "Are you a complete idiot? Did you think I meant a game of billiards?"

Clement said nothing. Whatever ridiculousness this Rocheron was up to he would regret, Clement promised himself.

Rocheron picked up a red billiard ball from the worn green baize, tossed it into the air and caught it. "Billiard balls."

"Well, you show some imagination anyway. The length of the table as the field of honor, then?"

"Suits me."

"Take your stance, youngster."

"Stop this!" Antoine shouted. "I won't allow it!"

"This is not your fight, my friend," Clement said, taking a white ball from the corner pocket. He considered the weight of the ball and without so much as a glance at Rocheron, he said, "Rules? Conditions?"

One of the gentlemen holding a cue said, "*Monsieur* Rocheron, has the right—"

"Shut your mouth," Rocheron snapped, cutting him off. "On the count of three we shall see who is the better man."

Clement nodded. But that name. Rocheron. It was familiar now. He'd heard it or read it only the other day. But he could not place it. No matter. He would show this rogue, this miscreant, the error of his ways. And he would have his three hundred and fifty *francs.* He needed that money.

"Begin the count," Rocheron ordered, glancing at the gentleman with the cue.

Clement locked a steady gaze on his adversary.

The gentleman with the cue wiped his mouth with the back of his hand. "One."

Clement heard the dryness in his voice.

Rocheron smirked. A drop of sweat trickled down his temple.

Clement held the ball behind his back, twisting it twice with his fingers, considering its weight as well as the lesson he intended to teach this ignoramus, this popinjay who understood nothing about the honor of play . . .

"Two."

. . . of the vulgarity of bad debts, the decency of gamesmanship, the blunder of keeping him from the delectable and accommodating Marisene . . .

The gentleman doing the count tried to swallow, licked his dry lips and the word "three" caught in his throat.

In one swift movement, Clement saw Rocheron roll his left shoulder and bring his right arm up. The red billiard ball hurtled past his head, hit the wall a few feet behind him and dropped to the floor, thudding sharply.

Clement heard Antoine cry, "Foul! The count was not complete!" as the white billiard ball flew out of his hand, hurtling with more force than he had expected. It struck Rocheron squarely in the throat. Clement saw his eyes bulge out, his mouth stretch wide open, gasping for breath that would not pass. Rocheron staggered back clutching at his throat and fell to the floor.

Antoine and several other gentlemen rushed to Rocheron's side. Clement pushed his way past them to see for himself. The gold stickpin in Rocheron's loose cravat appeared awkwardly bent. A round red swelling spread across his throat. Panic showed white around his eyes as he struggled for breath, his choking rasps coming in shorter bursts, his body convulsing, his hands reaching out as though grasping for sweet air.

"Do something!" someone cried.

"Tell me what to do and I will!" someone else answered.

A final guttural rattle escaped Rocheron's quivering lips. His eyes glazed over. His body stilled. Rocheron was dead.

Clement heard the front door open. Looking up, he saw the coachman run out of the *cercle*.

Antoine took Clement's arm and pulled him away. "You must leave. Right now. Do you have any money?"

"About fifteen *francs*. But he owes me three hundred and—"

"I know. But this man you killed is Tristan Rocheron."

Clement shook his head.

"He's the son of the Imperial Prosecutor."

"Merde," Clement whispered. Now he recalled the name. "Why didn't you tell me?"

"I tried to but you cut me off. And I saw that look in your eye. You had a point to make."

"Well, he was a damn fool. A point of honor was at stake. And three hundred and fifty *francs*. Would someone see to that money, please?"

The man who did the count checked Rocheron's pockets.

"In this case, a point of honor will make little difference to the Imperial Prosecutor," Antoine said.

"Eight *francs,*" the man said, holding the coins in his hand.

"That's all?" Clement said, stunned.

"I checked his purse."

"Bastard!" Clement shouted. He spied the bent diamond stickpin holding Rocheron's cravat. It would more than cover the debt. The gold watch fob and watch would do nicely, as well.

"Don't even think about it," he heard Antoine say. "They will add theft to the charges."

Damn it! Clement knew his friend was right.

"That coachman is probably on his way to alert the local *gendarmes,*" Antoine said. "You need to go, right now!"

"But everyone here saw what happened. They heard his challenge."

"Yes, and we also heard him call you a cheat, and you called him a coward. The vagaries of this duel will only work against you."

"He's right," one of the other men said. "You need to go, Clement."

Another man said, "We'll confound the *gendarmes* as long as we can."

Clement blew out a breath and nodded. He understood his predicament. He and Antoine were at the door, and Clement suddenly returned to the faro table and collected his deck of cards. "Can't leave these behind."

Outside, early morning light showed over the tile rooftops. "How much money do you have?" Antoine asked.

Clement opened his purse. "Eight *francs.* A run of bad luck lately."

"Anything at home? The bank?"

Clement's chuckle was mirthless. "You know me. I have it. I spend it. This night I came in feeling lucky."

Antoine nodded and thrust his purse into Clement's hand. "Twenty *francs.* All I have." He gave Clement a wry smile. "Bad night for me, too."

"Thank you, my friend," Clement said. "I will repay you as soon as I can."

"Don't trouble yourself about that. Get as far away from the city as quickly as you can. Don't come back."

Clement felt the hard grip of his friend's hand as he took his and heard the gravity in his voice as he said, "You can't come back. Ever."

Chapter Two

Peering from around the corner of a closed millinery shop, Clement saw two *gendarmes,* armed with rifles, bayonets fixed, standing watch at the triple-tiered entrance of the Orleans railroad station. They eyed any pretty ladies exiting horse-drawn cabs, but he could not tell with certainty if they had been alerted to be on the lookout for him. Other *gendarmes* might already be inside searching the trains.

Clement studied the five large windows on the second tier. No *gendarmes* watched from them. A single gable with an ornate stone façade housing a large clock face jutted out from the sloping roof. The clock had stopped, the hands pointing up at twelve. At the base of the gable, carved into the stonework, was a single word in block letters: Depart. It dares me and mocks me, he thought bitterly, leaning back out of sight.

Church bells pealed nearby. Eight o'clock. It had taken him almost three hours to make his way from the north side of Paris down to the southeast side, carefully avoiding the widened boulevards and gas lamp–lit avenues, part of an ongoing citywide restoration. Fortunately, there remained plenty of sinuous alleyways and narrow winding streets to accommodate a man who needed to remain in the shadows, unseen, anonymous.

Against his better judgment, he had detoured to *Le Artois* to ask Marisene for money. To beg, if necessary. Of course, whores were in the business of taking money, not giving it away, but he was desperate. His desperation turned to panic when Madame

Perot told him that his Marisene was no longer engaged at her establishment. An Austrian count had come in only a few nights ago and, well, he and Marisene departed yesterday for Salzburg. "The old count was a most charming man," Madame Perot had said. "He compensated me quite handsomely for Marisene. Still, she will be missed. Her expertise with men made both of us a lot of money." She had paused, giving him a concerned look. "Aren't you feeling well, *Monsieur* Grantaire? You look ill." That's when he had bolted from the room, proving this had been a gamble he should have left unventured.

But what to do now? He had no idea how far his twenty-eight *francs* would take him. Germany to the east? Or Belgium? One of the Italian states in the south? He didn't care where at this point as long as he got out of France. And today would be better than tomorrow. No doubt a reward would be offered soon enough. One hundred *francs*. Two hundred, maybe. Every set of eyes, on every corner, out every window, would be on the lookout. He would be dragged before a judge within hours. Thrown in prison, or worse! All because of Rocheron. Stupid little bastard.

The hearty aroma of fresh bread from a bakery a few doors down only added to his dilemma, as he had not eaten since late afternoon the previous day. He jammed his arms over his growling stomach and held his breath, hoping no one had heard.

Carefully peeking around the corner again, Clement swore a silent oath on seeing two mounted *gendarmes* ride up to the two on foot. They conversed. The two on foot shook their heads. One of the mounted *gendarmes* continued to speak to them. The other turned, looking his way.

Clement jerked his head back. Too quickly! He must have been seen! He listened for accusing shouts and galloping horse hooves on cobblestone, ready to run for his life. But all he heard was a tense, eerie quiet. A cool, late September breeze chilled his clammy skin.

The creak of a nearby door opening spun him around with a gasp. The sight of the man in a blue uniform froze him to the spot, but this uniform was not that of the *gendarmes.* The blue coat was similar, but the trousers were red, not white. Four red chevrons were sown to the top of his left sleeve. And two gold stripes with red edgings affixed on both his lower sleeves. A sergeant. His graying hair swept back, an older man, heavyset. Clement watched as he tapped his clay pipe on the heel of his shiny black boot. The sergeant glanced at Clement. He seemed unconcerned at what Clement thought certain was his obvious suspicious behavior and stepped back through the doorway. He reappeared a moment later placing a large sandwich billboard on the street and returned inside. The colors had weathered but the billboard showed a tough-looking soldier standing defiantly in a blue uniform coat and red bloused trousers brandishing his rifle, a white kerchief fluttering from the back of his white kepi hat. A cluster of palm trees was tucked in the background. A proclamation in bold black letters stated:

Adventure Calls
Join the French Foreign Legion

Clement cast another look at the railroad station. The mounted *gendarmes* had disappeared. The other two were still at the front entryway. The odds had improved somewhat, he thought, and he remembered his cards. They had almost always provided him good fortune. He reached into his coat pocket, the fine edge of the cards at his fingertips. A high card and he'd make the walk to the station. He felt the fateful card between his fingers, prepared to draw it out, but snatched his empty hand from his pocket as he was startled by a gravelly voice.

"You look like you could use some *café.*"

It had come from the open door at that storefront, the one

with the "Adventure Calls" billboard. Clement moved toward it, checking furtively for any *gendarmes.* He could smell the smoky richness of the *café.* It lured him closer. Clement eased his head around the doorway.

"Come in. It's all right." The sergeant sat at a small table, his legs crossed, a cup of *café* steaming in front of him. He motioned to a pot sitting on the glowing coals of a corner fireplace.

"Help yourself," he said.

Clement took an empty cup from a small wooden shelf and filled it from the pot. He noticed the only other chair sat on the opposite side of the table. With a nod of his head, the sergeant invited him to sit. Exhausted and on edge, Clement enjoyed this respite. He sipped his *café.* It was bitter, more so than he was used to, but he told his host it was quite good. The sergeant grunted his appreciation and refilled his cup.

Clement saw it was a small space he'd been invited to share, fairly clean but Spartan in its furnishings. Besides the table and two chairs, a shelf with stacks of paper and a few ledger books stood behind the sergeant. Streaks on the windows from half-hearted attempts to wash the soot off of them filtered the sunlight. But he could still see the billboard standing outside through it.

"You have the look," the sergeant said.

"Pardon?" Clement said.

"A legionnaire." He raised his cup indicating the advertisement.

Clement grunted. "Not me," he said, setting down his cup.

The sergeant shrugged, took out his pipe and tobacco pouch and began to load the bowl.

Clement glanced at the advertisement again. "Are you in the legion?"

"Three years. They brought me out of retirement from the army." He pointed to those four chevrons on his left sleeve.

"Twenty years I served France. Five years for each chevron."

Clement nodded to be polite. He finished his *café,* thanked the sergeant and said he should be going. At the doorway he hesitated, checking the street for *gendarmes.*

"That look. You still have it," the sergeant said.

Annoyed, Clement turned. "What? What do you mean?"

The sergeant held his pipe in his mouth. With a flick of his thumb, he struck a match, held the bright flame over the bowl and drew in breaths until it was lit. Sitting back in his chair, he blew out a stream of blue smoke and said, "The look of a man who needs to start a new life."

Clement stared at the sergeant, wondering what he knew, how he knew it. His heart pounded.

"You might make it to a train," the sergeant said. "But I'm guessing you have only a few *francs* and they will not get you far these days."

Clement wanted to run.

"Sit," the sergeant said, motioning to the chair.

Go, Clement thought. Time is running out.

"I don't know what you may have done," the sergeant said, "and I don't care. But to those *gendarmes,* you will look like the guiltiest man in Paris."

A moment passed, and something drew Clement back to the table. Something promising. He sat down. "What do you mean, start a new life?"

"The legion," the sergeant said, "gives every man who joins a fresh beginning. A clean slate."

Clement heard footsteps approach and leapt out of his chair, fear coursing through his veins. Two women carrying baskets filled with flowers passed by. Blowing out a deep breath, he sat down again and saw the wry smile on the sergeant's face.

"Some say the legion even wipes away sins," the sergeant said.

Sinning had been Clement's life. Though baptized a Catholic, the only houses of worship he'd entered in years were those that ministered to gambling, drinking, whoring and any other hedonistic desires that beckoned. He'd given God little thought, doubted he even existed. But here, at this moment, Clement realized a clear and unmistakable offer of salvation. That salvation meant escape.

"All right," Clement said, "I'm listening."

"Enlistment is for two years."

A long time, Clement thought. A damn long time . . . That ridiculous duel . . . And this sergeant. It's as though he knows me, what I'm thinking . . .

"First, you'll go to Aix-en-Provence for several weeks of training. We'll see to it you get there without incident. After training, you'll be sent to the garrison at Sidi-bel-Abbes."

"Where's that?"

"Algeria."

"That's Africa!"

"Ah, *oui.* It's also a French colony but, more importantly, the home of the legion. And consider this while you calm yourself: you will be out of France. Gone. Untouchable. The legion will be your home. In two years, memories can fade and things will be forgotten. Lives change."

Exhausted, hungry and with bad prospects at best, Clement knew the sergeant made good sense. Maybe there was a chance he could come back one day. Antoine had said never, but maybe one day. "How does a man join up?"

The sergeant spoke while he retrieved a sheet of paper, an inkwell and pen from the shelf behind him and arranged the items on the table. "All kinds of men have joined the legion. A Russian general who made a drunken joke at the wrong party, a defrocked Austrian bishop with a weakness for certain ladies, a Dutchman of dubious reputation. Some join to escape wives, debts, a misunderstanding with the law."

The sergeant made no glance or gesture toward him, Clement noted.

"Some join because they're hungry and have nowhere else to go. We have men who break the Ten Commandments and live by the Seven Deadly Sins because no one else will have them. We have all kinds because life is filled with calamity. But, to a man, they are loyal to the legion and each other."

"Sounds like the kind of company I could use right now," Clement said.

"Very good. Oh, and did I mention that Frenchmen are prohibited from joining the legion?"

Clement frowned. "But, you're French."

"*C'est vrai.* All of the officers and non-commissioned officers of the legion are French, but soldiers in the legion, they must all be foreigners."

"I don't understand," Clement said.

"Thirty years ago, France decreed that foreigners could no longer serve in the French Army. Radicals from Holland and mercenaries from Prussia were seen as troublemakers, undesirables. France wanted them gone, out of the country. An enticement was needed. And so, the legion was formed. The king and his ministers decided Frenchmen in the French Army would defend the French homeland, and foreigners in the legion would fight Arabs in France's colony in Africa. After all, who would have to explain the deaths of strangers fighting for France to French mothers and fathers?" The sergeant shrugged. "Now you know everything. Only foreigners can join the legion. Those are the rules. No exceptions."

"Damn it" caught in Clement's throat.

"So, think carefully before answering my questions," the sergeant continued as he took his pen from the inkwell and prepared to write. "First, where were you born?"

Clement understood. Salvation was still within reach. "Brussels," he said.

"Belgium. Good," the sergeant said as he wrote on the paper. "And your French is excellent. Your name?"

Clement opened his mouth to answer and hesitated. Should he give his real name?

"Did you know your father?" the sergeant asked without looking up, unfazed, like he'd done this a hundred times before.

"Of course," Clement answered, perplexed.

"His first name?"

"Oh, ah, Victor."

The sergeant wrote it down. "Your last name?"

Clement tried to think of something. His mind was a jumble. Outside, a horse-drawn cart went by.

"Cheval," the sergeant said as he wrote. "Your age?"

A horse . . . ? Clement blurted out, "Twenty-seven."

"Victor Cheval, sign here," the sergeant said, pushing the paper toward him.

Flummoxed, Clement took the pen and hastily scrawled his strange new name where the sergeant pointed.

"Congratulations," the sergeant said and stood, extending his hand. "The legion takes care of its own."

Clement, still trying to grasp all that had happened, shook the sergeant's hand. A new name, he told himself. A new life . . . Two years. I'll be back in two years ready to imbibe heady wines and rich foods . . . Wear the most elegant clothes and gold jewelry . . . And women. Sweet, exquisite, voracious women who will lock me in their bedchambers with them, each for at least a week . . . Yes, everything will be fine again.

★ ★ ★ ★ ★

1863

★ ★ ★ ★ ★

Chapter Three

CAMERONE, MEXICO

Clement sat down hard in the thick grass, propped his rifle inside the crook of his arm, removed the floppy sombrero from his head and wiped the sweat from his face. It would be another blistering day in this tropical hellhole. Then he counted, as he had done every day since joining the legion, the time he had remaining before his enlistment was up. Today, April 30, meant four more months and twenty-two days.

That last day could not come soon enough. After almost a year and a half spent in Algeria, he'd gotten used to the stinging desert sand, and then his unit was ordered to this festering abyss called Mexico. "Emperor Napoleon III, has decreed that Mexico must pay the monetary debt it owes to France," the garrison commander had announced to the men. Yet, no one could recall the reason Mexico had borrowed the money in the first place anymore. But the emperor wanted it back and had sent both the French Army and the legion to Mexico to demonstrate his resolve. At this moment, sitting at this fetid roadside, Clement wished the emperor were there so he could tell him what he could do with his resolve.

The only good thing Clement could muster from being in this wretched hole of a country was that someone had figured out that the uniform long, blue coats and heavy, red trousers of the legion wouldn't do in this jungle terrain, so shorter coats and white, canvas trousers had been issued before they set sail across the Atlantic Ocean.

It was a little past seven in the morning. The song of the cicadas was already thrumming. Clement and the sixty-four other legionnaires that comprised the two platoons of the 3rd Company, 1st Battalion—half its strength, as yellow fever had decimated the battalion—had been on the march for six hours through the dark of night. They had covered some twenty-two miles following a rutted dirt road that lead from legion headquarters at the village of Chiquihuite, situated at the edge of a high jungle plateau, down to the hot, humid flatlands.

"I told you this would be a leisurely walk to get the blood flowing," laughed Sergeant Morzycki, Clement's platoon sergeant. "And didn't I promise it would be easier without haversacks packed with tents and blankets and shovels strapped to your backs? And no ambulance wagon to slow us down, either. Hell, we'll be back at headquarters by noon as long as the convoy's not late."

Clement was too tired to care. All that mattered was they had reached their objective, an open scrub patch called Palo Verde alongside the road near a water hole. This was where they were to rendezvous with the supply convoy coming from Vera Cruz. Their orders were to escort it to headquarters. That meant going back up the road they'd just trekked. It was bad enough at night, what with predators like snakes and jaguars searching for food. However, in the daytime, that road was mile after mile of scorching, steaming, God-forsaken shit. But right now, the column would enjoy their morning coffee. It didn't matter how hot and miserable any day began. That morning coffee was a tradition in the legion, one Clement had come to relish.

"Third squad, up off your asses," Morzycki barked. "Kurz and Groux, water barrels. Burgiser and van Opstal, pots. And you two," Morzycki pointed at Clement and his friend Dekker, "the platoon can't have coffee without fires to boil water."

Grumbling, a legionnaire's prerogative, Clement and Dekker started gathering firewood while Kurz and Groux headed for the water hole to refill the barrels they had taken off the two pack mules. To prepare the coffee, Burgiser and van Opstal came around to each man, large blackened pots in hand. Clement poured a portion of water from his canteen into a pot. He wasn't worried that his canteen was half-empty now. All of the men's canteens were no doubt low after this march. But they'd fill them again from the barrels once that detail returned from the water hole.

Dekker added his complement of water to the pot and rubbed his tired eyes. "I hate this damn country," he said. "The yellow fever makes us puke our insides out. These people despise us. The women are ugly as sin. This sun beats us unmercifully and the humid air saps the strength. But you know what I hate the most, Victor?"

Clement, who'd long ago gotten used to his new name, knew what was coming. It had been this way since they landed at Vera Cruz three months earlier. He added kindling to the burning tinder and asked, "What do you hate, Dekker?"

"That goat piss passes for wine here."

Legionnaires nearby laughed and offered their agreement to Dekker's statement. Another asked Sergeant Morzycki, who was going by, if he thought they would meet with any hated Mexican *juaristas* this day.

"With any luck," Morzycki said. "And be ready if we do."

"We've been ready and waiting," the legionnaire said. "For weeks."

"Our fight will come," Morzycki said. "We're legionnaires. And if a fight doesn't come to us soon, we'll make one."

Clement joined in the enthusiastically profane appreciation that greeted the bald Polish sergeant's words of encouragement. Though keenly aware he had not seen battle, as many in the unit had at places like Magenta and Crimea, Clement was accepted by his fellow legionnaires because they shared one thing: they were all outcasts, men without a country. A breed set apart. It's what made them different from other soldiers. That was the *esprit* of the legion.

Clement had embraced that *esprit* along with discovering a change within himself. Of course, his libertine ways had not diminished. Drinking and whoring and gambling were as much a part of the legionnaire's life as had been his before joining up. The shanty inns and shadowy fleshpots of Sidi-bel-Abbes beckoned all legionnaires. But marching in a heavy, woolen uniform carrying a full sixty-pound pack and rifle across the torrid sands of the Sahara had taught him stamina. Building roads through that torturous desert had toughened his resilience. Dealing with Arabs who hated the French and wanted them out of their country had hardened his spirit. His vocabulary had been expanded, too. He knew how to say *shit, bastard, son of a whore* and *god damn it* in German, Polish, Russian, English and Spanish.

Most importantly, though, was proficiency with his 1857 percussion rifle. He could tear open the cartridge paper, pour the black powder down the barrel, ram the stubby .58-caliber, cone-shaped bullet called a minié ball home and fire with remarkable accuracy nearly five times a minute. At best, most legionnaires managed three shots a minute. And Clement's proficiency had been accomplished under fire against Arab bandits.

The coffee had boiled and Clement and Dekker sat down to enjoy it.

"My rifle in my hands and coffee in my belly," Dekker said with satisfaction, wiping drops of coffee from his bushy moustache with waxed, pointed ends. "Let the Mexican cowards who call themselves soldiers come now."

"Very true," Clement chuckled. His friend was older and had been a sergeant in the Prussian Army. As he told it, a "disagreement" with an officer resulted in his "departure." That mysteriousness resulted in speculation that he was a wanted man. It was compounded by the fact that he was known only as Dekker. He'd given no first name when he enlisted.

Clement sipped his coffee and looked out over a sea of sombreros. Most of his fellow legionnaires had adopted them in place of their issued kepis. Even with the extra-long, white Havelock affixed to the back to cover the neck, the cap didn't offer enough protection from the blazing Mexican sun. But the men carried their kepis within easy reach on their belts. The kepi was *de rigueur* battle dress.

"How about a game while we're waiting?" Dekker asked. "Give me a chance to win back some of my money."

"You don't have any money left," Clement said.

"You know I'm good for it," Dekker said. "I feel lucky today."

Clement knew his friend was good for his debts, and he paid on payday without fail. He was also a terrible card player. But it would pass the time. Clement reached into his pocket and pulled out the worn deck of cards he kept with him, the same one he'd almost left behind that night in the *cercle*. They reminded him of Paris, and the new life he looked forward to having there again soon.

As he shuffled the cards, Clement glanced over at where Captain Danjou and Lieutenant Vilain and Lieutenant Maudet, Clement's platoon leader, were having their coffees under a lone, dying magnolia tree. They were studying a map. They wore their kepis. Officers always did. Vilain was a slight man with a blond moustache. Maudet was thicker with dark hair. The battalion adjutant, Captain Danjou, had taken command of the company only the day before. Clement knew him to be a good officer, strict but fair. A brave one, too. He had lost his left hand in an explosion during the Crimean War. A wooden hand, with moving fingers no less, was affixed to the stump. A white glove covered it. It struck Clement as preposterous yet elegant somehow.

There was a warning shout from a posted picket. Clement saw Danjou raise his field glasses. In the distance, a cloud of yellow dust rose above the tree line to the west, moving north. It couldn't be the convoy; it would be coming from the east.

"To arms! To arms!" Danjou shouted, drawing his pistol.

Clement shoved the cards back into his pocket and he and Dekker and the rest of the company dumped out their coffee, grabbed their rifles and assembled for action. Before leaving camp the night before, each man had been issued sixty rounds and cartridges. Clement felt confident that would be enough for whatever came.

Danjou ordered the company into the trees north of the road. It was Mexican cavalry, irregulars armed with lances, he told them.

Clement wondered why the company didn't stand and fight. In the open, legionnaires could cut down a cavalry charge easily. As though reading his mind, Dekker said, "It's smarter getting into these woods. We don't know how many of them there are."

They moved rapidly through the woods, back toward the tiny, deserted hamlet of Camerone they had passed earlier that morning. All that was left were three crumbling outbuildings with roofs caved-in. A hundred yards further stood an old adobe hacienda. Clement guessed the captain was making for it as it had high walls surrounding a large courtyard facing a two-story farmhouse. The place looked ramshackle, unattended, probably for years from what Clement could tell. But it might serve as a good fortress to fight from while waiting for the supply convoy and its armed escort.

Emerging from the tree line, the hacienda lay off to the left below them on the other side of the road. And, to their right, waiting on a hillock, were around two hundred and fifty Mexican irregular cavalry. Besides their long lances, they also carried pistol carbines slung across their backs. Clement recalled Morzycki saying those carbines had a tendency to misfire. They also wore short jackets with what appeared to be silver buckles all over them, as well as bandanas around their necks and wide-brimmed straw hats and sombreros.

"You ever see so many fancy-looking *peons* on horseback before?" Dekker asked.

"Not until today," Clement said. He estimated the distance between the company and the hacienda at three hundred yards, and the cavalry at less than a hundred yards away from them. The cavalry would be on them before they got halfway to the hacienda.

A shot rang out. A legionnaire went down, wounded. Clement heard him cursing.

"Battle square!" Danjou shouted.

Clement and the other legionnaires threw off their sombreros and donned their white kepis. They formed the battle square with dispatch, ten men kneeling to each side. Twenty other men were kept in reserve to reinforce the lines.

"Fix bayonets!"

The men drew the long blades from their scabbards and affixed them to the lug under their rifle barrels. The bayonets gleamed in the sunlight.

"At last. We have a fight," Clement said, a smile crossing his face. To his right he heard Dekker's evil chuckle. In the center of the square stood Danjou, holding his pistol at his side. With him were Lieutenants Vilain and Maudet armed with rifles. Behind them someone tended the angry, wounded legionnaire, who wanted to get into the fight. Two muleteers were trying to calm the mules.

Clement licked his lips. Time ticked by. The horsemen on the hillock made no move. What were they waiting for? Four minutes passed. Five . . .

He heard Morzycki as he moved behind the line. "Keep steady," the sergeant said, his voice low. "We'll give these childish Mexicans a taste of a hollow-based, .58-caliber minié ball that'll put a hole the size of a Christmas ham in his gut."

Danjou gave the order to move. Maintaining a loose formation and readiness, the company followed the road and advanced toward the hacienda.

Clement heard a shout in Spanish. The Mexican cavalry started toward them at a walk.

"Steady. Keep moving," Danjou ordered.

The gap closed. Clement kept his finger alongside the trigger guard so as not to fire prematurely.

The cavalry split, forming two columns. They mean to encircle us, Clement thought. Another shout. The points of their lances dropped. They spurred their horses into a charge.

The square halted, ranks reformed, rifles raised. Clement saw the Mexican cavalry coming directly at his line. Danjou reinforced the rank behind Clement with ten more legionnaires. Clement picked his target. Now it comes.

"Front rank. Fire!" Danjou shouted.

The deadly volley of minié balls found their marks. Clement saw riders fall, horses crumple, lances gouge the earth.

Clement reached into the ammunition pouch strapped to his side and pulled out another paper cartridge and round to reload. Dekker was only a second behind him.

"Rear rank. Fire!"

The rifles thundered. Black smoke wafted past Clement as he rammed the minié ball home. He aimed, as did the others, waiting for the order. Part of the cavalry veered off. The rest pressed on, surrounding the square, pulling their carbines and firing at the legionnaires.

"Fire at will!"

Clement pulled the trigger and through the smoky haze caught sight of the rider falling backwards off his horse as his minié ball struck him in the head. Rifle fire roared from the other sides of the square. Clement got off three more rounds before Danjou ordered the men to cease fire. The company had suffered no new casualties that Clement could see. He heard the mules bray. Lieutenant Maudet shouted, "Hold them!" Others yelled, "Look out!" Clement turned. The mules had broken loose of the muleteers and bolted through the line, men ducking out of their way. Clement watched in disbelief as the mules disappeared into the woods. Strapped to their backs were all of the extra ammunition, food and water barrels.

"Move!" Danjou shouted.

The company followed him across the road and down into a ditch running parallel to the road. The ditch ended a few hundred feet from the hacienda, but thickets of spiky cactus as tall as a man peppered the length of the ditch. Clement had seen this cactus growing all over since he'd arrived. The Mexicans called it *cacto del infierno.* The legionnaires called it bitch needles. What in the hell was the Captain thinking leading us into this? Clement wondered. One thing was certain though, the Mexicans' horses wouldn't charge into these damn bitch needles. But the Mexicans could fire on them from the top of the ditch, yet they hadn't. Where were they?

The men moved as best they could through the prickly maze. The barbed needles broke off and stuck into their short jackets and light trousers and white leggings as they brushed against them. Needles caught in hands but got picked out quickly. Branches grew out like green tentacles. The men slashed at them with their bayonets and mashed them down under their thick-soled shoes, creating a path for those behind them. Danjou, Vilain and Maudet urged the men forward. "Keep moving! Don't stop!"

Just beyond the top of the embankment near where the ditch ended, Clement could see a hedgerow of more bitch needles. The captain was headed for it.

Moving close to the edge of the ditch where the cactus wasn't so thick, Clement found the dirt hard and the embankment slippery. A Mexican rider suddenly appeared at the top of the other side of the ditch and leveled his carbine at him. Clement raised his rifle, lost his footing and fell to his knees. He scrambled up. He would not die on his knees! A shot fired. The Mexican fell sideways from his saddle. Clement spun around and saw Dekker, his rifle smoking.

"I couldn't let you go to hell without me!" Dekker said.

"We'll meet the devil together!" Clement grinned.

A carbine fired. Dekker went down, his legs knocked out from under him. *"Gott verdammen!"*

Clement turned, raising his rifle, scanning the top of the embankment. A rider thrust his carbine into the air and cried, *"¡Viva Mexico!"* Clement shouted back, *"!Viva la Legión!"* and blasted him off his horse.

Dekker was tying a tourniquet around his bloody right thigh as Clement got to him.

"Bad?" Clement asked.

Dekker shook his head. "Hit meat, not bone."

Clement helped him to his feet. They moved through the thicket, Dekker's arm over Clement's shoulder. More riders, Clement wasn't certain how many, appeared at the top of the ditch and fired their carbines and threw their lances at the company. Legionnaires returned fire. Black gun smoke, screams and curses rose up into the hot, stagnant air. Clement wiped his eyes. The black powder smoke stung, making it hard to see.

A legionnaire in front of Clement fell dead, a lance through his neck.

"*¡Pendejos!*" Clement shouted. There wasn't time to reload and he needed to get Dekker out of this hellish pit. And he realized the firing had stopped. He looked up. The Mexicans had vanished.

Danjou was at the top of the embankment by the cactus hedgerow. "Follow me! This way!" He waved his gloved, wooden hand, beckoning them on.

Out of the ditch, Clement and other legionnaires rallied behind the hedgerow and reloaded their rifles. Using a couple of kerchiefs, Clement bandaged Dekker's wound. "I'm no doctor," he said. "That's the best I can do." Finding their squad, Clement asked about the Mexicans. Legionnaire Burgiser said, "Those cowards rode off as soon as we started up out of the ditch." He didn't see where they went.

A handful of their comrades lay dead among the bitch needles. Scattered around the top of the ditch, Clement counted a score of Mexicans dead or dying along with them. Wait! About a dozen legionnaires were being herded off at lance-point into the tree line near the hillock where they first saw the Mexicans. Half of the legionnaires were carrying the others.

"They must have gotten separated and trapped in the thicket," Maudet said bitterly to Danjou.

His jaw tight, Clement glanced at Danjou. The captain's face was a grim mask. No one said a word. All were keenly aware there was nothing they could do for their comrades at this point. Except wish them a hasty death. Stories of Mexican butchery were well known.

"Report," Danjou said.

"Forty-six men present, sir," Maudet answered. "Eight wounded. None serious. Shall I send a detail to retrieve our dead from the—"

"Captain!" Vilain exclaimed, cutting off Maudet and pointing toward the woods behind them. "The trees."

As Clement turned, he saw Mexican cavalry forming at the tree line two hundred yards away. Another attack!

Danjou ordered the men into a double firing line.

"¡Assalto!" a Mexican in the center of the line shouted and drew his saber. The riders spurred their horses into a gallop and lowered their lances. The leader held his saber pointed straight ahead.

"Steady," Danjou called out.

Kneeling, Clement chose his target, the son-of-a-bitch with the saber. Dekker stood in the rank behind him. They could feel the ground shake.

"Steady!"

One hundred yards. *"¡Viva Mexico!"*

Clement licked his lips. He felt surprisingly calm.

Fifty yards. *"¡Viva Juarez!"*

"Front rank. Fire!"

A wall of smoke and flame erupted. Clement saw dozens of riders hit by the fusillade, including that saber-pointing bastard. Horses reared. Some skidded into the ground, throwing their riders headlong into the dirt, their lances snapping in two.

"Rear rank. Fire!"

More Mexicans fell dead. Dust swirled. Riders yanked back on their reins. There were cries and confusion. The charge halted!

"Bayonets! Forward!" Danjou shouted, and the line surged at a run. Clement and Dekker and the rest of the company let loose savage war cries. They wanted blood! But the Mexicans wheeled their horses around and galloped away back into the woods.

"!Viva la France!" Clement shouted as the line halted. The rest of the company joined him. *"!Viva la Legión!"*

Taking advantage of the rout, Danjou ordered the men into the abandoned hacienda.

Chapter Four

"Merde," Clement said after he ran inside the courtyard. It was larger than he expected, about the size of an acre of land. The two-story farmhouse and an attached one-story storage annex sat at the north side of the courtyard. Both had pitched roofs with weathered, red tiles. A few gaping holes showed in the rooftops. At the southeast corner were the remains of a stable with a sagging, thatched roof. But the problems were obvious to every legionnaire. The ten-foot-high walls did offer protection, but while the Mexicans couldn't see in, no legionnaire could see out. The two gateways in the west adobe wall the company had rushed through had no gates. A section of the south wall that had likely been the main gate had collapsed. Four or five men abreast could come through it.

"Barricade the holes!" Danjou shouted. "Lieutenant Vilain, the west wall. Lieutenant Maudet, south wall."

Vilain and Maudet ordered their platoons into action. "Get planks, posts, rocks, anything! Hurry!" "Check the stable!" "Look in the farmhouse!" "Every fifth man cut firing slits into the walls!"

In the stable, Clement, Dekker, Burgiser and Kurz found a one-wheeled donkey cart. "A prize," Dekker said. They rolled it to the south wall breach and pushed it over on its side. Clement turned in time to see Morzycki climbing an unsteady-looking ladder to the roof of the farmhouse.

"Third squad, first platoon, on me!" Maudet shouted.

Clement, Dekker, Burgiser, Groux, van Opstal and Kurz ran to him.

"You men will cover the inside perimeter," Maudet told them. "You'll reinforce any weakness, any breach. The stable looks to be your best vantage point. Go!"

They ran to the stable and took up positions behind a low adobe wall. Maudet was right. They had the full sweep of the courtyard from here, from the barricade at the south wall across the east wall to the farmhouse and annex and along the west wall to the barricades there. Clement watched as three men pulled the farmhouse door down and carried it to the west barricade. He saw little remaining to use for cover.

"What's the progress with those firing slits?" Maudet shouted.

"Bayonets are no good for this, sir!" someone shouted. "We can't dig through. The walls are too hard and thick!"

"Captain!" Morzycki called down from the farmhouse roof.

"Report!" Danjou answered.

Every legionnaire could hear Morzycki as he shouted down to the captain. "Many sombreros to the west and south. They're dismounted. They appear to be waiting."

Loud enough for the company to hear, Danjou said, "We shall be ready to give them a legionnaire's welcome when they come to call on us."

The men laughed. It was exactly what they needed.

Bullets spit into the dirt at Danjou's feet. Another struck a legionnaire at the west wall barricades. Danjou ran toward the annex. Legionnaires scrambled for cover, anyplace to crouch and cling for protection.

"They're in the farmhouse!" someone yelled.

Clement saw half of Vilain's men at the west barricade turn and fire on the farmhouse. There was no breeze, so he also could see black rifle smoke hanging at the farmhouse windows, two on either side of the front doorway and three small windows on the second floor.

"How in the name of sweet Jesus did they get in there?" Dekker wondered.

"Snuck in somehow," van Opstal said. He was seventeen.

"Just shoot them," Clement said and took a bead on a window. "I think I heard three shots." He saw movement. A rifle barrel inched out. A silhouette appeared. Clement fired. The rifle barrel and silhouette snapped back.

"Good shooting, legionnaire!" Danjou called out.

Clement opened his canteen and took the last small swallow. He glanced at the others. "Anyone still have water?" He could tell from their faces they did not.

"Captain!" Morzycki shouted from the rooftop. "More cavalry!"

"How many?"

"Over a thousand! More coming! They're surrounding us!"

Clement let out half a breath as he watched for another shadow. That convoy and its armed escort better get here and damn soon, he thought. But right now he had to concentrate on the bastards shooting at them from inside the courtyard. Something moved at the middle upper window, a shadow in the one to the right. He fired, and so did Dekker and Burgiser. One of the bullets splintered the wooden window frame in the middle. But the other two hit their marks. Everyone in the courtyard heard screaming and cursing in Spanish coming from inside.

"I'll bet that one wishes he'd stayed home today," Clement said.

Dekker and Burgiser chuckled.

Reloading, Clement watched as Danjou, along with a squad of men from Vilain's platoon, charged through the farmhouse door. Shots echoed inside! Danjou and the squad rushed back outside. More shots! Two of the squad fell, both shot in the back. Danjou and the others cut over to the single-story annex.

Clement scanned the farmhouse windows and doorway. Wanting a target. He caught sight of movement to the left near the annex. Danjou, with pistol in hand, was making his way along the west wall. Good. The captain was all right. And Clement guessed they must have a good defensible position inside the annex. He could hear firing and French curses. Clement grinned. Danjou's squad must be giving the Mexicans hell and keeping any more of them from getting into the farmhouse.

Of course, Clement knew what the others were thinking. He was thinking the same thing. The convoy would make it with their escort of two hundred men from Vera Cruz. They had to make it.

He looked at the bodies of the two dead legionnaires in front of the farmhouse. Brave men. Good men. In the dirt. Face down. No way to get them out of there. Nothing to be done. Except to kill those Mexicans inside. How many were in there? Hell, it didn't matter. They would kill them all.

"The captain," Kurz said. "Coming this way."

Danjou was moving rapidly along the west wall.

"Give him cover," Clement said, scanning the farmhouse windows. He saw movement at a first-floor window and fired.

Danjou slid over the low adobe wall. "How are you men holding up?"

"Good, sir," Dekker said.

"There's not much time," Danjou said. "You know the situation. I ask each of you to take an oath, to swear, on your honor as legionnaires, that you will not surrender this day. You will fight to the death."

Without hesitation, each man agreed. Clement still hoped that the supply convoy with its armed escort would arrive, bugles sounding the charge, drums beating a battle tattoo.

Danjou pulled a small bottle from inside his coat. Clement

saw it was less than half full with what looked like red wine. The Captain uncorked the bottle and held it out to him. "For every man's honor," he said.

Clement understood. He took the bottle and said, "On my honor." Then he put the bottle to his lips and took only a drop or two on his tongue. The wine was hot.

Dekker, Burgiser and the rest followed. On their honor.

Danjou thanked them and scurried to Maudet and the men at the south barricade.

Clement and the others scanned the windows ready to give their captain cover. No shots were fired from the farmhouse. The Mexicans were in there, though. What were they waiting for?

"*Gott verdammen* it's hot," Dekker said.

Clement's mouth was dry. He could barely make spit. The Havelock on the back of his kepi stuck to his neck. His whole uniform was sticking to him.

"Anyone know what time it is?" he asked.

Kurz had a watch. "Nine thirty."

Clement let out a breath. Where was the supply convoy? He wasn't one for prayer, but he wished God would get it here . . . and water . . . and food . . . The company had last eaten at midnight, right before setting out for Palo Verde.

"Captain!" Morzycki called out for the roof. "A man with a white flag!"

"Maybe they've come to surrender," Dekker said.

In the stable they couldn't hear what the Mexican outside the wall was saying. But Clement figured he must speak French because he knew Morzycki didn't speak Spanish. However, all the men could hear the message he relayed to the captain. "This captain says his colonel wants us to surrender. They have over two thousand men. We are surrounded. He says if we lay down our arms, our lives will be spared. He says we should accept our fate and not die needlessly."

Danjou nodded. "Tell him we have plenty of ammunition and will be happy to continue the fight."

Clement laughed. A cheer rose up from the company. He wondered what that Mexican officer thought of that.

Less than a minute passed. "Here they come!" Maudet shouted from the south barricade. "Fire at will!"

Rifles opened fire again from the farmhouse. Clement and the squad returned fire. Chunks of adobe flew off the farmhouse walls from the withering fusillade Clement's squad poured into it. The Mexicans continued to fire from their vantage point. Bullets kicked into the low stable wall. Burgiser's head snapped back, a bullet hole through his eye.

"Push them back!" Clement heard Maudet shout from the south barricade.

Black rifle smoke hung over the courtyard. The heat hammered down. Shouts and cries echoed around the walls. Men fell. Blood flowed.

Clement glanced at the east wall. No heads popped up. He guessed the Mexicans must not have scaling ladders. Must be why they were only assaulting the barricades.

Maudet and his men were still holding off the Mexicans at the south barricade with intense rifle fire. Clement heard Dekker say that Mexican bodies were piling up there. At the west barricade, Clement saw Mexicans had broken through one of the entryways using their lances. But those long lances were of no use in close. The legionnaires were at them with their bayonets. That was how legionnaires fought best! Clement wanted to join them. But he kept up his fire on the farmhouse.

Reloading, Clement saw Danjou. He had stepped back from the fray at the west barricade. He was shouting at the men, encouraging them. A Mexican broke through the barricade and charged Danjou. The captain coolly aimed and fired his pistol.

The Mexican crumpled to his knees, holding his belly and fell forward on his face. Danjou looked up at Morzycki, calling him, motioning him to come down.

The Mexican moved, raising his carbine to fire. Danjou didn't see him! Clement aimed his rifle and squeezed the trigger. The top of the Mexican's head blew apart.

And Danjou was hit! The shot came from the west barricade. He dropped his pistol and clutched his chest. He fell backwards to the ground, his left arm out at his side, his gloved, wooden hand open.

Clement reloaded, wanting to find the killer.

Morzycki made it down the ladder, jumping the last ten feet to the courtyard near the annex. At that moment, legionnaires came running out of the annex. "They've broken through!" one of them yelled. Three were shot as they made for the west barricade. Morzycki raised his rifle and killed the first Mexican coming through the annex doorway. He and the other legionnaires who had made it out joined Vilain's men. The Lieutenant ordered a squad to direct their fire on the annex.

Clement, Dekker, Kurz, Groux and van Opstal kept up a merciless fusillade on the farmhouse. Maudet added four of his men at the south barricade to help drive the Mexicans "from those damn windows." The fusillade was so intense Clement realized the Mexicans had stopped firing. Had they killed them all? He heard Maudet. "Cease fire! They're withdrawing!"

Clement drew in a breath. His lungs hurt. It felt like he was breathing in hot coals. Sweat and grime streaked his face. He noticed Groux wrapping a bandage around van Opstal's head.

"What happened to him?" he asked.

"Bullet grazed him," Groux said.

Clement nodded and then wondered if he was hearing things. He glanced around and realized everyone was hearing it. A bugle call sounded! The convoy! He wanted to cheer but his mouth was too raw and dry.

"Wait!" Maudet shouted. "That's not ours. It's a Mexican call."

Clement felt too weary to even whisper an oath. He noticed Vilain cover Danjou's face with his kepi. Out the corner of his eye, Clement saw Dekker cross himself. In the time he'd known Dekker it had never occurred to Clement that he might be a Catholic.

Shielding his eyes, Clement looked up into the sky. He guessed it was about noon. The sun was a great white eye, bloodshot by smoke and dust. He heard Morzycki's voice and saw him talking to Vilain, who was now in command. The sergeant reported fifteen legionnaires killed in the attack and a score of wounded. All but five of them could still fight.

"Let's go! There's work to do!" Morzycki shouted and set the men to work rebuilding the barricades, including using the bodies of dead Mexicans. Vilain announced the reason for the enemy's withdrawal. Mexican infantry had arrived. "Close to fifteen hundred more men. Regulars. Armed with rifles and bayonets."

Clement, Dekker, Groux, Kurz and van Opstal exchanged silent, grim glances. They all knew this would be a fight to the death now. Danjou had realized it. And in spite of his promise to Danjou, Clement did not want to die today.

"I hate this country," Dekker said and divided up the remaining ammunition from Burgiser's pouch between the squad. Each man got six rounds and cartridges apiece. When Clement took his share, he saw dried streaks of blood on Dekker's hands. Dekker told him he had gotten so desperate for something, anything to drink that he had stuck his fingers into his leg wound and licked off the blood.

Clement couldn't blame his friend. Hell, Clement didn't know what real thirst was before today. God, it was hot. He noticed Groux relieving himself back in the stable against the wall. Then he saw him lift his cupped hand to his mouth. He was drinking his own piss.

"Officer coming! Looks like they want another parley!" Morzycki shouted. Vilain told the sergeant to speak to the officer.

Morzycki climbed up one of the west wall barricades.

Down in the stable, Clement and the others couldn't hear the Mexican, but every legionnaire heard what Morzycki replied. *"Merde!"*

When the sergeant came down from the barricade, Clement saw Vilain pat his shoulder and smile.

Glancing at the others, Clement said, "The sergeant knows the short way to—"

He stopped. Van Opstal, his face bright red, slumped down against the wall. Heatstroke. His swollen tongue protruded from his mouth. Kurz moved to help him.

"¡Assalto!"

Shots rained down on the courtyard from the farmhouse. A bullet struck Kurz. He dropped on top of van Opstal. Dekker rolled Kurz over. He was alive but unconscious, shot through the jaw. Bandaging would have to wait. Dekker grabbed Kurz's ammunition pouch. "We need it now."

They returned deadly fire on the farmhouse windows.

"Front rank! Fire!" It was Maudet. Clement glanced over. Two ranks were aiming at the top of the barricade. "Rear rank, fire!" Maudet shouted. "Fire at will!"

Rifle fire and shouts and cries of the wounded on both sides filled the courtyard.

"Third squad!" Maudet shouted. Clement saw him signaling them to come fast. Clement, Dekker and Groux rushed in as the Mexicans broke over the top of the barricade, bayonets forward, shouting *"¡Viva Mexico!"* and *"¡Muerte a Francia!"*

Clement thrust his bayonet through the belly of a Mexican attacker. He pulled it out and smashed the butt of his rifle up into another Mexican's face, dropping him where he stood.

The platoon surged forward. Bayonets on both sides were bloody. Clement stabbed another attacker. A bullet buzzed by his head. Another clipped his sleeve.

"Forward!" Maudet shouted. "Drive them back!"

Climbing over the bodies of dead and wounded of both sides, the platoon furiously stabbed and clubbed the invaders, forcing them back over the barricade.

Clement was at the donkey cart when a Mexican with gold epaulettes on his shoulders, a red bandana around his neck and a raised sword in his hand jumped on top of it shouting, "*¡Matarlos a todos!*"

Clement jabbed his bayonet at him but the officer deflected it with his sword. Clement jerked his bayonet up and it crossed with the officer's sword as he swung it down. Clement pushed forward to drive the officer back but the officer drew his sword free. Somehow, Clement's kepi went flying off his head. He didn't feel anything at first but then something was getting in his left eye. Thick and wet. He couldn't keep that eye open. He knew he'd been cut. Ferocious violence swelled within him. He could taste it.

The Mexican leapt into the courtyard. Clement rushed him, shoved him back against the wall, his rifle braced hard against his throat. The officer, struggling to breathe, tried to slash at Clement with his sword. Clement screamed his war cry and pushed the rifle harder against his throat. He stared straight into the savage, dark eyes of the Mexican with his own hate and fury and saw the fear sweep into the Mexican's eyes. He had him now.

The officer dropped his sword, got his hands around Clement's rifle and pushed him away. Trying to catch his breath, the officer reached down to retrieve the sword, but Clement rammed his bayonet into his chest, pinning him to the wall. The officer expelled his last breath. The bitter smell of death bit into Clement's nostrils as he yanked the bayonet free.

The Mexicans broke and ran.

Clement wiped his hand over his left eye. Blood covered his palm. "*¡Hijos de putas!*" he shouted from over the top of the barricade. "Come back! We're here!"

Dekker and some of the others joined him with their taunts. "Is that the best you have?" "We're waiting, you bastards!" "Next time send your men to fight!"

Clement went to Dekker, wiped more blood off his forehead and asked, "How bad?"

"One of the bastards got you," Dekker said. "Sit down." Taking the red bandana off the officer Clement had killed, Dekker used it to clean the wound on Clement's forehead. It was about two inches across and not deep. But blood streaked his face. Dekker scooped up some dirt in his hand. They could barely make spit, so Dekker mixed the dirt with some of Clement's blood to make a poultice. Using his fingers, he applied it to the cut and then wrapped the bandana around Clement's head. At least it was something.

Clement peered over the barricade. Mexican dead were piled three and four deep in front of it. Their wounded lay helpless in the blistering sun. Some crawled across the open fields for the tree line where the Mexican forces regrouped.

"We won't give up and they won't give in," Clement said to Dekker.

"Such is war," Dekker said, and grunted. "Such is life."

They looked at each other and did the only thing they could do. They laughed.

Clement retrieved his kepi. The visor was split along the left side, the Havelock stained with blood. He put it on and saw two legionnaires pulling Groux's body from under two dead Mexicans. Clement and Dekker were all that was left standing of their squad from the second platoon.

Maudet ordered the men to rebuild the barricade. He told Clement and Dekker to check the perimeter.

Sergeant Morzycki reported to Maudet that Lieutenant Vilain was dead, a bullet through his forehead. Maudet assumed command. Twenty-one other legionnaires had been killed in the attack. That left eleven, including the wounded that could still handle a rifle. There were twenty-three legionnaires too badly wounded to fight.

"They're gone!" Dekker shouted. "The farmhouse! It's empty!"

Clement saw the smoke first. It was coming out of the windows on the second floor. "They set it on fire!"

It spread rapidly. No water to put it out. Billows of dense, black smoke surged out of the windows. Orange flames reached up through the holes in the roof. Within minutes the entire building was an inferno, adding to the miserable afternoon heat. A column of thick, black smoke rose into the cloudless, blue sky where Clement saw vultures circling.

"Legionnaires!" The shout came from the other side of the west wall. It was the Mexican officer again. Maudet joined Morzycki at the barricade. Clement went to listen.

"We're still here!" Morzycki answered.

"My colonel instructs me to tell you that you have nowhere to go. He asks you to surrender. There is no shame in it."

Maudet shook his head. Morzycki made no reply to the Mexican.

Clement, Dekker and the rest of the company still able to fight went through the ammunition pouches of the dead and wounded that hadn't already been scavenged. Seven rounds apiece went to each man to add to the few remaining in his pouch.

Maudet sent Clement and Dekker back to their position at the stable. Four legionnaires were stationed at the west-entry barricades with Sergeant Morzycki. Maudet and his three men were at the south barricade. All were exhausted. It had been over eight hours since the fight began. And flies were swarming over the dead and the wounded.

In the stable, Clement and Dekker had done what they could to bandage their comrades. Kurz, mercifully, was still unconscious. Van Opstal was delirious, moaning for water. His pathetic cries mixed with those of the other wounded and dying in the courtyard. They tore at Clement. "Water! Water . . . please." And he knew there was nothing to be done. Except to wait.

Captain Danjou's body lay where he had fallen in the middle of the courtyard. His kepi still covered his face. Fight to the death. He made the men swear it.

I cannot die here, Clement thought. I will not die here. They don't even know my real name.

Dekker swatted at flies buzzing around his wounds. "It's like a hammer on an anvil," he said, his voice hoarse. "And we're caught between them."

Clement was so tired he wasn't certain if Dekker meant the heat or the situation. What did it matter? His tongue felt thick in his mouth.

The Mexicans attacked again. Clement and Dekker aided Maudet at the south barricade. Volleys from the legionnaires at both barricades sent the Mexicans running. Each legionnaire had only a few rounds left. They all knew the Mexicans were trying to force them to use up their ammunition.

An hour passed. The fire had consumed the annex. The farmhouse continued to burn. Flies became more numerous. The coppery, putrid smell of blood and death hung thick in the stifling, tropical air. Blood soaked into the ground. It was smeared on the walls. The white leggings laced up over Clement's shoes were a dirty, sickening red.

"A bad omen," Dekker said as the wind came up, and from exactly the wrong direction. It blew the terrible, black smoke from the fire down into the courtyard. Clement and Dekker tried to stifle their coughs. They heard firing and shouting at both barricades. The Mexican bastards were using the smoke as cover.

Clement and Dekker aimed their rifles even though it was so hard to see.

"Any movement, shoot it," Dekker said.

A few tense minutes passed. More sounds of struggle. "Hold them!" It was Maudet on the right. Clement and Dekker heard footsteps running toward them. They aimed their rifles, ready to fire at anything coming through the smoke.

"Hold fire!" It was Morzycki. With him were legionnaires Bertolomo, Catteau and Maine.

"Coming in," they heard Maudet coughing. Legionnaires Constantin and Wenzel followed him.

"Anyone else, sir?" Clement asked.

Maudet shook his head, coughing.

Clement let out a breath. Only nine left standing. At that moment, Clement knew he did not want to die, in spite of his promise to Captain Danjou. Short of a miracle, though, these would be his final minutes. He hadn't prayed in many years. He couldn't remember the last time he had prayed, but he said a prayer now. I know I abandoned you a long time ago, God, but please, let me live through this. I spent my whole life sinning, but I promise I will change.

A shot cracked from out in the courtyard. The bullet bit into the wooden post inches above Clement's head. He wondered if God was sending him a message.

The men brought their rifles up. Shadows appeared through the smoke. The legionnaires fired. The shadows fired back and hastily disappeared into the smoky haze.

"Goddamn it," Maudet whispered, looking down at Morzycki.

Clement saw Morzycki sprawled on the ground behind the wall, a gunshot to the head. Bertolomo was wounded, his breathing ragged. A bloody hole in his chest bubbled. He died a moment later. Dekker checked their ammunition pouches. They were empty.

Clement looked at Maudet. He saw the resignation on his face.

"We swore an oath to the Captain," Maudet said, his voice rough and parched. "No surrender. We will attack them. Fire one volley and charge."

Clement reached into his pouch. Only one cartridge and minié ball remained.

"I'm out," Dekker whispered. "Anybody got one to spare?"

Clement handed him the cartridge and ball.

"Thanks," he whispered and noticed Clement not reloading. "Is this your last?"

"Go on. Take it," Clement said. "You've been a soldier all your life. You deserve it."

Dekker chuckled. "How about one last game, my friend? High card takes all."

Clement liked that. He took the deck of cards from his pocket and held it out in his palm facedown to his friend. Dekker made his choice. Ten of clubs. Clement showed his card. Three of diamonds.

"First time I've won in a long time," Dekker whispered, handing him back his cards.

Clement slipped the deck back inside his pocket. He smiled. He couldn't recall Dekker being lucky at cards at all before.

"Hell will be crowded today," Dekker coughed as he began loading his rifle.

Clement heard a soft, low humming. Unmistakable. It was a song. He'd never heard it before, but there was a strength to it. Courageous somehow. Dekker was humming. The Prussian kept his eyes on his rifle as he finished loading it. He lowered his head and finished the song. When he looked up, Clement saw the hard edge of the legionnaire in his eyes. Determined. Unafraid.

Clement knew that look well. He'd summoned it himself many times, especially this day. He knew he wasn't afraid of death. It was that he wasn't yet ready to die.

A breeze wafted through the courtyard. It cleared some of the smoke away and revealed a throng of slowly advancing Mexicans. Their bayonets were fixed and bloodied, hate etched on their swarthy faces.

"Honor and glory," Maudet said, his voice a rasp. "Follow me!"

They formed a line out in front of the low wall and aimed their rifles. Clement stood with his rifle ready for the bayonet charge. He repeated his prayer. Please, God, let me live and I promise I will change. And please, God, if I die, let me die on my feet.

The Mexicans halted. The front ranks raised their rifles, waiting for the order to fire.

Please, God . . .

"Fire!" Maudet rasped.

Six rifles spit fire. With bayonets leveled for the attack, the seven legionnaires charged forward.

Please, God!

"*¡Matarlos!*"

Please—

Clement felt the hot, searing bullet tear into his lower-right ribs as it spun him around into blackness.

Chapter Five

Clement could swear he heard humming. Dekker's song. It sounded far off, getting dimmer. Wait! Don't go, Dekker! He tasted dirt in his mouth. Thick. Gritty. He tried to spit it out. More dirt fell into his mouth. Dirt was in his nose. Covering his eyes! His hands! Arms! Legs! No!

He bolted upright and doubled over from the pain in his side. He wiped dirt out of his eyes and spit it from his mouth. Dirt clung to him. Face. Hair. Everywhere.

Looking up, he saw stars across the black night sky. In the subtle light of the quarter moon he could make out the walls of the hacienda over to his right. The fire had burned itself out. He could hear the night sounds, the buzz of insects, the grunting whoop of monkeys, a coyote howl in the distance. He was alive. Alive! He hadn't died! He'd survived! He tried to laugh, but his side hurt like hell, and he coughed on dirt. Using his fingers he wiped more of it out of his mouth. The bullet wound in his side oozed. Wait. He was naked, his uniform stripped off him. Even the red bandana he had wrapped around his head was gone. And his deck of cards from Paris.

Then he smelled it. Thick and pungent and rotting.

He saw an arm over his leg and pushed it off, disturbing more dirt, revealing part of a neck and face next to him. He brushed the dirt away. It was Dekker. Dead. What was this? He looked on his other side. Something was under dirt there, too. Brushing it off, he saw Morzycki's face.

The pain in his side overwhelmed him. It was like a hot poker jammed into him. He caught his breath. Looking more closely, he realized loose mounds of dirt and more limbs surrounded him. It was a big grave. The Mexicans had dug a large shallow hole in the ground. Only they hadn't covered all the bodies. And more naked bodies lay heaped in a pile nearby. Legionnaires. The Mexicans had taken their uniforms, their rifles. Stripped them of everything. Left them to rot. Bastards! And that heavy, rotting smell was death.

But Clement was alive. And he couldn't stay here. He would follow the road. He shivered against the cold night air. Rubbed his arms. He tried to stand but was too weak. He'd crawl. All the way back to headquarters in Chiquihuite. Twenty-two miles. Damn, it was cold. The heat of the day boiled you and the night froze you. But he would make it. He gripped the loose earth with his hands and pulled himself forward. He survived the battle. He'd survive the night. Get away from here. Keep going. He was a legionnaire. And legionnaires never surrender. They never . . .

Clement collapsed in the dirt. Hard. He heard the sound of tramping feet, the rattle of canteens. The Mexicans had returned! Get off the road! Hurry!

Hands took him by the shoulders. He felt himself being rolled over. And voices. He heard French voices. "Get him some water! Colonel! Over here! He's alive!"

Alive. The word had never sounded so sweet.

And he'd forgotten all about his promise to God.

The battalion surgeon was able to remove the bullet from Clement's chest. He told Clement he'd been exceptionally fortunate the bullet had broken a rib because hitting it had slowed it from travelling around his insides, quite possibly deflecting it from perforating vitals, "though a divine hand may have been at work in that instance, as well." Luck or the Lord mattered not to Clement. All he knew was that it hurt to breathe, eat, sit up and lie down. The surgeon had also sewn up his head wound. Eight stitches. "I'll take them out in a few weeks," the surgeon said. "But you'll have a scar there for good."

While recuperating, Clement also found out that the supply convoy his unit was to escort had turned back when local Indians warned it of a possible ambush. It was likely that the Mexican forces Clement's unit encountered were the very ones waiting to attack the convoy and thereby saved it.

Three weeks later, the day he was released from the infirmary, Clement was awarded the Medal of the Legion of Honor for bravery. Colonel Jeanningros, commander of the French Foreign Legion in Mexico, presented the green, white and gold medal to him at a ceremony on the small parade field at Chiquihuite. Clement still had it around his neck, hanging from a blood-red ribbon, when he was told to report to Jeanningros's command tent.

"Legionnaire Victor Cheval. It is an honor to shake hands with a hero of the battle of Camerone."

To Clement, the man shaking his hand looked like he could have been someone's grandfather. He had a full white beard and kind eyes. But it was his clothes that struck Clement as odd. He didn't wear the uniform of any French officer he'd ever seen. This man wore an ornate Mexican jacket of red and gold with fancy gold epaulettes on his shoulders and gold braiding on the sleeves. Two rows of medals hung across the left side of his jacket. The sombrero on his head was embroidered with gold-leaf filigree. He wore a saber at his side. An ivory-handled revolver with fancy engraving protruded from the front of his wide leather belt.

"Allow me to introduce myself," the man said. "I am Colonel Charles Dupin. Perhaps you've heard of me."

"I have heard the name, sir."

"I'm the commander of a special imperial cavalry unit, all volunteers, and I have come here to speak to you about a matter of some importance. The surgeon says you'll be fit for regular duty shortly."

"Yes, sir," Clement said.

"Your colonel tells me you'll be assigned to a new unit. That means you'll be guarding the convoy road again. Escorting supply columns. Fighting off ambushes. Fighting on the enemy's terms." He glanced at Jeanningros. "I know you would prefer things differently, Colonel."

"We all have our orders," Jeanningros said to him. "And good soldiers follow orders."

"Precisely," Dupin said, turning back to Clement. "My orders have been to find and destroy the bandits harassing our forces. I've enjoyed success these last few months. My three hundred cavalry move swiftly and hit hard. I'm here now to offer you the opportunity to fight that enemy on our terms. More specifically, I'm going after the swine that butchered your friends and fellow legionnaires. I want to know if you will join me."

Clement was stunned. "I'm a legionnaire, sir."

"And a damned fine one," Dupin said. "As you proved at Camerone."

"Thank you, sir. It's just that legionnaires fight best on two feet, not four." Clement saw both men smile. But a thought went through Clement's mind. Maybe he'd spoken too soon.

"You should know," Jeanningros said, "that some of your fellow legionnaires, the wounded from the battle, are being held as prisoners by the *juarista* forces. About twenty or so, I'm told. The Mexican commander has sent word they want a prisoner exchange."

That was a surprise. Clement wondered if that included those taken prisoner in the cactus copse, as well. "Do you know the names of the prisoners, sir?"

Jeanningros shook his head. "But one can only hope for their safety. I am skeptical of their offer. But that's another affair. The point here today is that Colonel Dupin is giving you an opportunity, one none of the rest of us in the legion have the luxury to consider. An exception would be made for you under the circumstances."

"Circumstances, sir?"

"Your unit no longer exists," Jeanningros said. "You would be assigned under detached service to Colonel Dupin's force. Legionnaires do fight best on their feet, but legionnaires fight no matter what."

"Join me," Dupin said. "Avenge the slaughter of your comrades."

"This would be for the honor of the legion," Jeanningros said. "It would be for all of us."

Clement said yes. It would indeed be for the honor of the legion and to avenge his unit that no longer existed. But the thought Clement had earlier had also influenced his decision, one he felt certain Dekker would appreciate. He had four months and one day before his enlistment would be up. With that much time to go, why march when you can ride?

Five days later Clement was riding north with Dupin's cavalry along the eastern foothills of the Sierra Madre Orientals. His side still hurt, but it was the first day Clement didn't feel saddle sore. But every day the heat and humidity hammered unmercifully.

Clement had turned in his legionnaire uniform, including his kepi, and now wore a red dolman, leather trousers, high boots and a sombrero. He was issued a short French carbine and a six-inch knife he was advised to "slip inside your boot." He was told that since they had no saber available for him, "kill a Mexican officer and take his." The revolvers, however, came courtesy of the British.

"This civil war the Americans are fighting is good for us," Lieutenant Boule told Clement when he handed him a Kerr's revolver. "British companies sell arms to the Confederates but Union ships blockade the Texas ports. So, British ships sail to the port of Matamoros and the Confederates smuggle the guns across the Rio Bravo into Texas. Except sometimes our ships must seize those British ships, believing the guns on board may be for the Mexican insurgents. We escort those ships to Vera Cruz where they wait while the Confederate government makes accusations and we object to those accusations until they pay us to return the ships. Meanwhile, the stores must be unloaded to be kept safe onshore. I liberated two hundred of these revolvers the last time I was in Vera Cruz."

Dupin's cavalry rode into a deserted village. They were on the trail of a force of Mexican irregular cavalry that local Indians had told Dupin was seen in the area. Clement was one of the sentinels posted to keep watch for troops and insurgents. He heard Dupin order his men to burn the village. The men laughed as they set fire to it. "Leave nothing!" Boule shouted. Clement hadn't seen this kind of warfare before.

The next day, they came across another deserted village. Doors hung loose. Fire pits were long cold. Clement was ordered to help burn it.

"There's no one here, Lieutenant," Clement said. "No one's been here for weeks by the look of things."

"We leave nothing for them to come back to. It's all these people understand," Boule told him sternly. "I should think you would understand that. Burn it."

Clement set his torch to several of the buildings. These are not honorable men, he told himself. They're brigands.

That night, Clement was told to report to Dupin.

"Lieutenant Boule tells me that you have 'concerns' about

how we operate," Dupin said. He held out a bottle of red wine to Clement who hesitated a moment, then accepted and took a drink.

"My concern, sir," Clement said, "is . . . Forgive me, may I speak freely?"

Dupin took a pull from the bottle and shrugged.

"My concern is that these actions may be questionable."

"Indeed? How so?"

"Our mission in Mexico—"

"Yes, tell me what our mission is," Dupin interrupted. "Why are we here?"

Clement knew he should tread lightly as Dupin seemed to be getting drunk. "Mexico borrowed money from France and has refused to repay it. The emperor sent us to force Mexico to make good on the debt."

"So, it's for the honor and glory of France that we're here."

"Yes, sir."

Dupin laughed. "Take another drink, legionnaire, and let me tell you about honor and glory."

Clement didn't want to drink, but took one to satisfy Dupin. A small one. He thought it wise to keep his wits about him.

"You're right," Dupin said, and took a pull on the bottle. "We are here for money. The emperor wants the money he loaned Mexico. But it's a trifle. Did you know that? He knows it. Our great emperor is no fool." He took another swig. "He doesn't care that Juarez ran all the priests out of the country. Or that Juarez is nothing but a thief. It's more than money the emperor wants. You know how I know this?"

Clement shook his head.

"Your Colonel Jeanningros told me. An envoy from Paris stopped at his headquarters for the night. He was on his way to Puebla to see General Forey. He had a battalion of French soldiers as escort. Your colonel invited him to have dinner. The envoy brought a case of champagne with him and offered a bottle to have with the dinner. They finished that one and opened another. The envoy got a little drunk and the colonel made some inquiries about his reason for coming to Mexico."

Clement watched as Dupin took another drink. Wine dribbled down his chin. He wiped it off on his sleeve.

"The envoy told him . . ." Dupin sniffed, "told him something very interesting. He had a letter from the emperor to the general. You know what the letter said?"

Clement made no reply.

"It instructed him to take the town of San Luis Potasi." Dupin chuckled. "San Luis Potasi has one of the richest silver mines in this country. And the emperor wants it. What do you think of that?"

"The emperor wants the money he loaned," Clement said. "Taking the silver mine would be a way to get it."

"Very smart," Dupin said. "Except the envoy said the silver is only the start. The emperor wants all of Mexico. The whole rotten pesthole. Another colony. That's right. It's not his silver and not his land but you and I will do everything it takes to see that he gets them. That's the glory and honor of France. Make no mistake, legionnaire."

Clement went back to where he'd laid out his bedroll. He knew this was the way of the world of kings and emperors, and there was nothing he could do about it. He wanted to throw up. Instead he counted the days he had left. Three months and three weeks. Somehow it felt like time was going backwards.

Chapter Six

The following day, Dupin's men rode into a village that wasn't deserted. Some thirty men fanned out through the surrounding woods as sentries and to check for possible ambush. It was evident to Clement that most or all of the villagers were already in the center of town having a celebration of some kind. They were dancing and singing. Some of the women had been making tortillas. A large pot of beans was bubbling over an open fire. But no matter now. The villagers were herded together around the stone well in the village center. There were about fifty people—men, women and children—most with fear in their eyes. When Dupin appeared before them on his horse in his gold and red finery, Clement saw many of the people cross themselves and whisper something to each other. He glanced over at the man next to him. His name was Lebiche.

"What are they saying?" Clement asked.

Lebiche grinned and said, "The Hyena. It's what they call the colonel in this country. He likes it."

Dupin said he wanted to see the *jefe*. A slight man with white hair and goatee came forward.

Clement noticed two boys, one around ten years old and the other a few years older, standing close by with their parents. Both boys looked anxious, the older one particularly so. The younger one wore a *serape* and started to reach out for the old man with his right hand, keeping his left under the *serape*. But his mother dropped her hand over his arm. Maybe the old man was his grandfather or an uncle, Clement thought.

Dupin spoke to the *jefe* in Spanish. Clement knew almost no Spanish but he heard Dupin say *"juaristas"* several times. The old man shook his head.

Dupin signaled Boule who threw a noose around the old man's neck and pulled him to a nearby tree. Boule tossed the rope over a limb and walked his horse, pulling the rope until the old man was up on his toes. Clement kicked his horse forward a few steps. He didn't like this.

Dupin barked again in Spanish at the old man. His eyes shut tight, teeth clenched, fingers trying to loosen the rope around his neck, the old man sputtered, *"No se."*

Dupin nodded at Boule who kicked his horse and raised the old man a foot off the ground. He struggled and choked against the rope.

Clement saw the small boy held back by his mother. She had tears in her eyes.

Suddenly, the older boy ran forward, shouting at Dupin. Pulling out his pistol, Dupin shot him down.

"¡No!" the younger boy yelled. The mother screamed. Her husband grabbed her arms to hold her back. She glared at Dupin. *"¡Bastardo!"*

The front ranks of Dupin's men moved their horses in closer, keeping the villagers back. Clement moved in with them.

Dupin grunted and motioned to Boule to lower the man. Boule did, but kept the rope taut once the man's feet were on the ground.

"No se," the *jefe* sputtered. *"¡No se!"*

Clement had had enough. "Colonel!"

Dupin jerked his head at him, the anger flashed in his eyes.

"These are not soldiers," Clement said.

"You will keep silent!" Dupin shouted.

"No, sir. We don't kill children and old men."

Dupin leaned forward in his saddle. "Let me make this clear, legionnaire. This is a different war we fight. This is how we get information."

"No," Clement said.

Several mounted men made a move toward Clement but Dupin waved them back.

"You disappoint me," Dupin said. "You think there are innocent people here? No one in this whole miserable country is innocent! Last night you called our actions questionable. What do you call it when these *juarista* bandits who call themselves soldiers take captured French soldiers, bury them up to their necks and then use their heads as practice for their lances? Tell me!"

"These people here are not soldiers," Clement said through gritted teeth.

"These people give aid to the *juaristas*!" Dupin shouted. "Every village. They're probably all *juaristas*! The women and children kill as easily as the men. They're savages. Only one way to deal with savages."

Dupin motioned to Boule who pulled the old man higher. His legs kicked, his mouth was stretched open trying to suck in air.

The younger boy broke free of his father and ran to the old man, grabbing his legs to try to hold him up, but the old man in his struggle kicked him away. The boy landed on his back.

"Colonel!" Lebiche called out. He was pointing at the boy. Everyone saw it. It was a legionnaire's white kepi on the ground next to him. He'd had it under his *serape*.

Lebiche dismounted and picked up the kepi. "Blood stains," he said harshly.

No one moved. Then Dupin spoke to Clement. "It's likely that belongs to one of your dead comrades. Need more proof? Still think they aren't savages?"

Clement didn't know what to think. Except that he'd started something and it wasn't going the way he hoped it would.

Dupin motioned for Boule to tie off the rope. As the old man struggled, Lebiche got back on his horse and went to Clement. He threw the kepi at him and said, "Did the Mexicans cut off your balls in that battle?"

Clement heard chuckling. The kepi bounced off his chest and fell to the ground. He kept his eyes on Dupin.

The old man's arms went limp and his body swung gently. Some of the villagers cried.

Dupin grunted with satisfaction. "This is what we will do now, legionnaire. We will burn this village, kill everyone here and throw their bodies in the fires. And you will keep your promise to your colonel to avenge the legion and kill this boy first."

Clement pulled his revolver. Anger swelled in him. He pointed his revolver at the boy still on the ground. His mother and father pleaded in Spanish, *"No, no. ¡Por favor!"* Clement cocked the hammer back, and turned the revolver on Dupin.

A number of Dupin's men instantly pointed rifles and revolvers at Clement.

Clement didn't flinch. He remained steady, unsure of what might happen next, but there would be no more uncalled-for killings while he drew breath.

A moment passed, and Dupin laughed. A big, loud belly laugh. "The hero of Camerone has a soft spot for Mexicans."

"No," Clement said evenly. "I have a hard spot for killers of defenseless old men and children."

Dupin sighed. "Don't you know I can only be killed with a golden bullet?"

Clement frowned. Was he mad?

"Listen to me, legionnaire," Dupin said. "The easy part will be having you executed for this insubordination. Every man here will gladly volunteer to serve on the firing squad. But because you are a hero, I will have to report that you died valiantly in battle. Anything else would upset the emperor. Heroes of the empire cannot be traitors."

A shout came from the western woods. One of the sentries came riding fast into the village. "Lancers approaching!"

Clement heard shots. Bullets peppered buildings. He saw one of Dupin's epaulettes fly off. Villagers scattered. Dupin shouted orders. The men spread out for the fight. More shots! Yelling! Clement felt a tug on his reins. It was the boy. He pointed and, still holding on to the reins, quickly pulled the horse toward the nearby woods.

Clement heard Dupin shout, "Get the legionnaire!"

Bullets flew past Clement as he entered the woods. The boy was speaking excitedly in Spanish. Trees and vines became thick but this boy seemed to know a path. They stopped and Clement saw the boy's parents. His father held a horse with a rope bridle but no saddle. He put the boy on the horse, handed him a cloth sack with a piece of rope tied around the end, a revolver as big as his arm and said something in Spanish. All Clement could recognize was "Matamoros."

"*¡Ándale!*" the man shouted and slapped the rump of the horse. The woman slapped Clement's horse. Clement hunkered down to avoid low vines and limbs.

They rode north the rest of the day and into the night, stopping to rest the horses every few hours, sometimes to walk them. Inside the sack were tortillas. Clement was glad the boy was not selfish about sharing them.

The boy spoke to Clement, his Spanish a rapid race of words. Clement could only gather that he was leading him somewhere, likely Matamoros since he mentioned it several times, though he had no idea how far they were from the town. But they were moving fast through thick forests and into the lowlands. This boy certainly seemed to know the way. Clement also guessed the boy and his parents were grateful to him for holding his ground against Dupin. It was their way of saying thank you.

At one of their rests, Clement asked the boy how he got the kepi. He had to find out. Using his hands he described the cap. "Kepi. Kepi," he said and pointed at the boy. The boy understood and pantomimed finding it on the ground. Perhaps a troop went by the boy's village and it was dropped, Clement thought. At least that's what he comforted himself with.

It was early afternoon the next day when they arrived at the outskirts of Matamoros. Dark, roiling storm clouds were building inland.

The boy pointed north. *"Tejas,"* he said, *"Tejas,"* and wheeled his horse around and rode back the way they had come. Clement watched him go, then looked at the town before him. Tall twin bell towers rose prominently over the center of town. Probably a cathedral from the size of those towers. Dozens of ships lay at anchor beyond the sandbars. Texas was on the other side of the big river. Choices lay before him. One thing was certain: he could not remain in Mexico.

He needed money. He sold his horse, saddle and rifle to the proprietor of a livery stable, but kept his revolver and the knife in his boot. Black faces, white faces and brown faces populated the town. There were plenty of saloons and whores and gambling. It was not unlike Sidi-bel-Abbes, except for the ocean and the ships.

Clement found many saloons near the beach. In one called El Dorado, the barkeep was an Irishman named Keough who spoke an atrocious French. Clement wanted wine. Keough said all he had at the moment was beer, whiskey and tequila. Clement settled for beer so as to keep his wits and asked Keough if there was a chance of signing on as a hand to one of those ships.

"There's a lot of people in Matamoros these days," Keough said and started wiping down the bar. "Desperadoes, adventurers, runaway Negro slaves, lost-looking Frenchmen, refugees from Texas and Louisiana. Most of them would like to leave here. Particularly the refugees." He indicated a large man sitting at one of the gambling tables. "That man has been coming in every day at the same time for the last two weeks. He came here from Texas. He's one of those refugees. German. Doesn't say much. Stays for three hours, orders beer, sits at that table, gambles a little, then leaves. I say he's waiting for someone."

"What do you mean?"

"After the Americans declared war on each other, some of those in the southern states didn't agree with breaking away from their northern neighbors. Had to flee for their lives, they did. Many of them crossed into Mexico." He cocked his head toward the German. "That includes an entire town of Germans from Texas. They'd just built their first church, God love them. I'm told they've written letters to President Lincoln for two years now asking for help to get out. Poor bastards. But I say maybe, just maybe, he's been told to be here to meet a contact. That and it's getting so I can smell the anticipation on him."

"How do you know all this?"

"This is Matamoros. Everybody knows everything about everyone here. I already know you're French and anxious to leave this wonderful country." Keough smiled.

Clement chuckled. "All right. But what about getting on one of these ships?"

"First thing you should know is that half the ships out there are Union warships waiting for the other half, which are Confederate blockade runners. Those blockade runners are loaded with cotton smuggled out of Texas, brought through here and bound for Europe. Sometimes the blockade runners slip through, but many's the night you can see the fires of sinking ships. I wouldn't advise those."

"I've heard ships from England come here," Clement said.

"That they do," Keough said. "And ships from France and Cuba and South America, as well. So there's a good chance you'll find a captain or a first mate in almost every saloon most evenings, including this establishment. And many's willing to discuss taking on an extra hand over a drink. Or two. But choose wisely."

Clement wondered why the hell Keough didn't choose to tell him that from the beginning. But now he had information and he was hungry. Keough brought him fried oysters, beans and tortillas. Clement watched the faro players while he ate, observing who played well and who didn't. He joined a game and spent a few hours playing. He did succeed in adding to his purse. One of the men at the table was the large German. Clement noticed him eying him suspiciously. After a few hands, the German left the game, went to the bar and waited, checking his watch periodically. Clement heard cracks of thunder rolling closer. It was getting darker outside. That storm he saw earlier was coming.

It wasn't long before a man carrying a cane entered. No one paid him any mind, except the German. The man with the cane went to him at the bar and they conversed briefly, nods were exchanged and the German left. Clement noticed Keough staying close by during their conversation. The man with the cane ordered whiskey. As Keough set it down, he caught Clement's eye and motioned to him.

With his sombrero in hand, Clement went to the bar and Keough put a whiskey down in front of him with a nod that said just take it. The barman spoke to the man with the cane in English. Clement didn't understand a word, but the man glanced at Clement, turned back to Keough and shook his head.

Keough said something else and the man shrugged and grunted something.

Keough set another whiskey in front of the man, then told Clement that this was Barlow, first officer on the *Chesterfield,* a Union warship anchored offshore. The ship had orders to take those Germans from Texas, about a hundred and fifty of them, to a safe destination. "It would appear those letters they wrote to President Lincoln must have worked," Keough said.

"So what is this to do with me?" Clement asked.

"Patience. I asked Barlow if there was room for one more. He looked at you and said no. I asked him if he might reconsider."

"And?"

"He said a monetary arrangement might be made."

Clement grunted. "A bribe."

"That would be correct."

"He wouldn't care to let me wager my passage in a game of faro, would he?"

Keough asked. Barlow shook his head once.

"How much does he want?" Clement asked.

"How much do you have?"

The arrangement was made. Clement gave him all his winnings from faro and the sale of his horse, tack and rifle, about two hundred American dollars, some of it in pesos, according to Keough who counted it up. Barlow told Keough where Clement was to be the next morning or he'd be left behind.

"Can I trust him?" Clement asked Keough.

"Do you have any choice?"

Clement understood. "Ask him where the ship is going."

Keough asked and Barlow answered and left.

"He said Baltimore," Keough said.

Clement had never heard of it. But at least he had a chance now. He'd be in America. He thanked Keough, who told him he could stay in the saloon until it was time for him to go. "This saloon never closes."

Deciding to stretch his legs, Clement stood and saw Lieutenant Boule standing in the front doorway looking directly at him, grinning. Clement asked Keough if there was a back way out of the saloon.

"Of course," Keough said. "This is Matamoros."

Taking the knife from his boot as a precaution, Clement slipped through the hallway and out the back door where Lebiche grabbed him from behind, knocking off his sombrero and wrapping an arm around his neck.

"The Colonel said to bring the deserter back alive," Lebiche said through gritted teeth.

Clement jammed his knife into Lebiche's thigh. The man screamed and loosened his hold enough that Clement broke free. Rain began to fall. Clement pulled out his revolver and shot Lebiche in the chest. This was about his life. No time to take chances.

With his revolver still in hand, Clement retrieved his knife and ran down the alleyway, forgetting his sombrero. He figured Boule would show up any moment. Rain fell harder. Lightning flashed close by. Thunder cracked, so loud it sounded like it was right overhead. Soaking wet, Clement came around to the front of the saloon. No Boule. He headed for the window to see if he was inside. Suddenly, the lieutenant came out the door and saw him.

Clement raised his revolver. Click! Misfire! He turned and ran. A bullet clipped the corner of the saloon wall as he ducked around it.

Cursing the rain that likely got his revolver too wet and caused the misfire, Clement ran. He needed to get away, to lose Boule. Another bolt of lightning lit up the sky. More thunder, so loud he winced. But in that brief moment, Clement saw the twin bell towers of the cathedral. Maybe he could hide inside.

He looked back down the street searching for Boule. The rain made it hard to see. The town plaza was ahead. The cathedral was on it. He crept forward. Peering around the corner he saw the large double doors of the cathedral were closed, no light in the windows. Maybe he could find some way in or—

"Don't move, deserter!" Clement heard Boule shout.

Clement saw him approaching up the street to his left. Boule had his revolver leveled at him from the hip. Clement couldn't take the chance that Boule's revolver would misfire. But he wouldn't go back to face that animal Dupin and his firing squad, either.

Boule stopped in the middle of the muddy street. "Drop the gun and the knife."

Clement saw no other choice at the moment. But he needed to play for time. "How did you find me?"

"You were seen going off with that kid," Boule said. "After we ran off the lancers, the Colonel hung the kid's mama to make her husband talk. He told us where you were going. And we all know Matamoros. Saloons are the first places we look for runaways."

Clement glanced over at the plaza, then down the street he'd come up, searching for something—a person, a dog—anything to distract Boule.

"But enough wasting time," Boule said. "You're a deserter and a disgrace and you murdered a good soldier back there at the saloon. I'm going to kill you right here, find a shithole to dump you in and tell the Colonel I had no choice."

"He won't like that," Clement said.

"I don't care," Boule said and took aim.

In that moment, Clement remembered that he had abandoned God after Camerone, God who had been generous enough to answer his prayer and not let him die. He was sorry, but he couldn't ask God to help him again now. It wouldn't be right. He knew he'd never see Paris again. Never have a woman again.

Boule pulled back the hammer on his revolver.

And Clement saw Dekker's face and the look in his friend's eyes before the final charge at Camerone. Determined. Unafraid. Clement knew he had nowhere to run, no gun to fight back with, no words to stop Boule. He straightened his back and looked death in the face. Determined. Unafraid. Strangely, the words of the big sergeant in Paris, the one who'd convinced him to enlist, came back to him. "Life is full of calamity." He knew what mattered now was how he faced it.

And he didn't blame God for what he was about to receive.

Boule's revolver sounded louder than a cannon. The bold flash blinded Clement. He felt himself thrown to the ground.

Rain pelted Clement's face. Had he been knocked out? How long? His back and head ached. But he hadn't been shot. Boule must have missed! But what threw him off his feet? Opening his eyes, he saw rain coming down so hard now it appeared like drops hit the ground and jumped back up. And there was something lying in the mud of the street. He picked himself up and took a closer look. It almost made him retch. The upper half of Boule's body was burned black. What was left of his sombrero lay scorched next to him. His revolver was seared to his hand, the barrel twisted into a strange angle. A bolt of lightning had hit Boule. Another lightning bolt made a jagged thrust across the sky. Clement looked up through the downpour. The cross atop the cathedral stood silhouetted in the intense brightness of the white light. He could feel thunder in the air around him. It roared in his ears. But he paid it no mind. Something had happened to Clement. Something had changed. Face death, face life. He believed he'd been granted another chance. He'd asked God for help before and then forgotten him. But God had not forgotten him.

★ ★ ★ ★ ★

1875

★ ★ ★ ★ ★

Chapter Seven

PENQUERO, TERRITORY OF NEW MEXICO

Clement swung the nine-pound sledgehammer again in a ferocious arc. He felt the jolt ripple up his arms when he struck the wooden post. Lord, he was tired. Old Aguirre, who had a patchy beard and a milky eye, was helping by steadying the post. Even with the hole they'd dug using a spade and an iron bar, that hard clay was unforgiving.

It was late October. The grasses had turned brown but an Indian summer had crept in the last few days. Though only mid-morning, the heat rose up off the ground in blurred waves, but Clement hardly noticed. No matter how hot it got, no day's heat could compare with that day in the hacienda at Camerone. Twelve years had passed, yet nothing about that battle or Dupin or Mexico had dimmed in his memory.

He swung the hammer once more and stopped to rest. Wringing wet from his floppy hat down to his brogans, he wiped the sweat from his eyes. Glancing out across the open rolling plains Clement saw a rider getting closer. He recognized the man wearing the wide-brimmed padre hat with the short crown and black shirt with the standing white collar around his neck and black trousers. A large gold cross hung at his chest. It was the bishop. No, he was the archbishop now. Clement last saw him that past June in Santa Fe when he attended his investiture as archbishop. The whole town had turned out for the ceremony and the festivities had lasted well into the night. And what a celebration it had been! The cavalry band from Fort Union had played on the plaza and people danced. Hundreds of *faralitos* illuminated the town and fireworks lit up the sky. The rider raised his hand. Clement returned the greeting and wondered what had brought the archbishop all the way out here. The annual tithes had been collected that past summer. And the archbishop surely hadn't left Santa Fe to ride over two hundred miles to Penquero for a social visit.

Clement told Aguirre they'd have to finish this task another time. Aguirre did not hide his relief. They'd already sunk two posts this morning and nailed the cross beam creating a new hitching rail. This was the third post and another to come for a second rail. Truth be told, Clement was glad for the interruption. Sinking posts was hard, exhausting work as evidenced by his sore back and calloused hands.

Using the ladle from the water jar nearby, Aguirre took a drink, removed his straw hat, poured the remainder over his head, then put his hat back on.

"You have your visit," Aguirre said. "I'll go up and pull the weeds, if you wish."

Clement said that would be a good idea and Aguirre nodded, took the wooden ladder from the ground, placed it against the flaking adobe church wall and climbed up to the flat roof.

"Be careful," Clement shouted up to him. "I don't want your wife giving me grief because you fell and broke your arm. Or worse!"

"If I fall, Rosa will give me the grief," Aguirre said and disappeared over the parapet.

Their whole conversation had been in Spanish. Clement had come to learn it over the years and spoke it pretty well now. Almost as well as he spoke French. And English.

He set aside the sledgehammer, removed his hat and wiped his sweaty face with a kerchief as he headed for his small house beside the old church. Once inside, he changed out of his soiled shirt and worn black trousers but left on his red-long-ago-faded-to-pink-flannel underwear, what with no time to properly wash up and change into his other dry pair. When he came back out in his black cassock, Archbishop Jean-Baptiste Lamy was tying his horse to the new hitching rail. At sixty, Lamy was twenty years older than Clement. He was a slight man physically but possessed a hale sense of humor. Though his hair was almost all iron gray and his face showed hard weathered edges, Clement saw that Lamy's dark eyes were sharply alert.

"Father Grantaire," Lamy said, "so good to see you. Making improvements, I see."

"Indeed, Your Excellency," Clement said and knelt and kissed the gold ring of office Lamy wore on the third finger of his left hand. "I'm pleased to see you, as well."

Brown, spiky-leafed weeds and strands of dead, reedy grasses fell from the sky. Looking up, Lamy saw more come flying over the church parapet. Clement and Lamy heard jaunty singing from above. A Mexican song.

"One of my parishioners," Clement said. "Let me put your horse in the corral with mine. There's a water trough. Your horse must be thirsty."

Lamy nodded. "An excellent idea." A clump of uprooted weeds landed in front of him. "In the nearly thirty years I've been here, one thing I've never gotten used to is that they pack these flat rooftops with dirt. I know it helps seal them, but only in this country have I seen weeds and flowers and grass growing on the roofs of houses and churches."

They spoke in French. It was about the only time Clement spoke his native language anymore. It was no secret that many of the priests Lamy had recruited to join him over the years in the Archdiocese of Santa Fe he had found in France, where he was from. Clement was one of the exceptions. Lamy had come through Baltimore on his way back to Santa Fe from France on a recruiting trip. While in Baltimore, Lamy visited the Saint Sulpice Seminary there with the intention of inviting priests to join him in the archdiocese. At about half the size of Texas, the archdiocese covered most of the New Mexico Territory and part of southern Colorado and southeastern Utah. Clement had heard that Lamy was always in need of more priests. Some who came west didn't like the wild, untamed country. A few developed unacceptable behaviors such as drinking and gambling and had to be replaced. But when Lamy had asked the newly ordained Father Clement Grantaire to come with him nine years ago, Clement eagerly accepted. He made one request. He asked if he could be assigned a parish far out in the hinterlands. That had surprised Lamy, who said most new priests waited in silence for their assignments. Clement said he was anxious to begin his new life in God's service. Lamy commended him, then chortled, calling Clement the most brash new priest he'd ever met and said he would certainly accommodate him but asked him why he wanted such a posting. Clement answered, "It seems like a good idea."

Clement knew part of his calling was to serve God and believed another part was to atone for his abandonment of God in Mexico and for his libertine ways. To find redemption. Accomplishing that meant being as far from temptations as possible. When he arrived at Our Lady of Good Tidings church and saw the village of Penquero, he thought he might have been too zealous in his request. The village, whose name meant keeper of orphaned lambs, was a handful of squat, adobe buildings that, along with the church, made up three sides of a square. The people called that dusty square the plaza. A stone community well sat in the middle of it. It was more than a far cry from his beloved Paris. But time had tempered his misgivings and he found a real happiness in helping the people of his parish, located near the eastern border of the territory a little north of where the Canadian River crosses the Texas state line. He helped them bring in their crops of corn, gave a hand to repair and replace adobe on their houses, gathered wood and cow chips so every home would be warm in the winter. He also baptized the newborn children, heard their confessions, blessed the marriages of the young, administered the last rites to the dying. Yes, Clement needed all of this, accepted it, to feel that he was accomplishing the work he'd come here to do: not only God's work, but also repaying the debt he owed God. God had something in mind for him, Clement was certain. Otherwise, why would He have saved his life, twice? But Clement did ponder, from time to time, if this was all God intended for him.

His atonement was a different matter. He knew enough not to succumb to any temptations of the flesh. Penquero was a town of families mostly, all Mexican. Daughters were virtuous and Clement took his vow of celibacy seriously. There was also the conversation he'd had with one of the priests assisting Lamy in Santa Fe shortly after he'd arrived in the territory. That priest told him that certain behaviors, "sins of drunkenness and sloth and any of the other Seven Deadly Sins," would be dealt with harshly by Lamy. "However," he warned, "should you succumb to any lustful dalliances in your parish, your parishioners may very likely save the bishop the trouble and deal with you themselves." Clement didn't know if that statement was based on actual experience in this new wilderness or not, but he knew he would avoid testing its veracity.

Of course, Clement also accepted he had his weaknesses that he carried with him. There were often moments of desire, and he would combat them with prayer. The struggle for redemption was constant.

"May I offer you some water?" Clement asked as they went inside the house. It was a simple room with a hard, dirt floor. A small crucifix hung by the door. A blanket stretched across the middle separating the kitchen from where Clement slept on a wooden cot. They sat at the table and Clement poured Lamy a cup of water from a chipped clay jar.

Clement set a loaf of bread, a dish of honey and a plate down for Lamy, but he politely declined, saying the heat had taken away his appetite. He did take another cup of water. As he drank, Clement noticed the archbishop's hair had become grayer and his face more drawn in those few months since he'd last seen him.

Even so, the water and rest and shade from the sun seemed to revive Lamy, who got right to the reason for his unexpected visit. "I have come to ask for help because I need money. Not donations, you understand. I am asking for loans. Work has come to a standstill on the cathedral. I need the men back. The stonemasons, the teamsters, laborers, everyone. They haven't been paid in nearly six months. Most have already taken other jobs. But this work must continue."

Clement had heard of work on the cathedral stopping before, once for over year. The reason was always the same: a lack of money. But this was the first time that Lamy had come calling seeking funds. Unlike the dozens of hospitals, schools and orphanages the archbishop had built or that were under construction across the archdiocese, the cathedral was the only one to be financed entirely by donations. But now Lamy was asking for loans. This was serious.

"I wish I could be of help," Clement said. "But this is a poor parish."

"Yes, I know," Lamy said, an edge creeping into his voice. "That's why I'm not asking for donations. I'm prepared to draw up and sign promissory notes. And I will pay a good interest rate on the loans. Is there anyone in your parish who may be able to help?"

"Two years of drought have dried up more than some of the creeks around here," Clement said. "My parishioners offer their services in lieu of coins in the collection plate. Like *Monsieur* Aguirre out there pulling the weeds from the church rooftop. His brother Emmanuel brought in a new baptismal font for the church that he had carved himself. The women take turns washing my vestments. I know that's not what you need but that's all we have."

Lamy took a breath. "I didn't mean to be abrupt with you, Father. Forgive me. I've been to so many parishes in these last weeks. The work has stopped. I must have the men back."

"I thought work had progressed well on the cathedral when I saw it at your investiture," Clement said. "It was a few years since I'd been to Santa Fe, but I heard people say it will be beautiful."

"Do you know what some in Santa Fe are calling it now?" Lamy asked.

Clement shook his head.

"Lamy's folly." He glanced out the window, then back at Clement. "It's not even half completed. The walls . . . You can see where the stained glass windows will sit, but that's as high as we've gotten. Volunteers hung the doors the day before my investiture as a gift. There's simply no money. I've done everything I can think of to find a remedy. I went back to France to raise money. I went to Baltimore and Chicago and St. Louis. I sold my carriage. It was a comfortable carriage, too. And I miss it. My backside misses it more, I assure you."

They looked at each other a moment and then laughed.

"It's true," Lamy said. "I'm not a young man anymore."

"Well," Clement said, "perhaps some of the merchants in Santa Fe would make you the loan."

"My credit is already extended with many of them. And understanding and patience have their limits. So many made generous donations when we began this work And others, good friends like Abraham Staab and Willi Spiegelberg, have since offered me more money. Mrs. Thomas Catron, a very sweet woman, offered me five thousand dollars. It was tempting, but I couldn't take it, not from any of them. It wouldn't be right."

"Catron," Clement said. "I know that name." He knew Catron was an important man but he also heard he was part of the Santa Fe Ring. Land speculation, mining interests and finance were its pursuits, and nearly always there was some black-hearted deviousness involved, or so he'd heard. Almost anyone who lived in this territory knew about the Ring.

"He's the United States attorney for this territory," Lamy said, and drummed his fingers once on the table. It was a gesture Clement had seen Lamy do before when he was troubled. If Lamy were a card player, that would be a bad tell.

"Is something troubling you, Excellency?"

Lamy thought a moment. "One hears stories. Suffice it to say that Mr. Catron is a . . . disquieting man." He took a drink of water and shot a furtive glance at Clement. "I did accept a gift of one thousand dollars from a brothel madam in Santa Fe."

Clement couldn't help but laugh. "How did that happen?"

"She waited for me in her carriage one night to come out of church. I recognized the carriage. It was mine before I sold it to her. She handed me the money wrapped in a red, silk handkerchief. I don't condone her profession, but she is one of God's children. And she asked no favor in return." Lamy chuckled. "But do you know what she told me?"

"What?"

"She said the money was insurance."

"Insurance?"

"She said she didn't know if there was a God, a heaven and a hell. But if there was, she wanted to be covered when she died."

Not even the madams Clement had known in Paris had

concocted such a contrivance, but he had to admit it had merit. "It's heathen in thought yet hopeful in spirit."

"A fine point, Father," Lamy said with a wry smile.

"I still wish there was something I could do to help you," Clement said. He meant it.

"I know you do," Lamy said. "It's just . . . I've spent over fifty thousand dollars on construction so far. I can't abandon it now. It has to be finished."

Clement noticed the faces of several children peeking over the windowsill and he motioned them away. They ran off, squealing with excitement.

Lamy looked out the window after them.

"I'm sorry for the interruption," Clement said. "Visitors here attract attention."

Lamy was still looking out the window, his thoughts elsewhere. A few moments passed and he said, "When I came to this place over twenty years ago, all I could see were mud huts. In Santa Fe, every building looked like it was about to collapse. And when I saw that crumbling stable of Bethlehem that passed for a church on the plaza, I knew at that moment I would build a cathedral, a proper house of worship, like the great churches back in France. Something grand. Something for all the people here." He indicated the children playing out in the plaza. "For them. And their children."

He turned back at Clement, who saw the half-smile on his face.

"I always say Providence will never abandon us and I believe that," Lamy said, "I must believe that."

"Where will you go from here?" Clement asked.

"I was going to go see Father Boucard in Mora and then on to Fort Union before returning to Santa Fe. The fort commander invited me to come for a visit. Perhaps I could secure a loan from him or his officers. He brought the post band to play at my investiture. They were quite good."

An idea struck Clement while Lamy spoke. "How much money do you need, Excellency?"

"At least a thousand dollars. Two would be better."

"May I ask how much you have with you?"

"Thirty-one dollars. Sadly."

It was worth a try, Clement thought. "If you will allow me to take that money and you remain here for a few days, I believe I can help you. My parishioners will see to your needs."

Lamy frowned. "Well, I—"

"It would be an honor for them. They already know you're here. The children spread the word quickly." He indicated the window. Peering through it, Lamy saw a number of curious people looking his way from out of their homes and shops.

"Tell me what you have in mind," Lamy said.

"I can't. I humbly ask that you trust me."

Lamy considered Clement silently, and handed him the leather pouch he had tucked inside his belt.

While Lamy went out to greet the villagers who had gathered in front of the church to welcome his visit with festive songs, Clement stripped off his cassock, trousers and flannel underwear, and washed himself at a small basin of water. Even though he knew he had many miles to travel across this hot dusty country, it didn't feel right or proper to him to start off feeling dirty and sweaty. He pulled on his other clean pair of flannel underwear, though they were even more faded and worn than the others, meaning that seams were torn and holes had appeared. A clean shirt, a black coat and black corduroy trousers followed. Nothing fancy. He'd purchased them in Santa Fe when he arrived in the territory. He already had a pair of brogans and his floppy hat. Along with two long, black priest cassocks, they were the only clothes he owned. He had no revolver. Priests didn't carry them. Besides, he didn't have enough money to purchase one. So far, he'd had no reason to need a firearm. He left behind his Breviary, the slim volume of prayers, mostly the psalms, every priest must read each day. It was to remind them of their vow to serve God. For what Clement had in mind, the Breviary had no place. As for not fulfilling his daily obligation to read the Breviary, he would make amends to God on his return.

He went to the small desk in the corner of his bedroom, opened the drawer and took out the worn deck of cards he kept inside. Using his thumb he fanned the deck once, smiled and placed it back in the drawer. He couldn't take the deck with him. It could draw suspicion he didn't need, like he was some card sharp. Of course, he no longer gambled, but kept them as a kind of remembrance of his good friend Dekker, who was never very lucky at cards. He'd picked them up when he passed through St. Louis on his way to the territory years ago. Sometimes at night when he couldn't sleep, he'd play faro against himself. The cards were comforting. Like the psalms.

Outside, Clement saddled his horse, a buckskin gelding he called Paris. Once he had the hackamore over Paris's head, he put Lamy's money pouch inside the saddlebag along with a few cold tortillas wrapped in a cloth. He hung his canteen around the saddle horn and tied a blanket roll on the back of the saddle.

Lamy approached him and asked, "Would you like to make your confession before you go?"

Clement nodded. As he had a long journey ahead of him, cleansing his soul by confessing his sins in the sacrament of confession was an advisable idea. Should he encounter some mishap, he would not want to be denied entrance to heaven due to some sin staining his soul.

Crossing himself, Clement leaned close to Lamy's ear and whispered. "Bless me, for I have sinned. It has been many months since my last confession. I have cursed on many occasions, usually when I am doing physical labors and I know that is no excuse."

"I understand. Go on," Lamy said.

"There are times I catch myself eyeing some of the women here. I pray and ask God to keep me strong, but my sin of lust is often. I know I have committed other sins, but I cannot think of them. Forgive me for that."

"We all wrestle with temptation. We are weak, but we are also God's children and God forgives us when we ask for forgiveness. Life is a constant struggle to gain the kingdom of heaven. For your penance say five Our Fathers and make a good Act of Contrition."

Clement silently recited the Act while Lamy prayed, asking God to forgive Clement's sins and grant him grace. Then Clement knelt for his blessing and closed his eyes. He felt the archbishop's hand, his left, gently on top of his head and knew Lamy made the sign of the cross with his right as he offered the blessing in Latin.

Rising to his feet, Clement faced Lamy's stern visage and could tell the archbishop wanted to ask him about his plan. Neither spoke, though, as Clement mounted his horse.

"Providence will not abandon you!" Clement heard Lamy shout as he rode away.

Clement prayed he would be right.

Heading west, Clement expected to cross Ute Creek shortly after noon. Only a sliver of moon would show this night, but he felt certain if he kept going into the evening and then got an early start the next morning, he'd cross the Canadian before midday and, with God's blessing, reach his destination by sundown. As he'd heard from old Aguirre and others, "When you see the flag, you're maybe a day's ride away. Maybe less."

Chapter Eight

About eleven the following morning Clement saw the flag. It was plain to see above the rolling, treeless plains to the west. At this distance it was hard to tell that it was the stripes and stars of the United States, but old Aguirre hadn't been exaggerating when he said the flag was *muy grande,* very large, and that the flagpole at Fort Union was over one hundred feet high.

Clement patted Paris's neck, gave him a kick and thanked God. He needed to reach the fort by nightfall. He'd dip down into a depression, lose sight of the flag for a brief time, ride back up and there it would be. Off to the northwest, a swirling column of dust rose up a hundred feet into the air. People called them dust devils here. Back when he was in the legion in Algeria, the Arabs said they were ghost winds. Then he smiled at the memory of Dekker who called them "evil women," because "they're completely unpredictable. She'll sway and beckon, and then she'll spin into you, lift you up and throw you down, laughing the whole time." Clement watched it dance and sway for at least half an hour before it vanished in the heat.

A few hours later and about eight miles out from the fort, Clement caught sight of a line of telegraph poles stretching north from the village of La Junta. They looked like toothpicks set out in a row. The telegraph line angled off to the southwest in the direction of Santa Fe.

Clement stopped in the village to water his horse. While Paris drank, he splashed water over his head to cut the heat and dust.

The Turkey Mountains rose up in the distance up ahead to the right. A rocky ridgeline jutted out of the ground on the left. It ran for miles, as far as he could see toward the horizon. Clement climbed back on Paris and continued straight for the flag.

When he finally saw the fort itself, it was across the rolling distance in the long light of the setting sun. As there was no stockade around the fort, he could make out several corrals. Horses and mules milled about inside two of them. Cattle were in a third one. Soldiers crisscrossed the fort grounds. The buildings were made of adobe with flat roofs and white columned porticos. Most had tall chimneys, one near each corner. But that flagpole seemed to reach toward heaven.

It was so dry; Clement knew he'd been trailing a dust cloud for hours. He wasn't surprised when, a couple of miles out from the fort, a mounted patrol approached. Three men. They ordered Clement to halt. Old Aguirre had warned him about this, too. *In thee, oh Lord, I put my trust,* Clement prayed.

"What's your business here, mister?" a corporal asked him.

Clement said he was passing through and had been riding all day.

"Where you coming from?"

"Down around Mora." He noticed one of the other soldiers eyeing Paris closely.

"You from Europe? France maybe?"

Clement nodded. In all these years, he'd never lost a bit of his accent. "That's right."

The Corporal grunted. "Thought so. You feeling sick?"

"No. Just hot and tired."

"How about your horse? He poorly?"

"He's like me, I'd say."

The soldier eyeing Paris nodded at the corporal. "Horse looks good."

"We got to be careful, mister," the corporal said. "Can't allow contagion near the fort. Man or beast."

"I understand," Clement said. "Any chance I could get something to eat there?"

"Find food at the sutler's store. Get something to drink at the Billiard Saloon. Just head on in real easy. Doc'll examine you before you're allowed on the post. Got to make sure you got no sickness."

Clement nodded and rode on. The Billiard Saloon. The memory of his billiard ball duel had never left him in all these years. Stupid as it was, he knew full well it had brought him to this place. In its own way, it had made him what he was now. That and the legion.

It would be close to dark before he reached the fort, but no matter. He needed the night for what he wanted to do. And this time now gave him a chance to consider his plan again, to get it straight in his head. He didn't wish to have to tell any lies, but he didn't see that he had much choice. Like saying he was from around Mora. He'd make his peace with God later about all of this. But for what he had in mind, he couldn't very well admit he was a priest. And he figured no one would recognize him. No one should since he'd never been to the fort before, and no soldiers had come to Penquero that he'd ever seen. He'd concocted a story about himself in case anyone asked. He kept it simple. And a name. He thought it best not to use his own in case someone came looking for him later. He had been Victor Cheval in the legion. It would do again.

Sergeant Amos Tully was in a foul mood, even though it was payday. A stocky man with a pockmarked face, he sat at a table in the Billiard Saloon. It was part of the sutler's store on the post. Beer was the only alcohol it served, and warm to boot. And there was word the price of a bottle of beer would be going up from fifty cents to a dollar. Tully took a swig of his beer, grimaced and cursed the day he joined the U.S. Cavalry.

Sitting at the table with Tully was his friend Red Howarth, the quartermaster sergeant. Howarth, his dour expression even more pronounced at this moment, was complaining that he'd been ordered to put names to all the graves in the post cemetery marked as unknown. "You know how many there are? One hundred and three. And there's no record to be found anywhere. My predecessors didn't even bother to keep a list. How am I supposed to identify those men? That's almost a third of the graves that nobody bothered to put a headstone on. Lazy bunch of—"

"Aw, Jaysus, I don't give a damn about dead men," Tully said, cutting Howarth off in mid-sentence. "I'm breathing and I got thirteen new greenbacks in my pocket right now. And I got most of my last two months pay locked up in my quarters and what I'd like to know is, when in the hell our illustrious post commander, his highness Captain Howard Ellis, is going to lift the restriction on Loma Parda."

"We all want the answer to that one, Amos," Howarth said.

"A thirty-minute ride's all it is," Tully said, disgustedly. "Six miles away. Ain't nothing."

"Get no argument from me," Howarth said.

"Hell, a man with a powerful thirst could walk to it in less than an hour." And Tully knew he was such a man. The siren songs of strong whiskey and loose women beckoned in the little village of Loma Parda. So did games of chance like poker, roulette wheels, three-card monte and faro. Gambling was against regulations at the fort, but it was rarely enforced. Tully glanced over at four troopers at a table across the room playing poker. Nobody cared. Not Tully or Howarth or the barkeep. The whole point was getting away from Fort Union, a place Tully considered about as exciting as a prairie dog hole.

A little fracas five weeks ago had soured the captain on granting leave to the men. It was all on account of Private Josey Pickler, who had the first poke of his life with one of the whores in the "hog ranch," the name the men gave to the best of the several whorehouses in Loma Parda. Pickler, a witless Nebraska youth, fell in love with that trollop and wanted to marry her and didn't like it when other men enjoyed her services. He got drunk as a fiddler's bitch one night, took a knife and killed a New Mexican man who was bragging on his conquest with that "little curly-haired strumpet with the pretty mouth down the hall." Pickler was arrested immediately by the Mora County sheriff, who was having his own needs tended to a couple of doors down that same hall. And he'd been none too happy about the interruption. The captain was informed early the next morning, but as the incident had occurred off the post, that made it a civil matter. To make things worse, the dead man had four brothers. They pulled Pickler from the jail the next night while the sheriff and the rest of the townspeople were putting out a fire that had mysteriously erupted at the abandoned church and shot him full of holes. The captain decided Loma Parda was "an evil place, a festering nuisance, a modern-day Sodom," and declared it off limits until further notice.

"Two things I know to be certain," Tully said. "First, the captain can kiss my arse. And, second, it ought to be a requirement that every man be properly acquainted with hard liquor and jiney poking before being allowed to enlist in the god damn U.S. Cavalry." He tilted his beer to his mouth and sucked down the last swallow.

The front door to the saloon opened. A man stood there. A civilian. His clothes were dusty. A sweat-stained, floppy hat covered his dark hair. Tully guessed him to be around forty.

"The sentry said I could get something to drink here," the man said. "I've been riding all day."

A Frenchy, Tully thought. Same as some of these black-robed

pape priests in the territory. But this one didn't look like most of those sorry bastards to him. They had a soft look, especially around the belly and the eyes. Not this man. He was lean and hard. When he took off his hat, Tully saw an old jagged scar on his forehead. He figured you don't get that preaching from a pulpit. "We got water," Tully said. "We also got something that passes for beer, if that would suit you."

The man went to the bar.

Tully heard jingling, like coins, as the man walked. He exchanged a look with Howarth, stood up and joined the man.

"Beer," the man said to the barkeep.

"It's piss-poor beer," Tully said, "but ain't nobody died from drinking it. Not yet anyway."

The barkeep set a bottle down. "That's four bits."

The man reached into his leather pouch on his belt, pulled out a gold dollar and set it on the bar. Tully heard other coins clinking against each other in that pouch.

"I'll have another," Tully said, digging into his pocket.

The barkeep set the beer on the bar for Tully and the man indicated the gold dollar he'd put down. "That one's on me."

"A prosperous man," Tully said, shoving his paper money back into his pocket. "Thank you kindly."

Tully took a swig from his bottle. Horse piss, he thought. But, more importantly, he wondered if this man might be enticed into a game of cards or maybe billiards.

"You like a game of billiards while you get your gullet wet?" Tully asked.

The man took a pull from his bottle. "No," he said. "Don't care much for billiards."

"Oh," Tully said. "Where'd you say you was headed?"

The man looked at his beer and grinned. "Haven't decided. Maybe Colorado."

"What's that accent of yours?"

"French."

"That archbishop or whatever the hell he is over in Santa Fe. I hear he's from France, or some damn place."

The man shrugged.

"What part of France you from?"

"Paris."

"Well now. How'd you end up in this godforsaken hole?" Tully lifted his beer to his mouth.

"A woman," the man said.

Tully snorted and looked at him with a narrowed eye. "Running from or chasing after?"

"Trying to forget," the man said with a half-smile.

Tully laughed. "Having any luck with that?"

The man shook his head.

"Give it time," Tully said sagely.

The man tipped his beer to Tully and took a swig.

"What's your name, mister?" Tully asked.

"Victor Cheval. You?"

"Sergeant Amos Tully." He shook Victor's hand, and did not let it go. "You ain't wanted for anything, are you? Running from the law?"

"No. I'm not."

Tully noted that this Cheval didn't try yanking his hand away. And he looked Tully straight in the eye when he answered. Tully figured he was likely telling the truth. It wouldn't help things having the civilian law ride in and arrest a wanted man in the Billiard Saloon. The way his highness the captain's mind worked, he would surely close it down, claiming it was attracting a bad element or some such damn thing. And this stranger did have money on him.

"Since you ain't a wanted man," Tully said, "maybe you'd be interested in a little friendly game." He called over to the troopers at the table. "What're you playing, girls?"

"Poker," one of the troopers said, "and all I'm getting is one bad hand after another. But you're welcome to join in, Sergeant."

"Well, Upshaw, maybe it's about time to switch your game," Tully said to the trooper. "Try a little faro. Don't have to concentrate so hard."

"Might do that," Upshaw said.

Tully looked at Cheval. "Care to try your luck?"

"That sounds tempting," Cheval said. "It's been a long time since I played faro." He turned to the barkeep. "Is there any chance of getting something to eat? I can pay."

"Got food next door in the sutler's store," the barkeep said. "Canned sardines and—"

"Won't be necessary," Tully said, cutting off the surprised barkeep. Tully was formulating a plan, and it meant making sure Cheval's money went on the gambling table, not in the sutler's cash box.

"I think we can accommodate this man," Tully said, nodding at Howarth. "What do you say, Quartermaster Sergeant?"

Howarth picked up on Tully's nod. He told Upshaw to get over to the mess hall and bring back a plate of food. "Anybody stops you, tell them I sent you."

As Upshaw went out, Tully turned to Cheval and said with a grin, "All right. Who'll be the bank? I got thirteen dollars I can put up. You?"

"I think I've got about thirty," Cheval said.

That was all right with Tully. Rules said whoever put up the best stake was the banker and that meant he dealt the cards. Besides, Tully was already feeling lucky.

While Cheval ate the slumgullion stew Upshaw had brought him, Tully told Upshaw and the other troopers to spread the word about a faro game in the Billiard Saloon. Within ten minutes two dozen men were at the bar, beer in hand, ready to play. Tully got two fresh decks of cards from the barkeep and handed them to Cheval. More troopers arrived as Cheval laid out thirteen spades face up from one deck on top of the table. He shuffled the other deck and wagering began in earnest.

An hour later, Tully had lost the thirteen dollars he had in his pocket. He'd also lost another thirty he had from previous paydays hidden in his quarters. He joined Howarth at the bar and ordered a beer. Howarth told him he'd lost half his pay, figured he'd have another beer and turn in.

"A lot of the men playing tonight," Howarth said. "A lot of pay is riding on that table."

That got Tully started on some figuring. There were about eighty enlisted men on the post. Nine were in the guardhouse. Three were laid up in the hospital. Fifteen on guard duty. A couple of the teetotalers didn't gamble. At eleven dollars a month for enlisted men, a dollar more for corporals and thirteen for sergeants, plus pay from the last two months, that comes to around . . .

Tully took Howarth outside. "I got an idea about how we can both make a tidy sum here tonight."

Howarth snorted. "I've lost enough already."

"This'll work."

"How's that?"

"Your quartermaster fund."

Howarth blinked at Tully. "I can't gamble that money."

"Ain't nobody going to know."

"No. You forget the inspector general is due any day. He'll be going over my books and the figures there have to add up to the monies on hand. That's money I'm responsible for. I have to account for every dollar."

"We don't need all of it."

"Can't do it," Howarth said, waving Tully off.

"You got more money sitting over there in your office than

you spend."

"That's right. That money's for the purchasing of—"

"I know what it's for," Tully said irritably. "And I also know every payday the paymaster gives you your allotment. How much money did you tell me you got in the quartermaster fund now? Over four thousand dollars, was it?" Tully pointed inside the saloon. "Damn near every trooper on the post is in there gambling his pay. I know Upshaw and his lot have gambled away two months pay already, each! There's got to be close to eight, maybe nine hundred dollars in there. Let's get some of that for ourselves."

Howarth looked away from Tully.

"It's not like I'm asking for all four thousand," Tully said. "We borrow a few hundred to make a few hundred more. Nobody's even going to know you took the money out of the fund. I'm telling you, I can break this Frenchy."

"I don't know," Howarth said with a grimace.

"Come on, Red. Any losses can—"

Howarth snapped his head back at Tully. "I thought you said you could break him."

"I can, damn it!" Tully said, trying to keep his voice down. "But I'm saying, if there's any losses, you can make them up by paying less for corn and hay and wood and anything else these yokel Mexes around here want to sell you. You set the rates. Who the hell else they going to sell to?"

"Too risky."

"We can win."

Howarth looked away and shook his head. "Can't do it."

"You're a gutless one, you know that? Look at them boys crowded at that table. They can't lose their money fast enough. That's the beauty of this. I can feel it in my bones."

"Wait, what about that money you got from selling all that old equipment?"

"That was last summer. That money's gone."

As a company sergeant, Tully knew well that Fort Union supplied every fort in the territory with equipment and provisions, from ammunition to turpentine. The reason was because he was one of four sergeants responsible for the loading and unloading of those supplies. And every few years, some of those supplies would be deemed obsolete. That past summer, old muskets, Burnside carbines, McClellen saddles, bridles, blankets and a slew of other pieces of worn-out equipment—everything from gloves to lariats to spurs—had been ordered sold at auction by Captain Ellis on account of replacement equipment coming in. The captain had even put ads in the newspapers, but almost no one had showed up to bid. The auction pulled in a paltry four hundred and two dollars. The captain had figured five or six thousand at the very least. And he might have gotten it had it not been for Tully coming up with the scheme to sell off over half of those goods between Albuquerque and Chihuahua, Mexico, with the help of the Lucero brothers, civilian freighters hired by the army to transport government stores. Yes, sir, a lot of folks had already purchased goods weeks before the auction. Of course, after paying the Lucero brothers and their teamsters and giving Howarth a cut for doctoring up the paperwork and turning the other way since all the goods came out of the quartermaster stores, Tully only cleared a few hundred dollars. But he figured it was better to have that in his pocket than the army's. And Tully had pretty much screwed and drank his share of the money away at the hog ranch within a couple of weeks. Of course, that had not been the first time Tully had used the Lucero brothers to transport and sell army equipment. He'd made that a going concern of his for the last three years, starting after the last visit by the inspector general. What had made him successful at it was that he'd been smart enough not to get greedy, which cut down on the chances of getting caught. But the threat of getting caught was the key to leveraging Howarth. Tully had to go for his weak spot.

"Well, you're probably right, Red," Tully said. "Taking money from the quartermaster fund isn't such a good idea."

"Now you're talking sense."

Tully chuckled. "You know, I heard there's a rumor been floating around."

"Rumor?"

"Damnedest thing. About a certain quartermaster sergeant's 'appendage' and its fondness for a lot of them whores at the hog ranches." Tully watched the blood drain from Howarth's face. "Well, it would appear them stories those whores told me about you and your, ah, 'friend' there 'tween your legs are true, then. What's that name they say you call him? Sergeant Major Happy Jack?"

Howarth shushed Tully. His furtive glances reminded Tully of a scared schoolboy.

"I did some figuring." Tully said. "All that poking you were doing didn't add up. Happy Jack costs you more money than your pay grade allows."

"First of all that doesn't matter now since the captain put Loma Parda off limits. And besides, I didn't take much," Howarth said, the worry evident in his voice. "And I always put it back in the quartermaster fund out of my own pay the next payday. And—"

"And someday the captain's going to have to rescind his order on Loma Parda. Even he'll realize you can't keep troopers away from hard liquor and loose women forever. He'll have an uprising on his hands soon. And if I know you, you and your 'Sergeant Major' will be busy making up for lost time. I'd say the quartermaster fund will be seeing a steep withdrawal."

"You'd turn me in?"

"I said no such thing. But word like that, well, it can get

around fast. Might give the captain the notion to keep closer tabs on the quartermaster."

"You bastard."

"That is a fact," Tully said. "Mama knew a lot of men. Now what about that money?"

Tully and a sulking Howarth went to the quartermaster's office. Howarth grudgingly opened the money bags he kept under the floorboards behind his desk.

"Why in the hell don't you get a proper safe to keep the money in?" Tully asked.

"Why in the hell don't you go to hell," Howarth grumbled.

Tully snickered, counted out two hundred dollars and they went back to the game.

A half an hour later, Tully sent Howarth to get another three hundred.

By nine o'clock, most of the men on the post had come in to try their luck. When Cheval put his leather pouch filled with greenbacks into his saddlebag, got on his horse and left the post shortly after that, Tully figured that Frenchy had cleaned out better than half of the troop. Including him.

Heading across the parade ground to their quarters, Howarth was apoplectic.

"Five hundred dollars!" he said, trying to keep his voice down. "How am I going to account for that?"

"That man was luckier than a man ought to be," Tully said and spit.

Howarth gritted his teeth. "Did you hear what I said? Five hundred dollars!"

"I heard you," Tully snapped. "Guess you and Happy Jack won't be going to the hog ranches for awhile."

"Sweet Mother Mary," Howarth whined. "What am I going to do?"

"All I know is losing is one thing," Tully said. "And feeling like I got cheated is another. That Frenchy son-of-a-bitch probably lied about everything. Goddamn it all to hell!"

Chapter Nine

Clement was well aware he'd won a sizeable amount of money and wanted to get away from the fort as quickly as possible. That Sergeant Tully's face was beet red when he lost the last of his money. And he lost quite a lot. He also drank quite a lot, too. The other one, his friend Sergeant Howarth, looked stricken during the last hour. Tully's winnings were up and then down, up and down again. It had been a long time since Clement had played faro, but he easily recalled other players like Tully who had let their vanity get the better of them.

After catching some sleep along a creek bed near La Junta, Clement woke at dawn. He needed food for the long ride home. But not before he counted his winnings. One thousand four hundred nineteen dollars. That should make the Archbishop very happy indeed.

With a grin on his face, Clement recited the twenty-third psalm in thanks. "The Lord is my shepherd. I shall not want . . ."

A light breeze wafted a savory aroma drawing Clement into La Junta. A moon-faced Mexican woman was stirring a pot outside an old adobe hut with a crooked doorway. Clement asked her if he could get something to eat. "I can pay."

She studied him a moment, then scooped a spoonful of the contents from the pot into a tortilla and offered it to him.

Clement took a bite. The flavors danced on his tongue.

"Oh, that is superb," he said. "What is this?"

"Lamb, sausage, chili peppers."

"I'll have another, please. What do you call this?"

She frowned. "Lamb, sausage, chili peppers. I told you."

He heard her grumbling about *"gringos pendejos"* as she stirred the pot. But he didn't care. He was hungry and this was delicious. He finished off the first one while she prepared the second.

"You need something for your travel?" she asked.

"Yes. Long way to go."

She handed him the second one and went inside the hut. When she came back out, she handed him a sack tied at the top with a piece of rawhide. "Cornbread. Fresh today."

"Many thanks," Clement said. He reached into his pocket for a few greenbacks he had put there from the winnings for just such an occasion. "What do I owe you?"

"Dollar. And half a dollar."

Clement paid her and she gave him change from her apron pocket.

He headed east, eating the second stuffed tortilla. Things were looking better. Maybe the heat would break today, he hoped and he prayed the twenty-third psalm. *The Lord is my shepherd.*

Within the hour, it felt even hotter than the day before. The blue sky was cloudless, from the black-crested mesas to the northeast to the tree-covered mountains in the west. That sky was beautiful, but the heat was relentless and the air didn't move. Around noon Clement rested. He poured water from his canteen into his cupped hand so Paris could drink. Tipping the canteen to his mouth, he took only a swallow. It felt good going down his throat. He wanted to make it home before midnight. Paris was a good horse, but pushing him to travel over a hundred miles in a day could ruin him. And it crossed Clement's mind that it would very likely take a toll on *him,* as well. But he needed to put this money into Lamy's hands. He had to keep moving. Do the best he could, with God's help. Mounting his horse, Clement offered a prayer asking God to see him home safely. "And a little rain, Lord, to cut this heat. Not for myself, but for Paris." Clement patted the gelding's neck. "He has a long way to carry me."

A few hours later, Clement was about a half mile from the Canadian River. He recognized the thicket of cottonwood trees straddling the riverbank where he had crossed the day before. He also saw a Mexican man wearing a sombrero, a brown shirt and sandals driving a herd of sheep across the river, coming his way. Clement counted about forty head or so. A black and white dog barked and nipped, keeping the sheep moving as they shook water from their wet, wooly coats.

Clement was glad for the break when the man stopped to speak with him. "*Por favor, senor,* could you tell me, am I close to Fort Union?"

"Keep heading west," Clement said. "You'll see the flag."

"Ah, yes, the flag. But how far?"

"Maybe five hours walking. When you see it, you'll be about a day out."

"*Muchas gracias.* Are you coming from the fort?"

"I was there last night."

"Did you see any sheep?" the man asked hopefully.

"No. Only cattle."

"That is good news," the Mexican said. "I sell these sheep at the fort. My village will have money. Would you have any food? I haven't eaten since this morning. I cannot pay, but I am hungry."

Clement grinned and took a couple of pieces of cornbread from the sack.

"Muchas gracias," the Mexican said, taking them from Clement's hand. He took a bite and made a contented sound.

He walked on past Clement, following his herd. "Watch out for the mosquitoes at the river. *Vaya con Dios.*"

"Vaya con Dios," Clement said. He turned, watching him go and made the sign of the cross with his hand, giving the man a blessing and offering a silent prayer for a safe and successful journey.

There were mosquitoes at the river. A swarm buzzed around him as he approached the sandy bank. He swatted at them and brushed them away from his ears. Paris shook his head and swished his tail to drive them off. And almost as soon as they appeared, they vanished. That's when Clement saw the man. He was standing by the big tree at the edge of a thicket. His back was to Clement. His chestnut horse, a mare, stood close by, ground tethered. He wore a faded blue coat and black boots. The coat was open and pulled back exposing a holstered revolver on his left. Butt forward. The man's hands were on his hips. He was peeing against the tree. Clement slowed down. That shepherd hadn't mentioned a man at the river, and Clement hadn't seen him ride up. No matter. He would pass to the other side of the river, fill his canteen, let Paris drink and be on his way.

That's when the man finished his business, turned and faced Clement, reaching across with his right hand to his left hip, gripping the gun butt and drawing his revolver. A white bandana covered his face below his eyes. Clement saw those eyes beneath the curled brim of his gray hat. They were blue, and full of menace.

Merde! Clement thought, pulling back on the reins. "Don't shoot," he said. "I have no gun."

"So now. French. Far from home, aren't you, frog eater?" the man said, his voice low and gravelly, like a growl. "Get off your horse. Slow. Drop the reins on the ground."

Clement did as the man said. He cared nothing at being

called names. He'd been called worse in his life. By staying calm he knew maybe he'd get out of this alive. But his life wasn't all he needed to get out of this. *The Lord is my shepherd.*

Using his revolver, the man motioned Clement away from his horse.

Clement stepped away a few feet.

"More," the man ordered. "Put your hands up."

Clement raised his hands as he backed away then stopped. He watched as the man went to Paris and opened the saddlebag on the right side. That put Paris between him and the man. There was nothing in that saddlebag.

The man came around to the other side. He kept his revolver pointed directly at Clement. "You don't carry a gun?"

"No."

"You're either the most trusting man in this territory or its biggest damn fool. Which is it?"

Clement shook his head. The man stared at him for a moment. Clement saw a look in his eyes and thought the man might shoot him right there. The man continued his stare and reached into the other saddlebag and pulled out the leather pouch. Clement watched as he opened it and checked its contents.

"You've done well," the man said with a chuckle and slipped the pouch back into the saddlebag. "You steal it?"

Clement shook his head again and the man raised his revolver and pulled the hammer back. The click seemed to sound so loud and sharp to Clement, as though the revolver was right next to his ear. He saw the cylinder rotate the cartridge chambers, and his eyes fixed on that black hole at the end of the barrel only a few feet from his face. "I won it," he said. But there was something . . . That cylinder . . .

"You shouldn't have any trouble making it all over again, then," the man said as he eased the hammer back into place, slid his revolver into the holster and turned to go to his horse.

"But it's not my money," Clement said.

The man spun around. "So you did steal it."

"No."

"Which is it? You a thief or a gambler or a liar? In some circles, there's no difference, so be careful how you answer me." He reached over and gripped the butt of his revolver.

Clement took a breath to keep his voice steady. "I did win it. And I need that money. Take my horse. Leave me my winnings."

"Well, now," the man chuckled. "You asking, or telling?"

"I'm asking," Clement said.

"You're a polite one, frog eater," the man said, releasing the gun butt. "But it won't do."

Clement watched as the man took Paris's reins and walked over to his horse. He hated the idea of pleading. He needed that money. And then he realized what was wrong when he was looking down the barrel of the man's revolver. The chambers in the cylinder were black. Empty. That gun wasn't loaded.

The man mounted his horse, still holding onto Paris's reins. And Paris shied away. The man yanked the reins and Paris pulled back harder, nearly unseating the man.

Clement charged, grabbing the man to yank him down, and a hard wallop on top of his head dropped him to his knees. Stunned, he got up on one knee and saw his hat on the ground nearby. Then the man stood before him, the silvery barrel of a revolver waving in front of his face. And he heard the man's voice. "You're a smart one. You figured it out. No bullets in my gun. Damn pack of wolves was after me last night. Used my last rounds to kill a couple and drive off the rest." Clement heard him chuckle. "But you pay attention close now, frog eater. You know your Scripture?"

Scripture? Trying to clear his head, Clement looked up. The bandana still covered the man's face.

"The cock has crowed three times," the man said. "Time to go to the garden and weep."

This bandit taking the Lord's words to Peter in this blasphemous way insulted Clement, but he still felt disoriented, dizzy. He saw the man raise his gun to strike him again. *The Lord is my rock.* Clement pushed himself to his feet and, at the same time, threw his fist, and hit the man square in the face. He heard a sharp crunching sound and felt bone break and collapse under his knuckles.

The man screamed an oath, brought his free hand to his nose, blood gushing over the bandana, went back a step, then clubbed Clement over the head with the butt of his revolver, harder than the first time.

Clement felt as though his legs had been jerked out from under him as he fell backward and hit the ground. Opening his eyes, he tried to focus on the man's face only inches from his. He saw the cold blue eyes. Fury swirled in them. Dark red blood spread out across his bandana.

Clement heard words but they sounded so far away. "You broke my nose, you son-of-a-bitch!"

Clement saw the man spit out a gob of blood and had the sensation of someone taking hold of him and being pulled up at his chest. His head lolled back. He tried to speak. "I nee . . . tha . . ."

It sounded like someone was shouting at him from far away again. Something about leaving him for the wolves to drag back to their pups to eat. His head hurt like sin.

"I nee . . . tha mahney," Clement said, the words slurring. Lifting his head, he saw the man raise his revolver up in his hand. He caught a glint of sunlight on the gun barrel, right before it came hurtling down at him.

Chapter Ten

Clement didn't know what jostled him awake. He was being bumped around though, and it was a cramped space, that was certain. His head rested on a rolled up duster. An old woolen blanket covered him. It smelled like a horse. Hard wooden boards lay beneath him and on either side. Above he could see the burnt orange glow of dusk in the evening sky. Hard creaking sounds of wood and wheels filled his ears, and, along with more jostling, he realized he was in the bed of a buckboard wagon. Lord, his head hurt. He reached up and felt a bandage. It wrapped around his head. The wagon dipped and threw him against the side of the bed. Hard. He let out a sharp groan.

"How you feeling?" he heard a smoky voice say.

He glanced up and saw the driver's back. All he could make out was a hat and coat.

"I said, you feel all right?" the driver asked, turning his head.

Clement couldn't see the face in the shadow under the wide brim of the hat. "Tired. Sore," he answered slowly, groggy. He felt a chill but then it passed.

"I'll bet you are. You got a couple of good-sized lumps and a bad cut. Rest now. Sorry about the tight space back there. No place else to put you."

Wanting to see where he was, Clement pushed himself up and gripped a long wooden box for support. It sat upright, on its side. That's what was taking up half the space in the wagon bed. His head felt like a tangle of cotton. He squeezed his eyes shut and hung on to the box until the tangle cleared. Opening his eyes, it took him a moment to focus. In the fading light of day, he saw a team of horses pulled the wagon and mountains rising in the distance. Glancing down, there was bold black lettering on the side of the long box: *Hold for R. Scott.*

"What is this?" he asked.

"Hannah," the driver said. "My sister. If there's judgment in the afterlife, she went straight to hell."

Clement wondered if he heard correctly. He was clutching a coffin? The black letters started swimming before his eyes. Another chill came over him. He gritted his teeth to try to stop them chattering. His shoulders shook, and suddenly, his whole body, from his head to his feet. Feeling his grip on the coffin weaken, he slid down onto his side and passed out.

Sergeant Amos Tully sat in the mess hall with his supper of beef hash, beans and bread, enjoying the tales Sergeant Nicholas Shumway told him of his adventures in Santa Fe. Shumway had returned that evening from a two-week furlough. He had butter-colored hair and a thick beard.

"The Palace Saloon," Shumway said. "You get there, ask for Arletta. Tell her you're a friend of mine. She'll take good care of you."

"I'll do that," Tully laughed. "You still planning to open a saloon the day you retire?"

"On occasion. Other times I think I'd do better to marry a rich widow."

Tully liked Shumway. He could hold his liquor, was probably the best poker player he'd known and told the most salacious stories. They'd served together in the war under General James Harrison Wilson. In Tennessee at the Battle of Franklin, their division had successfully repulsed a flanking attack by that Confederate devil, Nathan Bedford Forrest. What a glorious fight that had been. Their rout of Forrest saved the day for the Union forces. More significantly, it was also the day Tully had saved Shumway's life when he shot a rebel horseman out of his saddle as he bore down with his saber on Shumway, whose pistol had jammed. Shumway had always been grateful to Tully for that.

"I better be turning in," Shumway said.

"Come on now, it's still early," Tully said. "Wait and let me finish my supper and I'll buy you a beer at the Billiard Saloon."

"I got the duty tomorrow."

"Already? Ah, Kirby's a true horse's ass for putting you on without so much as a welcome back." Tully didn't like Lieutenant Kirby, the post adjutant. He didn't like the trim little moustache he wore. He didn't like his Massachusetts accent, which sounded like a wheezing concertina losing air. But mostly, he didn't like Kirby because Kirby was an officer.

"Bellah's in hospital, Cooper's on duty today and you've got a shipment to get out tomorrow," Shumway said, picking up his plate. "That leaves me to go polish my brass and shine my boots. The sergeant of the guard has to look sharp."

Tully took a couple more mouthfuls of food, when Howarth suddenly appeared next to him. Every time he saw Howarth it was a reminder of that damn French card sharp. To make matters worse, Tully knew this couldn't be good because Howarth looked like he was about to wet his pants.

"I need to talk to you right now," Howarth said.

"I'm trying to eat my supper here," Tully said.

"The inspector general has arrived," Howarth whispered urgently, grabbing a chair and sidling up next to Tully. "My quartermaster fund is shy five hundred dollars. Remember?"

"You hardly let me forget."

"Well, where am I supposed to get that money?"

Tully gave his friend a hard look. "I don't know."

"You don't know? I'm in real trouble here! You told me you'd have a plan!"

"Keep your voice down, damn it," Tully said, glancing around to see if any of the men were looking their way. "I wish I could help you. I wish that Frenchy son-of-a-bitch who cheated me would show up again so I could get that money back. But it's not looking very likely now, is it?"

"But you made me give you that money. You have to help me."

Tully didn't like hearing Howarth's whining. He also didn't see that there was anything to be done. The paymaster wasn't due for another three months, but what could he do, give him an advance on his pay? Not very damn likely! And nobody had five hundred dollars lying around, even if he was inclined to borrow it, God forbid. No, this was not good. Especially for Howarth . . . Well, just Howarth, come to think of it. After all, that five hundred was money Howarth was responsible for, not him. No one saw him take it. If asked for his version of the events of that night at the Billiard Saloon, Tully would recollect that Howarth was the one who shoved money into his hands begging him to gamble it for him. *And did you know this money was taken from the quartermaster fund? Absolutely not, and had I known, I would have advised Sergeant Howarth to return it forthwith.* No, this was all poor Red's problem. And if Red were to claim otherwise, saying Tully had lied and try to implicate him in his mishandling of army funds, well, there'd be no choice but to do his duty and tell what he knew about Red using those same funds at the hog ranches in Loma Parda. No two ways about it, Red was in deep trouble of his own making. That was plain enough.

"Damn it, you're right, Red. You know, the Lucero brothers are due here tomorrow to pick up shipments for Fort Stanton and Fort Seldon," Tully told him. "They usually carry cash money with them. Let me see what I can do." He saw relief spread across Howarth's face.

"Thank you, Amos," Howarth said in a quivering voice. "I knew you wouldn't let me down."

Tully patted Howarth's shoulder and watched him walk away. Yes, sir. It was too bad Red couldn't keep his pecker in his pants. Too bad he couldn't be trusted with army funds. Too bad he was such a disgrace. That's what everyone would say. Tully decided he would miss Red after he was court-martialed and very likely sentenced to that new military prison in Kansas at Fort Leavenworth. Misappropriation of funds was a serious charge, one Captain Ellis was a real stickler about. He took such thievery as a personal slap in the face. And it was too bad that, like him, Red Howarth only had a few more years to go before retirement. Yes, sir, too bad indeed.

The steady tick of a clock. The soothing aroma of chicken soup. The soft contours of a real bed. The fresh comfort of clean sheets. Clement wondered if he was dreaming. He opened his eyes. Overhead he saw the wooden beams of a ceiling. He tried to sit up but his head hurt and dizziness overtook him. Waiting a few moments, he felt a little better and managed to sit up and take in his surroundings. It was a log cabin. More than twice the size of his place. With a wooden floor. He counted four windows. The shutters were closed and latched. That ticking was a tall longcase clock in a corner. The hands read a quarter past eight. There was a table and chairs on the other side of the room. Looked like his clothes were lying folded on one of the chair seats. His brogans were under the chair. Two revolvers lay on top of the table. One was broken down into pieces, left in the middle of being cleaned, he guessed, seeing the rag and bowl setting nearby. Plates and cups were stacked in a hutch. A rocking chair sat by the stone fireplace. A fire burned in it. A kettle hung from a cast iron rod over the fire. The soup he smelled must be simmering in that kettle. And a coffee pot sat off to the side in the glowing embers. A double-barreled shotgun stood propped by the front door.

Glancing over at a chest of drawers near him, he saw a couple of framed photographs standing on top. Twisting around to take a better look at them, he realized that, except for the bandage still wrapped around his head, he was naked.

The front door swung open. Somebody's buckskin-covered arms appeared, carrying a pile of firewood. The man, his back to Clement, went to the fireplace and set the pile down. He wore a buckskin coat with the collar up and a printed blue skirt. Skirt?

Clement frowned. "Who . . . ?"

The skirt spun around and Clement saw her. As a priest, his mission was to see to the spiritual welfare of people, to offer guidance in this life against sin and temptation on earth for an everlasting life of peace and glory in heaven. He wasn't supposed to take note of a person's outward appearance. His responsibility was to their inner appearance, their soul. However, this woman, about his age, he guessed, with green eyes that twinkled in the firelight and reddish-blonde hair pulled back into a bun, was a beguiling sight in this roughhewn place.

"Oh, you're awake. Good," she said, her features going from startled surprise to pleasant relief.

It was the same smoky voice Clement had heard in the wagon. And he was aware he was sitting up in the bed, sheet and blanket covering only the lower half of his naked body. He slid back down, pulling the covers up, and realized the futility of his actions. He was naked and there was nothing he could do about it. Nor did he know how he got that way, because he surely didn't recall stripping off his clothes.

"You feeling better?" she asked. "You look better. I'm Rachel

Scott. Would you care for some coffee? Soup? Both?" She took off her coat and hung it on a peg by the door.

"Both," he said, clearing his head and trying not to stare at the graceful curves of her figure. As she turned, he also could not help but notice the revolver stuck inside the belt around her waist. "Is it day or night?"

"Night," Rachel said and closed the door. She set that revolver on the table with the others, then went about preparing his food. "You've been out all last night and today."

I should have been back at my parish by now, Clement thought. He opened his mouth to ask where he was, but Rachel kept talking as fast as a thought entered her head. Or maybe she was nervous. He couldn't tell which.

"Sorry about your clothes but I had to get you out of them. You were burning up with fever and they were wringing wet by the time I got you back here last night. I washed them. They're on the chair. Your fever broke this afternoon. So did the Indian summer. Chill's definitely on us. How about a little whiskey in your coffee? Help get you back on your feet. You got a name?"

"Yes. Uh, Victor Cheval." Clement hated to lie but felt he couldn't take any chances, given his circumstances.

He watched her take a bottle of Collier's whiskey, half empty, from the hutch and pour a shot into the coffee cup she had ready. She brought the cup and a bowl of soup over and set them on top of the chest of drawers.

"Now wait one minute," Rachel said. "I got something here should fit you." Opening one of the drawers, she reached inside. "Those flannel drawers of yours aren't fit to wear anymore. Torn seams. Holes front and back. These may do." She laid a pair of flannel underwear on the bed. "My husband's. Almost new. I sewed up the bullet hole. Don't know why I mended it, really."

With her back turned while she went to get a spoon and a

stool, Clement slipped on the flannel underwear. He fingered where she had sown up the bullet hole in the chest. And wondered what had happened to her husband and when he was coming back.

She returned and set the stool by the bedside, then arranged the coffee cup, soup bowl and spoon on top of the stool. "Eat what you want. There's plenty. Oh, I forgot a napkin."

He took a spoonful of soup. It was hot and savory. "That is good. Thank you."

"Glad you like it." She opened the napkin and laid it under his chin.

"Please tell me," Clement said, wiping his mouth, "where am I?"

"My house. Colfax County. Near Cimarron," she said, bringing a chair from the table over and sitting by the bed.

Clement had heard of Cimarron. A little town up north. It was on what used to be a big Mexican land grant a fellow by the name of Maxwell owned but sold a few years back, someone had said. Gold had been discovered on that land. A lot of folks had been lured by that siren song of quick riches. Clement understood that well enough. He'd heard Lamy, or was it another priest, say that more than a few Catholics lived there but the Protestants outnumbered them. Something about squatters, too . . . And Clement suddenly realized he had to be maybe three days ride from home and was already two days late. The Archbishop was no doubt very displeased with him. Nothing he could do right now. *C'est la vie.*

"And your husband. Where's he?"

"I thought I said. He's dead. Year ago next month. He was . . ." The words caught in her throat. She glanced down. "Sheriff said it was an accident. Drunken cowboys shooting up the town. Didn't find him 'til next morning."

Clement was about to say he'd say a prayer for him but

caught himself. Offering prayer might provoke questions he'd prefer not to answer. "I'm sorry to hear that."

As she nodded her thanks, Clement saw her push away the sadness that briefly clouded her face.

She let out a deep breath. "Now then, I hope I haven't embarrassed you about taking off those wet clothes you had on. I did my best keeping my eyes closed but it had to be done. Besides, I was married for twenty-two years. I know what a man naked looks like."

"You saved my life," Clement said. "Many thanks."

"That's fine," she said and considered him a moment. "I don't mean to pry but I couldn't help but notice a couple of old scars you have. One across your head. The other one, in your ribs. Looks like an old bullet wound."

Clement didn't know what she was after, or why. But he knew that "don't mean to pry" meant she wanted an answer.

"I'm guessing you got those fighting," she said. "In battle?"

"I did."

"Which were you, Yankee or rebel?"

Clement realized Rachel assumed he fought in the American war between the northern states and the southern states. He decided it best to keep things as simple as possible and he gave her what he thought would be a safe answer. It was a truthful one, too, at least as far as he saw his service in the legion in Mexico. "The losing side."

She cast her eyes down and drew her lips in, which made the corners of her mouth drop. She slowly nodded once and said, "I can understand your feeling. Did you own a place somewhere, and Yankees came in and burned you out, maybe?"

"Nothing like that," he said.

"I see," she said gently and raised her eyes at him. "Well, it's different for people who had land and lost it. I'm sure you had your reasons for joining the Confederacy. A lot of us did. But we got plenty of Yankees and a fair number of southerners in these parts. Most of us get along well enough, but a lot of southerners, around here anyway, they don't see themselves as losers. Hearing the word wouldn't set right with them."

"I understand," Clement said, certain she was telling him about herself.

"I hope so. Now, one other thing I need to ask. What were you doing out there on that prairie with nothing to your name?"

Setting down the soup bowl, he took a sip from the coffee cup. That shot of whiskey did help. "I'm a drifter, as you call it here. I came over from France."

"I gathered that. We got one of you French folks in town. Runs a saloon."

Clement smiled. "That doesn't surprise me."

"You'd like him, I expect. Friendly sort. Had another Frenchman here for a few years. A priest. Father Fourchegu. He got sent down to Sapello about a month ago. Supposed to start a new parish there, I heard."

Clement didn't know Fourchegu, but he knew Sapello was northwest of Las Vegas and about as remote a spot as Penquero.

"Did anyone come here in his place?" Clement asked, clearing his throat.

She shook her head. "Don't know when a new one's coming, either."

Clement decided it wasn't worth worrying about right now.

"So," Rachel said, "tell me what happened to you out there."

"A man robbed me at the river. He took my horse, my belongings, everything." He did not mention the terrible statement the outlaw made, perverting the Lord's very words to St. Peter.

"Get a look at him?"

Clement shook his head. "He wore a mask over his face."

"Too bad. Whoever it was gave you a couple of nasty cracks

on the head."

Clement grunted. "I broke his nose."

"You don't say," she said and smiled. "How do you know you broke it?"

"I felt it break when I hit him. He said so, too."

"And he didn't shoot you?"

Clement took another sip of coffee. "He said something about bullets and wolves but I don't remember." And he wondered what he was going to do about the Archbishop's money.

"You are one lucky pilgrim. If he's around these parts, a busted nose all swole up shouldn't be hard to spot. Probably a Texan. Only a Texan would leave a man to suffer like that and steal his horse, food, money and gun. Lowest form of critter on two legs."

"I don't carry a gun." As soon as he said it, Clement regretted it for it would likely create questions he did not wish to answer.

She stared at him a moment. "You don't carry a gun? What are you, a preacher?"

"No," Clement said, "I'm not a preacher."

"Well, you're either the luckiest man alive or the biggest fool walking God's earth."

It struck Clement that maybe he was both, being that he had won all that money and then lost it to a thief.

"I . . . I'm sorry," Rachel said, suddenly flustered. "I shouldn't have said that." She stood and dragged the chair back to the table. "Your business isn't mine. Just surprising is all. Only people I know without a gun within reach in this country is the Reverend McMains. And he *ought* to carry one." She sat down and picked up the cylinder of the revolver she'd been cleaning earlier. "Like this Army Colt. These were my husband's guns. Not that they did him any good when he got killed. Now you go on and finish your supper. Let me know if you need anything."

Clement watched as she took a rag and started wiping the cylinder off. An awkward silence followed.

"I'm not angry with you, Rachel," he finally said.

She looked up from her cleaning.

"I'm . . ." Now it was his turn to be flustered. He tried to think of something to break the tension. "Tell me what brought you to this place."

"Oh," she said and took a breath. "Well, after the war, me and my husband, Ethan, and my mama, we left Missouri for a new start. That longcase clock there was about all we had left after the Kansas Red Legs burned us out. It was Mama's. Anyway, this territory seemed like a good place. We got here, land was available and we were able to buy a few cattle with the last of our money. Herd grew and things got better for a time. Mama died a couple of years later." She indicated the photographs on top of the chest of drawers. "That one on the right is Ethan. I like keeping it close. He served the Confederacy."

Looking at the picture of Ethan alone, Clement saw he was a bearded man with a somber expression. He held a Colt revolver crossed over his chest and his other hand rested on the butt of another revolver in his belt. He wasn't dressed in any uniform, though. Except for the revolvers, he looked like any farmer. Clement had heard about bands of Confederate border guerillas during the war while he was studying in the seminary in Baltimore. The newspapers called them all murderers and arsonists. Clement chose not to ask her about it. The other photograph was a wedding picture. It showed Ethan standing behind Rachel, his hand on her shoulder. Ethan wore the same expression in that one, too. Looking closer, Clement thought he caught a hint of a smile on Rachel's face.

"Ethan didn't want me to smile. Said it was a serious moment, but I couldn't help it," Rachel said. "That was a happy day for me. If you don't mind my asking, you married, Mr. Cheval?"

"No. And . . . Victor. You can call me Victor."

"Fine. Any other family?"

Clement shook his head. "None." He thought he remembered Rachel saying something about a sister. "You?"

"Sister. Hannah. She's dead," Rachel said as she set down the cylinder, picked up the barrel and rammed a cloth into it using a small rod. "Wasn't worth a damn. Coffin's in the barn."

Clement thought he'd blundered bringing up the subject, but Rachel seemed to warm to it.

"Had to go all the way to some hell hole in west Texas to fetch her. Hadn't seen or heard from her in years but she had a will and my name was in it. One last way to needle me." Rachel shook her head disgustedly and continued cleaning the gun. "When I showed up to get her, I found out she'd been a member of the United Friends of Temperance. Didn't surprise me. She was always passing judgment on people. Apparently she'd taken it upon herself to get all the saloons in town closed. Some folks didn't care for that. It didn't help she was disagreeable and ill tempered her whole life. Always wore a scowl. Never knew why. She was reading her Bible walking through town when she passed by a new saloon they were building. A brick landed on top of her head. Bad luck, they said. Killed her on the spot."

Clement thought sure he heard her chuckle. "Why did you have to go bring her back? Couldn't they bury her there?"

"The town refused to bury her. I know what I said earlier about Texans, but I couldn't fault them for that. They knew her well enough. The undertaker told me he put extra fluid in her on account of waiting on me. I also heard they had a big celebration. Half the town was drunk by dawn day after she died."

She stopped cleaning the Colt and looked at Clement. "I

know Mama wouldn't want Hannah buried among strangers. She'll be buried at the cemetery in town. Mama's buried there. So is Ethan. I'll be buried next to him. But I'm not having Hannah buried anywhere close to Mama or me. She always treated me like dirt, and for no reason I knew. If I had my way, I'd stick her in a hole out behind the barn."

Clement thought he heard a noise outside.

"Hadn't been for her, my helper around here wouldn't have run off," Rachel continued and picked up a scrap of paper from the table. "I found this on the door when I got back. Listen to what he wrote. 'Miss Rachel, Have gone to find my fortune. Signed, S. Worden.' "

"What does that mean?"

"Means he took off for Baldy, where there was word of another gold strike right before I left. I was gone nearly two weeks on account of that damn Hannah. Only—"

Clement raised his hand. "Listen," he whispered.

A horse whinnied, followed by what sounded like a pail getting kicked and clattering across the ground.

Rachel jumped up, ran to the door, grabbed the double-barreled shotgun and rushed outside.

Trying to get to his feet, Clement felt wobbly.

A gunshot rang out and a bullet thudded into the wooden door. Dropping to the floor, Clement heard the sound of men laughing.

"We're going to burn you out, *mujer*!" a Mexican voice shouted.

His heart pounding, Clement took a deep breath, made a dash to the table, picked up the revolver Rachel had set down earlier and checked to make sure it was loaded. Slipping on his brogans, he went out the door, ducking quickly out of the light thrown through the open doorway and tried to see where Rachel had gone. Laughter came from the right. He turned and heard the loud blast of the shotgun. And more laughing.

"You want to make a stand, you got to learn to keep on your feet!" another voice taunted, high and reedy.

Coming around the corner, Clement saw Rachel scramble up from the ground and reach for the shotgun a few feet away. She seemed unhurt. Clement guessed she must have slipped somehow and dropped the shotgun. It went off when it hit the ground. She ran toward the barn where two men on horseback waited. One of the men wore a sombrero and held a burning torch while the other one, in a slouch hat, lit his torch from it. Bandanas covered their faces.

Slouch Hat, winding his arm to toss his flaming torch into the barn, shouted, "This is what happens to little fools what won't listen!"

Torchlight caught Rachel's movement as she ran, yelling at the men, "Get out of here, you cowards!"

Raising his arm, Clement cocked the revolver. The heaviness of it felt odd, yet his grip on the handle and the curl of his finger around the trigger was strangely familiar, as though only days had passed since he'd held a gun, not years. He asked God to keep his hand steady, his aim true and pulled the trigger.

The bullet kicked into the hard dirt in front of Slouch Hat's horse. The horse reared, right before Slouch Hat let his torch fly, throwing off his toss.

"Aw shit!" Slouch Hat shouted.

Clement saw the torch twirl wildly as it arched up, hit the crossbeam at the top of the barn entrance and drop harmlessly to the ground. Slouch Hat cursed trying to control his horse.

"*¡Cabron!*" Sombrero shouted and threw his torch into the barn. "*¡Vamanos!*"

Clement fired again and hit Slouch Hat in the arm. He heard Slouch Hat cry out, saw him hunker down, kick his horse hard and ride off.

Rachel raised the shotgun and let loose with the other barrel as Sombrero galloped away after Slouch Hat.

"Bastards!" Rachel yelled as Clement came running up. She grabbed his arm. "Help me before the barn goes up!"

They rushed inside. Clement saw Sombrero's torch on top of Hannah's coffin, still in the wagon bed. Flames had caught, scorching the dry coffin wood black. Thickening dark smoke rose toward the rafters. Rachel grabbed an empty burlap sack lying on top of the feed bin. Clement got to the wagon first and snatched the torch off the coffin. Using both hands, Rachel swung her sack over and over, smacking the coffin, beating out the flames.

"There's water in a couple of pails there," she said pointing at a pile of hay inside the opposite doorway

Clement handed her the torch, grabbed a pail and doused the smoking, charred wood.

"That was lucky," Rachel said, catching her breath. "I couldn't afford to lose my wagon." A horrified look crossed her face. "The corral! My horses!"

Taking the torch from her, Clement hurried with her to the corral where she was relieved to find four horses still inside, though the gate was wide open.

"They tried to run them out, that's for sure," she said, swinging the gate closed. "Good girls," she called to the mares and turned to Clement. "We better get inside. I'm cold and you're in nothing but your drawers."

Clement didn't feel cold, in spite of the frosty breath coming out of his and Rachel's mouths. His heart still pounded from all the excitement and danger. "What was that all about?"

"For a man who doesn't carry a gun, you did some pretty fair shooting," she said, stepping briskly toward the cabin. "Too bad you didn't drop at least one of them. You sure you're just a drifter?"

"I'm not anybody," he said, keeping up with her, lighting the way with the torch. He didn't tell her he hadn't meant to hit Slouch Hat, but it happened. Like a reflex he couldn't help. He didn't know whether to thank God for it or ask for God's forgiveness. What was certain was that shooting at those two bandits had very likely saved Rachel's life as well as her place. What was it Lamy had called out to him? Providence will not abandon you. But Clement still wanted to know about those two *criminels.*

Back in the house, he tossed the torch into the fireplace. That's when he noticed that both his hands were steady.

"Look at this mess," Rachel said annoyed, brushing at the dirt and grass stains down the front of her blouse and skirt. "If I hadn't tripped I'd've peppered at least one of those scoundrels."

Clement wanted answers. "Who were those men?"

"Hired guns. Some of them wear badges," she said simply as she warmed up her coffee.

He gave her a puzzled look. "I don't understand."

"I mean some of the sheriff's deputies are hired guns. Didn't get a good look at those two. For all I know, they could be the same ones who served me with an ejectment notice last week, then came back that night and shot at my house while I was fixing my supper."

"Deputies shot at your home *and* tried to burn your barn down?"

"It's how things are around here. They figure giving them a badge makes it legal, keeps them protected. They're making up their own laws. The—Oh, I forgot. You don't know about Colfax County. We got a war here."

"What do you mean a war?"

"You ever heard of the Santa Fe Ring?"

"I've heard the name," Clement said truthfully.

"A bunch of no-good lawyers and politicians who run this territory. Real sons-of-bitches, in my opinion. Excuse my language. The Ring's got everybody from that spineless Governor Axtell to judges and sheriffs all in their pockets. They buy their loyalty. They buy the elections."

Clement was about to ask how she knew, but Rachel kept talking.

"We had an election here last month. This Melvin Mills is the new representative in the legislature for this county. He's a lawyer. Beat a good man named Frank Springer. Springer was no friend of the Ring. That horse-faced Mills is. Word is our sheriff and his deputies brought in Mexicans from around here into town to vote. Some claim money was exchanged for their votes. But that's not even the worst of it. Lot of folks say the Ring's got blood on their hands."

"What do you mean?"

"I mean murder. They had Reverend Tolby killed. A decent man. A good Methodist. He was our minister." She took a drink from her cup.

"Why would they want to kill him?"

"He called the Ring out. Wrote letters to the *New York Sun* newspaper in New York City. Called it a many-headed monster. Said they were all thieves and liars. Then last month, shortly after that election, Reverend Tolby was found in Cimarron Canyon between here and Elizabethtown shot in the back. Twice."

"Maybe it was a robbery."

"None of his belongings were missing. His horse was found tied to a tree and they found his saddle in the creek some six, seven hundred yards downstream. The horse didn't tie himself up, and that saddle didn't float all that way by itself, neither."

"Were any arrests made?"

Rachel huffed. "Not a one. Sheriff Chittenden's a Ring man."

"How can you be so certain this Ring is behind it?"

"You know about the Maxwell land grant?"

"I've heard some things."

"The Spanish and Mexicans had land grants when this was their land. A man named Lucian Maxwell bought this grant years ago. His father-in-law had something to do with it, I think. It was actually two land grants side by side. Lot of land."

"How much land?"

"I'm getting to it. When gold was discovered on his land up around Baldy Mountain, prospectors came. Then ranchers and farmers brought in sheep and cattle. It was good land. Some people have been here almost thirty years. Mr. Maxwell asked for rent from most folks but he didn't try very hard to collect. Told Ethan and me to raise a good herd. Never asked us for a nickel in rent."

"I understand. But what's all that have to do with this Ring?"

"It was five years ago Mr. Maxwell sold his land, every last acre. Some English syndicate bought it. They set up the Maxwell Land Grant and Railroad Company. Of course, there's no railroad here yet but I guess they expect to get a good size piece of one, once it does. Anyway, those British boys want us gone first thing so they can portion up and sell this land to the highest bidders. Making a profit is the way of things. For some, it doesn't matter how."

The bitterness in her voice stung Clement. And making a profit at any cost had a sadly familiar ring. Like something Colonel Dupin told him down in Mexico a lifetime ago.

"We told those British we weren't leaving. This is our land. They called us squatters, said we were trespassing. We dug our heels in. And them, being four thousand miles away, needed some local lawyers to help them run things including running us off. Guess who they hired?"

"Ring lawyers."

"That's right. Thomas Catron and Stephen Elkins are the leaders."

Clement remembered Lamy had called Catron a disquieting man. "Catron's the United States attorney."

"Yes, he is. And Elkins is a damn Yankee, and it shames me to the bone that Tom Catron is from Missouri and served in the Confederacy. Damn him to hell."

She slammed down her cup and coffee sloshed over the rim.

Clement watched as she took a cloth to clean it up and then refilled her cup, adding a splash of Collier's.

She continued. "Those two must have had their mouths watering when they saw the land survey when Mr. Maxwell sold his grant. Claimed it was almost two million acres. That's close to half of this county. We figure Catron and Elkins and Mills and the rest get a cut from the British boys for every one of us they run off. The sheriff started handing out notices of ejectment. 'Either buy your land from the company or vacate,' he said.

"A few folks left. Said it was wasn't worth the trouble. And nobody's got the money to buy, if they were so inclined, which none of us are. Then some fellow from the land office in Washington decided last year that the grant was all public land. That meant we didn't have to leave. And now, Catron and that damn Yankee Elkins, who, by the way, was made president of the Maxwell Land Grant and Railroad Company by the damn British and now just happens to be the territorial delegate to Congress, are offering bribes and making promises to crooked congressmen and anybody else they need to in Washington to get that public land decision overturned. At least that's what Reverend McMains says. I told you about him."

She raised the pot at him, offering more coffee.

Clement shook his head. "He's the one you said ought to carry a gun."

"I did," she said and sat down. "He was Reverend Tolby's assistant. Took over after he was killed. Reverend McMains is trying to get help from Washington. Writing letters and such. He's sworn to find every person involved in poor Reverend Tolby's murder."

"I still don't understand what any of that has to do with his killing."

"I told you. He called the Ring out. That's when we started getting the midnight visits. Homes shot at, buildings fired, stock run off. Reverend Tolby wrote another letter to that New York newspaper and they published it, too. Named Catron and Elkins as responsible parties. I thought they'd bring a libel suit to try to shut him up. They had him killed sure as I'm sitting here."

"I wish you well with your fight," Clement said. "I truly do."

She stared down into her coffee. "During the war, Jayhawkers came in and ran us off our land. Burned us out. Left us with almost nothing." She looked up at him. "When we settled here, my Ethan said nobody would ever run us off again."

Clement saw the determination in her eyes and the fine color in her face. This was a handsome woman. Very attractive. The kind of woman he could . . . He closed his eyes and prayed. *Lord, please help me. Quickly. Amen.*

Chapter Eleven

Melvin Mills had a long face with deep-set eyes. His brown hair was lacquered into place with Bear's Oil. He was also in a foul mood. He'd been summoned to Santa Fe for a meeting earlier in the week with Thomas Catron. Upon his arrival, he was told to go to the New Era Chop House and Restaurant. Mr. Catron was waiting. At the completion of that brief meeting, Mills was instructed to return to Cimarron forthwith on the next stage, which happened to be departing in twelve minutes. Instead of enjoying a few nights in Santa Fe as he'd hoped to do, he snatched up his valise and carpetbag and ran for the stage depot. He stewed about his meeting with Mr. Thomas Benton Catron all the way back to Cimarron, a two-day trip with an overnight stopover in Las Vegas.

It didn't help that the stagecoach ended up running five hours behind schedule due to a broken axle, putting Mills into Cimarron at half past nine this night. His black coat and trousers, green vest, black bow tie, and white shirt were dusty and wrinkled. He'd been wearing these same clothes for the last four days and nights. A meal stop for tortillas stuffed with questionable meat and fried in lard had resulted in greasy drippings on his shirt and vest that did not improve his disposition. Stepping from the stagecoach, he accidently knocked his derby off his head. It landed in a pile of horse shit. That's perfect, he thought, as he got a wet rag and wiped it off as best he could. While he didn't have far to walk from the Barlow and Sanderson

Company Stage Line office to his house one street over, it did nothing to alleviate his misery.

Rowdies were enjoying a loud time drinking and gambling in Schwenk's Hall across the street. Fortunately, the light from the large windows at Schwenk's allowed Mills to make his way along the street, as there was no moon this night. There was just enough light that he could see the outline of his adobe house, and not far beyond it, the stone jailhouse. Actually, it was the ten-foot high stonewall surrounding the jailhouse. Only the peak of its pitched roof was visible over the top of the walls. Mills wondered if Sheriff Chittenden was inside and still up. He wanted to talk to him. But he decided it would have to wait because his foul mood darkened as he recalled, for the hundredth time, Catron's words as he walked into the back room of the restaurant to face his boss, his benefactor, the man who was making his life hell . . .

"This is your fault."

Catron's voice was low and sharp.

Mills knew he'd better tread lightly as he halted abruptly in front of the linen-covered table where Catron sat, a tumbler of Jameson in his right hand. His left rested on top of a folded newspaper. A platter of oysters on the half shell lay within reach. They looked delicious, and Mills was very hungry after that long stagecoach ride with occasional stops for beans and bread. But it was clear to him that Catron, a large man who, he once heard Stephen Elkins say, had the ruthlessness of a Roman emperor, was not inclined to invite him to eat.

Mills watched Catron take a drink of whiskey and wipe away a couple of amber colored drops clinging from the underside of his heavy moustache with his index finger. That whiskey looked good to Mills, too. But he wasn't about to ask for a drink. Not now. Seeing the glare in Catron's eyes, Mills knew better.

"Mr. Catron, I don't—" Mills began.

"Shut your mouth," Catron snapped.

Mills did. There was nothing else he could do. There were three things Catron did not like: being interrupted, being argued with and, in particular, being wrong.

"I get you elected to the legislature as the representative for the Colfax district," Catron said. "You had one thing to do. Put a scare into that Reverend Tolby. Make him stop writing those letters, I said. And you have him murdered. Shot in the back, no less. And not once. Twice."

"I did what you—"

"Did I tell you to speak?"

Mills stood still. His jaw tightened. He felt like some schoolboy being scolded. His scalp itched. He dared not scratch it.

"Your stupidity has turned this Tolby into a martyr," Catron said. "Your actions have thrown more light on us here." He opened the newspaper. "This is the New York Sun. *From last week. Listen closely. 'It is said that a few days before his death, Mr. Tolby had vigorously and publicly denounced some members of the Santa Fe Ring for their offences against society. The preacher boldly announced his intention of writing up the Ring rascals and exposing their nefarious actions for the eastern press.' "*

Mills wanted a drink. Desperately.

"Pay particular attention to this part," Catron went on. " 'No legal evidence thus far proves that the recognized leaders of the Ring had any connection or knew such an atrocious crime was in contemplation, yet it is impossible to make the majority of people in Cimarron and vicinity believe that they are guiltless, and the feeling against all persons who are supposed to be connected in any way with the operation of Catron, Elkins and Company is bitter in the extreme.' "

Catron laid the paper down and leaned back in his chair. Mills felt his heart racing.

"Do you know what you're going to do about this Tolby business?" Catron asked.

"I'm going to get Cruz Vega and Manuel Cardenas out of the territory," Mills said, trying not to let his nervousness show.

"No," Catron said and downed an oyster. "You're not going to do a damn thing."

Mills blinked, confused. "But, they shot Tolby."

"Fortunately, Sheriff Chittenden seems to be a capable man and has seen to making a creditable show of attempting to find the killer. Let him handle it. He knows what he's doing."

The insult directed at him in that last statement was vividly evident to Mills. And he was aware of the bitter truth of the statement, as well. Sheriff Chittenden knew full well Tolby was going to be murdered because Mills had met with him and Judge Longwell in the Cimarron jail the day before it was to take place. Mills and the judge had explained to Chittenden that his newest deputies, Vega and Cardenas, had agreed to carry out the deed. There'd even be a bonus: the mail carrier from Elizabethtown to Cimarron was suffering from the ague, so Mills told Florencio Donaghue, the local mail contractor and a good Ring man, that a couple of deputies were going to E-town the next day and they'd be pleased to pick up the mail satchel there and deliver it to the Cimarron post office. However, when the murder was being committed, Chittenden had seen to it to be miles away on the stage road running north between Elizabethtown and Pena Flor with Deputy Rinehart, following the trail of a couple of bandits who'd been robbing the Elizabethtown Express Coach along that stretch for nearly a month. He and Rinehart found and killed the two robbers, Clinton McKinney and Robert Keyes, alias "Coal Oil Bob," collected the one thousand-dollar reward the grateful folks of E-town had offered for them, and didn't get back to Cimarron until almost a week after Tolby's killing. Yes, sir, Chittenden knew exactly what he was doing, all right.

“Now, tell me what in the hell possessed you to give this task to a couple of Mexicans?” Catron demanded.

“I had . . .” Mills began and took a breath, “I had put out the word that men with particular talents were needed in, ah, Colfax County. They’d be made deputies. You remember you and I and Judge Longwell had discussed this arrangement earlier to deal with the squatters.”

“Yes, yes. Go on,” Catron said, annoyed.

“Vega and Cardenas arrived in town. From Colorado. Said they’d heard about the offer. I told them we had a prickly situation, explained the necessity of action required and they said they could take care of it.”

“They took care of it, all right,” Catron said.

The contempt in his voice struck Mills like a slap across the face.

“Did you or Longwell tell them to at least make it look like a robbery?” Catron asked.

Mills wanted to tell Catron that he and the judge had followed his instructions. He wanted to say, You told us to make Tolby stop. You said Tolby was a gnat that needed to be swatted. You said make certain he writes no more letters. That’s what you told us, you son-of-a-bitch. *Mills wanted to tell him all of that.*

Instead he said, “No, we didn’t.”

“Idiots and imbeciles,” Catron said, looked away and took another swallow of his Jameson.

Mills knew he needed to try to save the situation, and himself. “Vega and Cardenas aren’t going to say anything, Mr. Catron. They know what would happen if they did.”

“You better be right. For your sake.”

Mills nodded but said nothing. He waited, and time seemed to stand still.

“Mexicans,” Catron finally said distastefully. “The only good thing Mexicans did for this territory was give us the golden opportunity to take their land. And the only good thing you can do now is to get out

of my sight, get back to Cimarron and get those squatters off that land."

Mills walked up the steps of his front porch, slid the key into the door lock and entered his house. Dropping his carpetbag and derby on the bench inside the door, he took his valise and walked directly to his office, the wooden floor creaking beneath his shoes. His office was where he kept his liquor and he wanted to sit quietly, relax, enjoy his drink and try to forget about his humiliation by Thomas Benton Catron.

Going into the dark room, he struck a match and lit the lamp sitting on the corner of his desk. Taking the Remington derringer from inside his coat, he placed it on the desk, sat down and jumped, nearly pissing his trousers seeing a man sitting in the chair across from him. The man had his legs crossed, relaxed. He wore a gun belt. One gun on his left hip. Butt forward. He had short, sandy hair and hard, blue eyes. His nose was horribly swollen and crooked, the wide bruise black and yellow and ugly.

"You must be Mills," the man said.

"I am," Mills said, still scared. "And who are you?"

"Dixon Poth. I heard you were looking for men."

"The right men. How did you get in here?"

"Back door was unlocked. You should be more careful."

Mills nodded. "All right." He indicated Poth's nose. "What happened to you?"

"Nothing."

"Doesn't look like nothing."

"Nothing that concerns you," Poth said evenly.

The disquieting tone in his gravelly voice and the hazard implied in his words sent a chill through Mills. "Fine," he said, reaching for a lower drawer where he kept a Colt revolver and a bottle of Jameson.

"If you're thinking about having a drink, go ahead," Poth said. "But don't even think about reaching for that hog leg. I unloaded it while I was waiting for you." He opened his right hand, revealing the bullets, and dropped them on the desk.

Poth was obviously resourceful, Mills decided as he opened the desk drawer and pulled out the bottle of Jameson. "Drink?"

Poth shook his head.

"Well, I'm having one," Mills said, needing to calm his nerves. He took a glass from the drawer and poured himself two fingers. Taking it all in one gulp, he set the glass down.

"You've had your drink," Poth said. "Tell me about this job."

"There are squatters on this land. We want them gone. You'll wear a badge, report to the sheriff."

"You want it to look legal."

"The fact is it is legal."

A moment passed. "You said *we* want them gone," Poth said. "Who's *we*?"

"The Maxwell Land Grant and Railroad Company. A business venture in England owns it. They have asked us to act in their interest."

"And who is this *us*?"

"A small group of businessmen here in the territory." Mills poured another two fingers into his glass.

"Payment?"

"Twenty-five a week."

"Gold?"

"Greenbacks."

"And?"

"And what?" Mills asked, and took a sip of whiskey.

"You said this job was legal."

"Yes."

"The law is on your side."

"That's right."

"It has been my experience that my services are retained when the law has failed."

Mills smiled. "This is about taking steps to enforce the law."

Poth stared at him. Mills waited. His smile dissolved.

"Before I let myself in to your house," Poth finally said, "I stopped for a drink and a meal at Lambert's Saloon up the street. There was quite a bit of talk among the men there. About the law. About squatters. About public land."

"Regardless of what you may have heard, things are moving ahead. The rightful parties purchased this land. It is theirs, free and clear. The squatters are trespassing and must go."

"It isn't so much about what I heard. It's what I know."

Mills wondered what he was up to.

"I know about you and your partners. You're well-known in certain circles. I'm known, too. During the late war I was called the spawn of the devil. Others said I was an avenging angel. I still hear those names to this day. Some say you and your partners are shrewd businessmen and smart politicians. Others claim you're rapacious thieves and back-stabbing swindlers."

Mills shifted in his chair.

"But, like me, you and Catron and Elkins and the rest know it's best to keep those who oppose you off balance, until you're ready to strike. Am I wrong?"

Mills nervously tapped two fingers a couple of times on the desk, still unclear as to Poth's game.

"Tell me, if you believe me to be wrong," Poth said easily.

"You aren't wrong."

"Now that we have an understanding, let me return to the subject of payment. All agree that you and your partners are getting wealthy through your 'ring' of legal business ventures. Like you, I enjoy what I do because, like you, I have been able to make a very good living at it."

Now Mills understood. Poth was angling for more money.

Well, he'd get the rate he'd set for all the new "deputies." He leaned back in his chair. "The payment is twenty-five dollars a—"

"Fifty," Poth cut in, "for every squatter I convince to leave under his own power. One hundred for each one who refuses to listen to reason."

That last statement, *refuses to listen to reason,* struck Mills with a dread that he'd never sensed with Vega, Cardenas or the other one, Zeke Wilcox, whom he'd hired for this work. And until Catron's order to eliminate Tolby, this "work" meant using whatever methods were most expedient in driving these damn squatters off this land. But at this moment, Mills thought he had the means sitting right across from him to settle this squatter business. He felt a charge of anticipation because none of those others possessed the quiet menace of Dixon Poth. What was it he said he was called? The spawn of the devil? That was what was needed to clear the Maxwell Land Grant of the interlopers, the squatters and the troublemakers. And if Poth's methods worked, Mills knew he could convince Catron that the extra money was well worth the expenditure. Mills was certain, too, that success in removing these squatters would get him back into Catron's good graces, and *that* was paramount.

Reaching into a side desk drawer, Mills pulled out a folded piece of paper and slid it across his desk to Poth.

"That's a list of who you start with."

Poth opened the paper and read the list.

"You shouldn't have too much trouble finding them," Mills said. "They—"

"I hunted Missouri Bushwhackers for five years my own way," Poth cut him off, placing the list inside his coat pocket. "I'll find these my own way."

"As you wish," Mills said. "Oh, I almost forgot." He reached back into the drawer, found what he was looking for and held it out to Poth. "Your deputy sheriff's badge."

Poth took it. Mills watched him hold it in the palm of his hand, like he was weighing it. Poth grunted and shoved it into his pocket.

"Is there a good hotel here?" Poth asked.

"The National."

"You'll pay for my room."

It wasn't a question. Mills nodded, figuring he'd make up for the extra he'd pay for Poth's room by padding the charges of the next clients who came to him for legal services.

"The beds, they ticky?" Poth asked.

"Haven't heard any complaints."

"Safe?"

"You won't have any problems."

"No. Does it have a safe? For valuables."

"Uh, no," Mills said. "I don't believe it does."

"You have a safe?"

"No. I, I did but the combination lock froze up on it. I ordered a new one. From Chicago. Should be here in a couple of weeks. In the meantime, I had the blacksmith build this for me." Mills went to the closet behind him, opened the door and revealed a strong box. It protruded out from the wall at waist level and looked like it was inside a cage. L-shaped braces of pig iron bolted to the adobe wall formed a resting place for the box. Other iron braces wrapped around the box in a U-shape, further securing it to the wall. A padlock hung on the front of the strong box, and another padlock dangled on the front of the cage to secure the hinged iron lid.

Taking a pair of keys from his vest pocket, Mills unlocked the cage and box. "If you have valuables, they'll be safe in here."

Mills watched Poth reach down by his chair. When he came back up, he placed a leather pouch on Mills's desk.

"It's a lot of money," Poth said. "Over a thousand dollars.

When this job is finished, I'll come back for it. I'll also count it before I leave."

Mills wanted to tell Poth he could trust him, but somehow he knew it would make no difference to this man.

Poth left the office, the wooden floor moaning under his boots as he walked down the hallway.

Mills listened for the front door to close. When it did, he sat back down, exhausted. Sweet Jesus on the cross, he thought. A moment later, it occurred to him that Poth's expression had never once changed during their conversation.

Chapter Twelve

Sheriff Orson K. Chittenden woke with a start. Someone was pounding on the door of the jailhouse. A stocky man, Chittenden threw his feet over the metal bunk he kept in a corner in the front office and felt for his boots. He'd fallen asleep earlier fully dressed. The oil lamp on his desk was still lit. The pounding on the door continued, getting more persistent.

"I'm coming!" he shouted, scratching his craggy face.

Getting to his feet, he tucked in his wrinkled shirt as he crossed the stone floor to his desk where he'd left his pocket watch. One thirty. He rubbed the sleep from his eyes. His hands were beefy, his knuckles scarred from numerous boxing bouts over the years, most of which he'd won.

"Open the door! It's us!" It was a Mexican, his voice low and urgent.

"Cardenas?" Chittenden called out.

"Sí."

"Give me a minute."

Not one to take chances these days, Chittenden drew his Colt Dragoon from the holster hanging on the coat rack nearby. Using his other hand, he slid the wooden plank that barred the door from its braces and pulled it open.

"What in the hell happened?" he asked at seeing his deputy, Manuel Cardenas, wearing a sombrero and holding up another deputy, a hatless Zeke Wilcox, whose right arm was a bloody mess hanging in a sling. "Get in here! Take him back to a cell."

Cardenas half-dragged his companion across the floor, past the cast-iron stove at the entrance to the cells and into the first cell, leaving blood drops behind them. All four cells were empty, a lone cell on one side faced the other three.

Chittenden locked the door, grabbed the lamp and followed the two.

"Sorry, Sheriff, I didn't . . ." Wilcox murmured as he lay on a cell bunk and wiped his good hand over his sweaty, grimacing face.

"All right, Cardenas," Chittenden said, "what is this? I told you two to scare a few folks and raise a little hell, not get shot."

Cardenas removed his sombrero. "He needs a doctor."

"I can see that," Chittenden said. "Tell me what happened first."

"We went to the Scott place—"

Chittenden's face flushed bright red. "She shot at you? Tell me you didn't shoot her."

The man on the bunk moaned loudly.

"Settle down, Wilcox," Chittenden said.

"We did what you tell us," Cardenas said. "We go to her place. We call her out. At the barn, we have our torches. She comes out, and so does a man."

"What man?" Chittenden barked.

"*No se.* But he shoots and hits Zeke."

"And you didn't shoot her. You shoot at him?"

Cardenas shook his head and shrugged. "No, no. We no shoot nobody. Like you told us. The fire, it didn't catch. We got away. But Zeke, he is hurt bad."

"Yeah, yeah," Chittenden said. "Go get Doc Longwell. Be quiet about it. Tell him to bring his bag."

Cardenas left and Chittenden fumed. Who the hell was the man out there at Rachel's? He heard Wilcox moaning and asking for water. He tossed out some old coffee from a cup, filled it with water, gave it to him and took a closer look at his arm. Cardenas had cut off Wilcox's shirtsleeve above the elbow and used the sleeve as a tourniquet. The bandage around the elbow was soaked in blood. The arm was bent at an odd angle, too.

Chittenden sucked in a breath and blew it out. Bet it hurts like sin, he thought.

"It's throbbing bad," Wilcox moaned.

"Doc's on his way," Chittenden said and brought him some more water.

Chittenden liked Zeke Wilcox. He knew how to follow orders. He'd also been the only deputy to stay on after Chittenden's election. The other four deputies had quit. Perhaps they decided to seek their fortunes elsewhere, or maybe they didn't like the new sheriff's face. Whatever the reasons, they were of no consequence to Chittenden. What did matter was that they were gone and new deputies were needed. His first hire was Isaiah Rinehart who had ridden with him in the war. Because of that, Chittenden felt he could trust Rinehart. It was shortly thereafter that Mills took it upon himself to put out the word for men with "particular talents." Chittenden had taken a dim view of the idea altogether, given that he recognized the line between men who understood pushing to make a point, as Rinehart and Wilcox did, and those who were only too willing to simply draw and fire. But, hell, you couldn't tell Mills anything. Not a damn thing. He knew it all. He knew best. Prissy bastard. However, having no other men lining up to become deputies, Chittenden had grudgingly gone along with Mills and Longwell and approved the hiring of Cardenas and Cruz Vega. Of course, their idiotic blunder in killing Tolby had created a shit stew as far as Chittenden was concerned, but so far he'd managed to keep the lid on that boiling kettle. For a Mex, Cardenas had turned out to be pretty reliable if told exactly what to do. And he'd sworn to Chittenden that he didn't shoot Tolby, that Vega had fired both shots and that he'd acted only as a lookout. Chittenden hadn't decided if he believed him or not. Of course, the fact that Cardenas was there acting with Vega made him just as guilty in Chittenden's eyes, but still, he had come to allow respect for that Mex. As for Vega, Chittenden was not impressed with that cocky little back-shooting chili picker.

"Thanks for coming, Doc," Chittenden said when Cardenas returned with the potbellied Doctor Robert Longwell, the only medical man in Cimarron. He had heavy jowls and thick sideburns. Chittenden thought his face looked like a stirrup. In his hands Longwell carried a black bag and a kerosene lantern. He'd been elected as a judge in Cimarron last month, the same time as Mills and Chittenden. If Chittenden needed Longwell's medical expertise, he called him Doc. If it was for a legal proceeding, it was Judge. Chittenden hoped to always stay on Longwell's good side, in the event he ever got a bullet hole or brought up on some legal malfeasance.

Longwell took a pair of spectacles from his coat pocket, cleaned them with a handkerchief, put them on and examined Wilcox's arm. Between Wilcox's howls and whimpers, Longwell came to his conclusion. "I need to take that arm off," he said.

"No," Wilcox cried. "You can't."

"I have to. The distal humerus and olecranon and—"

"The what?"

"The bones that meet up to let you bend your elbow," Longwell said. "They're shattered at the joint."

"Fix it," Wilcox begged.

"I can't," Longwell said, slipping his glasses back into his pocket. "There's nothing left to put back together, nothing to mend. That bullet saw to that."

"Please," Wilcox said, reaching feebly for Longwell with his good arm.

"We need to get him to my home," the doctor said, not noticing Wilcox's reach as he turned to face Chittenden.

"Let's get him to his feet," Chittenden said to Cardenas.

"No, he's too weak," Longwell said.

"Pick him up," Chittenden instructed Cardenas and he and the Mexican each took an end of the blanket Wilcox was lying on and carried him between them to Longwell's house. Longwell lighted the way with his kerosene lamp.

They placed Wilcox on a table in Longwell's examination room. Chittenden watched Longwell roll up his sleeves, wash his hands and then take a bottle of chloroform from his medicine cabinet.

"Don't, don't take my arm," Wilcox pleaded. "Please! Sheriff, Manuel! Don't let . . . don't let him do it! Stop him!"

"Hold him down," Longwell instructed Chittenden and Cardenas. "I don't want him thrashing about."

Longwell poured some of the chloroform into a clean cloth and quickly covered Wilcox's nose and mouth. After a moment of struggling, his body went still.

"You don't need to wait," Longwell said. "This won't take long and he's out."

"I want to talk to you," Chittenden said. "I'll wait."

He and Cardenas went out to the parlor at the front of the house. He asked Cardenas if there was anything else, anything at all, he had to tell him about going to Rachel Scott's place that night.

"No," Cardenas said. "I told you everything."

"That man you said was with her. Did you get a look at him?"

"No."

"You sure it wasn't that fellow who was working for her had come back? What was his name? Worden?"

"No se."

"This man, he say anything?"

"I didn't hear nothing," Cardenas said.

"All right," Chittenden said, annoyed. "What about the others? Any trouble?"

"No. We shoot at the Buchanan house and run off his horses. Then we go to the Knott place, set the fire to the smokehouse, just like you tell us."

"And nobody saw you?"

Cardenas shook his head. "We no wait to see. We going next to burn the cornfield of Low's but then Zeke get shot."

Chittenden let out a sigh. "Here's what you're going to do. You're going to Willow Springs."

"Raton Pass? What for? There's no troubles there."

"Well, you're going to look around and see if you can find any."

"I don't understand."

"I want you gone for awhile. That shooting bothers me. Can't take the chance of having you recognized. You leave right now and you don't come back until I send for you, you understand?"

Cardenas shook his head, but said, *"Sí."*

After he left, Chittenden waited another hour until Longwell came out, a cigar stub clenched between his teeth and wiping blood off his hands.

"Well?" Chittenden asked.

"Arm's off, sewed up and bandaged. All I can do right now. His days of working for us are over."

"You'll keep him here, right, till he can get back on his feet?"

"Of course," he said and struck a match and relit his cigar. "But how'd he get shot?"

Chittenden told him Cardenas's story. Longwell pondered it for a few moments before he spoke.

"Cardenas was certain they weren't seen?"

"He says no."

"Buchanan may decide to git," Longwell said, scratching his whiskers. "Got those four kids and a new whelp still on his wife's tit. Knott, he's tougher. Going to take more convincing. Hard convincing, more than likely."

Chittenden nodded.

"Rachel Scott, though." Longwell grunted. "That didn't work out the way you expected."

"No," Chittenden said, his jaw tight. Nothing was working out the way he wanted with Rachel.

"It's none of my business, but you ask me I'd say she's not—"

"Stop right there," Chittenden cut in.

Longwell raised his hand in an apologetic gesture. "Any idea who this man out there with her is?"

Chittenden shook his head. But he would find out, that was certain.

"And you served them all with ejectment notices?"

"Them and six or seven others between here and the Ponil. And I had my deputies go back later and take a few shots at their houses, run off stock. Just like we did before with some of these other hardheads."

"You, me and Mills will have to figure out how we can offer more 'encouragement' to force these damn squatters out."

Chittenden knew he was right. And he'd give more thought to what that encouragement would be. But at this moment, the fact that Rachel Scott had a man at her place was more than troubling. It gnawed at him. Deep in his gut.

Chapter Thirteen

Clement woke before the sun was up. Rachel had insisted he sleep in the bed. "You need it more than me," she'd said. "I'll sleep in the rocking chair. Won't be the first time. Especially since Ethan's passing."

The bandage around his head had come loose so he pulled it off. Feeling around his head he was glad the lumps were gone, though one still felt tender. He slipped out of bed, went to the window, released the latch and opened it enough to look out. The brisk cold air stung his face. A dusting of white frost covered the ground. The sky held that last deep blue flintiness of twilight as it gave way to the first light coming over the pine treetops to the east. He'd once heard some folks in Santa Fe say that this land was an enchanting place. At times like now, he had to admit, that was indeed true.

Rachel stirred but didn't wake. Clement saw she was huddled under an old blanket. Moving to the fireplace to get a fire started, he couldn't help looking at her. The bun in her hair had come undone, leaving a few locks of reddish-blonde hair framing her face.

Busying himself with the fire, he knew that he had to get started back to Penquero, and the Archbishop. Empty-handed, sadly. The only thing to do when he got there would be to explain what had happened. The whole truth. How his good intentions were defeated. Short of finding that thief or one thousand dollars lying around somewhere, what else could he do? He hated the thought of it, hated that he had let down the Archbishop. But, more immediately, he needed to get a horse. He crossed himself and said a prayer asking God for help.

He also decided he could not stand the idea of that coffin out in the wagon bed being up on its side. Whether Rachel's sister was the harpy she said she was or not, decency dictated that the dead should be treated with respect. When he got to the barn, he dropped the wagon tailgate, pulled the coffin part way down the bed and started to ease it over, but it slipped out of his grip and landed with a loud bang. Bad as he felt about disturbing the body, at least the coffin was set properly in the bed now.

Returning to the cabin, the sunlight had already begun melting the frost. Inside of an hour, it would all be gone.

Rachel slept for another two hours and told him he should have woken her but she was grateful for the rest. She let him use her husband's razor to shave the several days' growth of beard off his face while she prepared a breakfast of eggs and bread and bacon.

Sitting down to eat, Clement tried to think of how he could get a horse. Ask her for the loan of one of hers? Did she have money he could borrow? None of this sounded good to him. If he borrowed her horse, he'd have to bring it back and that would take him away from his parish yet again for several days later on. Any loan he'd have to repay, but where would he get the money for that?

Rachel spoke. "I could use some help taking my sister's coffin to the cemetery. I'm hoping Reverend McMains can do the service today."

Clement wondered what she would do if the Reverend was unable to perform a burial service this day. As if she had read his mind, she answered his question.

"And don't worry if he can't. Mr. Carey'll hold the coffin."

"Mr. Carey?"

"Owns the livery stable in town. Usually has an empty stall. Owes me a favor."

Clement frowned. "But, it's your sister."

"If that coffin sits here, it can't get buried. Better if it's in town."

Two things were apparent to Clement. First, a dead body needed to be buried, and second, Rachel's mind was made up. "Considering all you've done for me, I'm happy to help." A horse would have to wait, at least for a while.

The longcase clock chimed nine o'clock as Clement and Rachel went out the cabin door and headed for the corral to fetch the horses and hitch them to the wagon. He and Rachel each carried a revolver. She had insisted. "Way things are these days."

The cabin, the barn, the corral and a couple of outbuildings lay in a clearing surrounded by pine trees that rose up the rocky hillsides. A creek meandered nearby. The remnants of a flowerbed lay off to the side of the cabin. Shriveled petals of purple and yellow lay scattered about among the leafless stems. Clement smiled at the thought that the promise of spring would bring color back to the sad little spot.

"Cold this morning," Rachel said, rubbing her arms through the sleeves of her blue, plaid, flannel dress. "Winter's coming."

Movement caught his eye. He saw the two men on horseback emerge from the woods before Rachel did. He halted, took her arm and placed his other hand on the butt of the revolver he'd stuck in his belt.

"It's all right," she said. "They're friends." Rachel raised her hand in greeting.

They met at the barn. Clement guessed the men as being close to his age, maybe a few years younger. One wore a gray coat and a dark, trim Van Dyke beard that accented his sharp features. The other rider had a full beard and bushy eyebrows. He wore a black coat, vest and tie along with a wide-brimmed straw hat, his curly hair poking out from underneath it.

"Hello, Reverend," Rachel said to the man with the straw hat. "And you, Clay Allison. Haven't seen you in awhile. This is Victor Cheval. Victor, this is Reverend Oscar McMains and the tall one here is Clay Allison."

Both men dismounted and shook Clement's hand. Clement noted that Allison's handshake was stiff and reserved. The man also stood ramrod straight, but that did not disguise an obvious limp. McMains, though, appeared amiable enough.

"Welcome, Mr. Cheval," McMains said. "You're a stranger hereabouts."

It struck Clement that Reverend McMains's voice, with its deep honeyed tone, suited him as a preacher.

"I ran into some difficulties," Clement said, "and Rachel was kind enough to lend me a helping hand."

"He got waylaid out on the prairie," she said. "I happened by is all. Now, what brings you two by this morning?"

"I have a letter," McMains said, reaching inside his coat, "and I want to ask you if you would sign it."

"Is this one going to Washington or the newspaper?" Rachel asked.

"Washington," he said as he unfolded the letter. "To the newly appointed Secretary of the Interior, the Honorable Zachariah Chandler. Listen to this part. 'We, the undersigned residents of Colfax County in the Territory of New Mexico, declare that for a wealthy and influential foreign corporation to successfully defy and override an authoritative and valid executive order of 1874, requiring the so-called Maxwell Grant to be treated as public land, is deplorable and unconscionable. We ask for your help in resolving this situation forthwith as the aforementioned foreign corporation has retained, as their representatives in this county, attorneys who are members of or are affiliated with the Santa Fe Ring, and have asserted a legal posture that in actuality thrives on corruption, fraud, mismanagement, plots and murder.' "

"Give it here. I'll sign it," Rachel said.

Clement noticed Allison watching him, studying him, like he was sizing up an opponent.

McMains took an inkwell and pen from his saddlebag. "I'm hoping for at least two hundred signatures."

"Looks like about fifty already," she said as she signed the document.

"Sixty-two now," McMains said and thanked her, taking the letter from her hand and placing it back safely in his coat.

"I see Bill Low signed. You just coming from his place?"

"That's right."

"Haven't seen him in a while."

"He's fine. Got his winter corn planted. Says the problem now is keeping the critters out of it."

Clement noticed McMains glance over at Allison, but Allison was still eyeing him.

"Bill always brings me a bushel or two of his winter corn," Rachel said as Clement realized she was speaking to him. "He's real proud of it. And it's good, too. Lives about three miles from here on the creek. If you saw his place you wouldn't think much of anything would grow there. It's mostly rocks. But he somehow always manages to coax that corn up."

"So, Mr. Cheval, how long will you be with us?" McMains asked.

"I'm not certain. Not long, I think."

"I see," McMains said. "And when did this fortuitous rescue by Rachel take place?"

"Three days ago," Rachel said.

"Oh," McMains said.

"I was coming back from Texas. Picking up my sister's body. I want to have her buried. Soon as possible."

"Of course," McMains said, taking his pocket watch from his vest and checking the time. "Let me think. I need to make a few more visits out this way for signatures. If I can't perform the ceremony this afternoon, I know I could tomorrow. After Sunday services. God wants us to keep the Sabbath holy, I know, but sometimes, well, I have to believe he'll grant us understanding. Would that be acceptable?"

"It would."

"Can you bring the coffin in to town today?"

"I can. And, I want her put on the far side of the cemetery."

"I don't understand."

"Don't want her buried near Mama or Ethan."

"But, she's your sister."

"It's what I want."

"That's not very Christian, Rachel."

"That may be. But that woman wanted nothing to do with me or Ethan in life, and I surely don't want her around me after I'm dead."

Clement saw the determined look on Rachel's face, as well as McMains's disapproving countenance. In his years as a priest, Clement had never come up against such a situation. Nothing so adamant. Families had disagreements, but when it came time for burying, differences were usually put aside. But this . . . Maybe it was this place. Maybe it was Methodists. Whatever it might be, it was surely different.

After a moment, McMains sighed and relented. "I'll see to it."

"Thank you, Reverend."

"Oh, did I mention that I might have a lead on the murderer of Reverend Tolby?"

"That's good," Rachel said. "You'll get proof, won't you?"

"Oh, yes, I'll have the proof."

"We need justice done."

"It will be. I promise. By the way, did you hear about George Buchanan?"

"No," Rachel said.

"Some scoundrels set fire to his barn and smokehouse last night. He lost them both. His wife is beside herself for the safety of their children."

"He's not leaving is he?"

"Word is that he's packing up."

"I'm sorry to hear that. I had visitors here last night." Rachel told them about the two masked men trying to burn down her barn and showed them Hannah's charred coffin still in the wagon bed. She shot Clement a look, and he knew she was wondering how the coffin had gotten righted but she didn't say anything. Clement also noticed one of the charred lid boards had started to warp and was coming loose. "Victor was a big help running them off," she continued. "Hit one of them. He kept a cool head."

"Chanceux," Clement said. "How do you say? I was lucky."

"That a fact," Allison said, his tone surly. He had a Southern accent. They were also the first words he had spoken.

Clement saw Rachel frown at Allison, and she said, "Indeed it was." She turned to Clement. "Clay has a ranch. Down on the Vermejo River, near the Canadian. He gets used to giving orders there, and sometimes forgets his manners."

It didn't seem to Clement that Rachel's words had much effect on Clay Allison.

"What do you do?" Allison asked him. There was a challenge in his voice.

"Passing through," Clement answered simply.

"How'd you get here again?"

Clement was about to answer but Rachel jumped in. "I found him, left for dead. A thieving Texan robbed him. Took his money, saddle, horse, everything. But he busted that Texan's nose."

"Good for you," McMains said, turning to Clement. "Robbery in any form is not only a sin, it is uncivilized and there is no excuse for it. How much did the thieving cur get?"

"About fourteen hundred dollars," he said and noticed the stunned looks on Rachel's and McMains's faces. Allison's features hardened.

"I've had luck with cards," Clement added quickly.

"I'd say you have," Rachel said.

"And I say God's judgment will be swift and severe."

"I appreciate that, Reverend," Clement said. "By chance, you haven't seen a man with a broken nose, or somebody working at hiding his face? Maybe in the last few days?" The odds were long, he knew.

"Can't say that I have," McMains said.

"So you're a drifter, a gambler and a fair hand with a firearm," Allison said to Clement, limping a few steps away from his horse, his eyes still fixed on Clement.

Clement shook his head. "Lucky."

"Well, I'm a shootist by profession," Allison said. "And luck's got nothing to do with it."

"A shootist . . . ?"

"Means he's good with a gun," McMains said.

"As he's proved many times," Rachel said sternly, cocking her head to one side and giving Allison a hard stare.

"Perhaps this is my fault for not explaining sooner," McMains said. "Mr. Allison offered to act as my escort today. We are all aware of the dangers lurking in our midst in these treacherous times."

"If I have given offense, I apologize," Allison said to Rachel. "Anymore I am wary of strangers. New faces around town and elsewhere are not to be trusted. There are even those who live among us who can't be trusted, as you pointed out in your story of your night visitors. Like the Reverend said, these are treacherous times." He shifted his eyes back to Clement. "And I put no scheme past the Santa Fe Ring. They'd sell their own mothers to a Kansas City brothel if they thought they could make a dollar from it."

"I'm telling you," Rachel said, "Mr. Cheval here is no Ring man. If you'd seen him last night, you'd agree."

"He is a stranger to me, and I say again, I put no scheme past the Ring."

"He fought in the war, Clay. Same as you."

"Indeed," Allison said, swiveling his head toward Clement. "I rode with General Nathan Bedford Forrest. Saw my share of fighting in Tennessee. And I don't recall many frog-talkers. Come to think of it, I don't recall a one."

"That's enough," Rachel said. "He helped me save my place."

"If you trust him, fine," Allison said, looking again at Rachel, then shifting his gaze again to Clement. "But I don't trust him, so you best stay clear of me, Mr. Cheval."

Flustered, McMains said, "Well, we should be on our way."

Rachel crossed her arms and glared at Allison. After he and McMains rode out around the barn, she snatched two bridles hanging on a post and headed out the open rear of the barn for the corral.

"If you'll get the harnesses ready, I'll get the horses," she called back to Clement.

He nodded. There were times he knew it was best not to say anything. This was one of those times.

Going to where the harnesses hung on the wall, he noticed a mallet on a bench along with a few loose nails in a can and grabbed them with the intention of repairing the charred coffin lid. Setting one of the nails in place, he was about to drive it in when he heard raised voices outside.

"Just who do you think you are?" he heard Rachel say.

"I'm telling you that man in there is lying to you." It was Allison's voice.

"What makes you think so?"

"Man claims to be a drifter and claims to be that lucky at cards? Something's not right, and you need to be careful."

"You're the one needs to be careful."

"Is it that you refuse to see or simply cannot see that he's hiding something?"

"What I see is a man who risked his life to help me."

"My God, you're sweet on him."

"Stop this foolishness!" It was McMains. "He's probably hearing everything you're saying."

"You go on now, Clay Allison," Rachel said, her voice lowered but the anger clear. "And I'll tell you something else. You better be thanking the good Lord every day for Dora McCulloch. She's a good woman and I'm surprised she doesn't run off and find herself a new beau because there are times you are not fit to be around."

Clement admired the fact that Rachel had spirit and was unafraid to show it. And he had to give Allison grudging credit for his perception. Clement had lied and continued to lie to Rachel, though not for the reasons Allison believed. But Clement was perplexed about the possibility that Rachel might have feelings for him. Was it true? She'd said nothing, but he hadn't seen her face. Well, it didn't matter. He was living a lie, and he needed to leave and return home, to his parish. He couldn't allow himself to think about anything else. At all. Especially Rachel.

He heard them ride away and finished securing the lid of the coffin, then waited for Rachel to return. Some minutes later, she came in leading two bay horses. From her expression, he could tell she was still upset.

They began harnessing the team to the wagon. Clement

thought it best not to say anything. Rachel finally spoke when they were nearly finished.

"Did you hear all that?"

"Some, yes," he said.

"You just don't pay any mind to what Clay Allison said. Thinks he knows everything. He served with General Forrest all right. But before that he got booted out of the Confederate Army. Kept having some kind of fits, so they cut him loose. Got dropped on his head or kicked by a mule as a boy. That's what I heard, anyway." She tied off the reins around the wheel break by the seat. "Somehow he managed to join up again. But I swear, sometimes that man's not right in the head."

"I appreciate you telling me," Clement said.

"Well, I need to go back to the house and get some things."

"I'll come with you," Clement said. "I want my coat."

"Another thing," she said as they headed for the cabin, "keep your distance from Clay. He tends to drink and is unpleasant once he's drunk. And his temper does not require alcohol."

"I could see that," Clement said.

"It's no lie. A few years back, a man named Kennedy got arrested over in Elizabethtown for killing and robbing guests who stayed at his place in Palo Fletchado Pass. It set something off in Clay. He and some of his friends rode over to E-Town, yanked Kennedy out of jail, tied a noose around his neck, and Clay dragged him behind his horse up and down the street for over an hour. People in town were too scared to stop him." They entered the cabin. Clement picked up his coat and took her coat from the peg where it hung. She went to the chest of drawers. "Kennedy was long dead," she continued as she took a small, blue, canvas bag from a drawer. "They say Clay cut off his head and put it on display but I can't swear to it. Wouldn't want to."

Clement handed Rachel her coat and they walked back to the

barn. She was quiet and seemed preoccupied. Clement hoped he'd never have to face Allison.

Taking an old blanket from a box inside the door, Rachel climbed up to the buckboard seat and placed it there. "You know how to drive one of these rigs?"

"I have done so a few times," he said.

She offered him the reins. "Go ahead."

"How far is it to town?"

"About seven miles. Road's kind of rough in places."

Clement snapped the reins and the wagon lurched forward.

As they cleared the barn, Rachel asked, "You notice that limp Clay has?"

Clement nodded, heard her giggle, glanced over and saw the impish smile on her face.

"He tried stealing government mules from Fort Union. Yankee soldiers chased him. He got so riled up in all the confusion, he accidently shot himself in the foot."

Chapter Fourteen

Sheriff Chittenden stepped through the gateway of the stone-wall surrounding the jail, squinted at the bright morning sunlight and adjusted his hat and buttoned his coat against the cold air. He had changed into a fresh shirt. His gun belt rested low on his hips. He was hungry. The corn dodgers and coffee he'd had at his desk earlier wasn't enough. He also needed to talk to Mills about new ways to encourage these squatters to vacate the county. And he knew he ought go see how Wilcox was doing and what Doc Longwell had to say about him. But finding out about this man at Rachel's place was still foremost on his mind. If he had to run some son-of-a-bitch away from Rachel, best to do it on a full stomach. Maybe he could get a stack of flapjacks at—

"Sheriff Chittenden!"

Chittenden turned in the direction of the shout and saw Mills, wearing his bowler hat, walking his way. But the man with him caused Chittenden to instinctively place his hand on his Colt Dragoon. It wasn't the revolver with the butt forward that the fellow wore. It was the bandana covering his face like he was some kind of bandit. Who in the hell was that and what in the hell was Mills thinking now?

"I need a word," Mills said. "In private. The jail empty?"

"It is," Chittenden said, glancing from Mills to the stranger and back to Mills, relaxing his grip on his revolver. "But I'm on my way to breakfast." Hell, Mills can wait for me, he thought.

"This won't take long," Mills said, brusquely walking past him toward the jail.

As the stranger went by him, Chittenden noted the coldness in his eyes. And he felt certain that under the bandana, the stranger was smirking at him. Chittenden didn't cotton to that. Not at all.

Back inside the jail, Chittenden removed his coat as Mills asked if he had any fresh coffee. Chittenden indicated the pot on top of the cast-iron stove. He'd made that coffee three, no four days ago, but as Mills was inconveniencing him, he saw no reason to inform him of the coffee's age. "Help yourself."

Knowing that Mills was a stickler for neatness and cleanliness, Chittenden watched bemused as he went to the stove, took a couple of tin cups from a nearby wooden shelf, frowned disapprovingly, pulled out a handkerchief and tried to swab out cooked-on residue from the bottom of the cups. Filling both cups with coffee, he handed one to the stranger.

Taking his chair behind his desk, Chittenden thought of telling Mills about Wilcox losing his arm. It was Ring business he was doing when it happened. But he wasn't about to say anything in front of this stranger.

Chittenden glanced from the stranger to Mills as Mills pulled the only other chair in the room up in front of the desk, sat and crossed his legs. The stranger leaned against the wall by the stove. When he pulled down the bandana to drink his coffee, Chittenden raised his head at the sight of the broken, crooked nose and ugly purple bruise that spread across it. Well, Busted Nose, guess you ain't so tough after all, he thought as Mills spoke up.

"Mr. Catron has informed me that ejectment proceedings against these squatters must be accelerated. He is tired of waiting."

Mills took a sip of coffee. The corners of his mouth turned

down in distaste and he quickly set the cup on the edge of the desk and cleared his throat.

Chittenden would have chuckled about Mills not liking his coffee if he hadn't been trying to figure out why in the hell Mills would be talking about Ring business in front of this busted-nose fellow. He pointed at the stranger. "Who's this?"

"Ah, I should have introduced you before. Dixon Poth, Sheriff Chittenden."

Poth didn't look up from his coffee as he took a sip.

Chittenden had heard of Poth, and he hadn't liked one bit of it. During the Civil War, Chittenden had joined the 2nd Colorado Cavalry. When his unit arrived in Missouri to relieve Kansas troops, the name Dixon Poth was as well-known and, in many circles, as reviled as that Confederate guerilla fighter William Quantrill. Chittenden had done his share of killing in the war. Killing that was called for to preserve the Union. But the slaughter of women and children? That was part of Poth's reputation.

"I believe Mr. Poth may be the answer to fulfilling Mr. Catron's wishes," Mills said.

"And how's that?" Chittenden asked.

"Mr. Poth is here to help us. He will act as a new deputy."

Chittenden pondered Mills a moment. "I don't believe he will."

Mills chortled. "You what?"

"We don't need him."

Mills straightened himself up in his chair. "I'm not so sure you appreciate the situation."

"Well, I'm not so sure you heard me then. I don't want him."

Mills pressed his lips together, and then said, "This is not a pissing contest, Sheriff. We require more decisive action. Your hit and run tactics against these squatters have resulted in only two squatters leaving this county in the last three months. Two squatters." Mills held up two fingers and shook his head dolefully. "That's unacceptable. The owners in England won't tolerate it. Mr. Catron demands better. Judge Longwell agrees. I spoke with him earlier this morning."

"I don't care. I don't want him," Chittenden said, looking at Poth, who took another sip of coffee.

"It doesn't matter what you want," Mills said and crossed his arms.

Chittenden looked at Poth. "You mind waiting outside?"

There was something disturbing about Poth's lopsided grin. But he pushed himself away from the wall, covered his face with the bandana and left, closing the door behind him.

"All right," Mills said, "let's hear your objection."

"He's not the sort we want."

"He is precisely what we want. Think of him as a . . . specialist."

"Specialist," Chittenden said. "Is that what you're calling assassins now?"

Mills shifted in his chair. "He's what you need; what we need to do this job."

"Not Dixon Poth," Chittenden said.

"Let me remind you again, Sheriff: your methods are not working. More direct action is called for."

"Direct action, you say. Seems to me the last time we tried that resulted in Tolby getting killed. That was our first mistake. And let me remind you that, so far, I've been lucky at keeping McMains and some of these other do-gooders around here from figuring that out."

"The Tolby matter is an unfortunate situation. And Mr. Catron feels you are handling it well. He told me he has full confidence in your abilities to find the perpetrator of that foul deed, whomever it may be."

"Good. So we don't need Poth. I'll handle things my way.

Now, I'm going to go get my breakfast."

"Mr. Catron also said his patience is running out. Time is running out. He wants these squatters gone. Deputy Poth will address that."

Chittenden snorted. "Sounds to me like you want to be the sheriff of this county. You should've run for the job."

"It sounds to me like you've forgotten that you and me and Judge Longwell were all elected to do a job. And that job is whatever Mr. Catron says it is."

Chittenden knew the little dandified, slick-haired pipsqueak was right. Damn it! But this wasn't over. "Using Poth is a big mistake. We need to drive these people out, not put them in the ground."

"The decision has been made, Sheriff." Mills stood up. "Deputy Poth!"

The door opened and Poth stepped inside, lowering his bandana.

"We have an understanding," Mills said to him.

"No, we don't," Chittenden said, shoving back his chair and getting to his feet. And Poth pulled one of his revolvers. Chittenden froze, the revolver pointed right at his stomach.

"Slow down there, Sheriff," Poth said calmly. "I've accepted a job. What I do will all be legal, just as Mr. Mills says it needs to be. If anything's not legal, there won't be anybody around to dispute it. And I don't care if you like it or not."

Keeping his anger in check and his hand away from his revolver, Chittenden had no doubt Poth would shoot him if he gave him any further provocation. That look in his eyes was unmistakable. This was the spawn of the devil, all right.

"Sounds like you've upset your new deputy, Sheriff," Mills said. "Probably best if you let him be. He obviously knows his job. Do you still know yours?"

Chittenden said nothing. He wanted to take Mills by the

throat and beat that smug smile off of his face. Instead, he watched Mills and Poth leave and pull the door closed. No, this wasn't over. Not by a damn sight.

Ten minutes later, his appetite for flapjacks having soured, Chittenden had shoved a couple of handfuls of corn dodgers into his coat pocket, gone out, saddled up and was looking forward to the ride to Rachel's place up on Ponil Creek. It would give him time to consider how to deal with Mills and Poth. As well as this man out there with Rachel. *That* was the first piece of business he intended to settle. As he reined his horse around, a big miner from the Ute Creek area named Evans came riding up at a gallop. Evans was one of the hundreds of miners claiming squatters' rights. These miners were a tough lot, too. This had to be important to bring one of them calling in such a hurry.

"You gotta come quick, Sheriff!" Evans shouted.

"What is it?" Chittenden asked, annoyed.

"Floyd Kunkle," Evans said, breathing hard, a chaw of tobacco bulging in his cheek.

"Oh, shit. Don't tell me he's killed Josh Teague."

Evans shook his head, spit out a gob of brown tobacco juice, and said that Floyd had gotten drunk, good and drunk, and snuck-up and clobbered Teague with a piece of stove wood. "They got Teague to the doc's at E-town. Says he's going to live. But a bunch of them miners up there, they say they've had enough of the whole Floyd-Teague feud and are going to hang him. He's holed up in his cabin."

"Anybody tell Deputy Rinehart?" Chittenden had sent Rinehart to E-town the week before to hand out ejectment notices around the Baldy area.

"He's with Floyd in Floyd's cabin. When the boys brought Teague into town, somebody told your deputy and he got out to Floyd's quick and was in the process of arresting him, right before the mob showed up. He's holding them off for the time being. Now I don't know if Teague jumped Floyd's claim or not. And I ain't no friend of Floyd's or Teague's, or that Ring you work for neither, but I don't hold with vigilante justice. Figured you best come."

Not one to take chances these days, Chittenden discounted the possibility that this could be a bluff to lure him out for an ambush for the simple reason that nobody particularly liked Floyd or Teague.

But hell's bells! Floyd Kunkle's place was in the opposite direction he wanted to go. Damn it! Rachel and that son-of-a-bitch out there with her would have to wait. Chittenden kicked his horse and he and Evans rode out of town.

Chapter Fifteen

"Cimarron's a Mexican word," Clement heard Rachel say. "It means wild. Doesn't exactly fit though, does it?"

They were coming out of the woods along the rocky foothills when Clement got his first glimpse of the small town of Cimarron. It was considerably larger than Penquero, but Clement agreed: wild was an odd word for such a quiet looking place. What he saw was a varied assortment of buildings made of stone, wood or adobe strewn over the bleak, brown prairie broken by a patch of cottonwoods along a creek north of town. A line of telegraph poles stretched up from the southwest to a small building at that end of town and then extending north toward Colorado. Some of the larger buildings, many with pitched rooftops, sat along two parallel roads. Situated on a slight rise off to the west was the whitewashed Catholic Church with its cross atop the pointed, wooden spire. The church seemed no larger than a chapel to Clement. Rachel pointed to the imposing four-story, stone structure near the town center, the tallest building around. "That's the grist mill Mr. Maxwell built. Indians come there to get their grain and meat from the local agent. There's some wish the Indians would go away."

"Why? Have they done something?"

"There's been reports of cattle stolen. And my neighbor, Bill Low, he claims they've been stealing corn right out of his fields. Can't say as I blame him if it's true."

Clement caught sight of the cemetery as they drew closer. It sat about a quarter mile outside the town on a sloping piece of brown, lonely ground. Going past it, Clement counted at least three dozen tombstones. Some tilted at precarious angles. There was a scattering of crude, wooden crosses in evidence, as well.

"What's that over there?" Clement asked. "It has a wall around it." He also noticed an outhouse off on the far side.

"The jail," Rachel said, her disdain evident. "I don't see the sheriff's horse. Must be out trying to run decent folks off their land, I expect."

Clement sensed there was something about the sheriff that vexed her, something much more than these evictions and this Ring business. The people of his parish often brought their problems to him, wanting his advice, his counsel and his solace. Sometimes, he'd discovered, people came to him and tried to hide or mask their intent, saying maybe a "friend" was having troubles. Others couldn't admit there was a problem, yet it was clearly there. Rankling them. Festering down deep. He wasn't about to push it, but he was ready should she want to talk.

A few people greeted Rachel with a nod or a "good morning" as Clement drove the wagon along the main street, the coffin bumping and rattling in the bed. He also noticed a quizzical frown or a cocked head in his direction, though he paid them no mind. And, as far as he could tell from glancing out the corner of his eye, neither did Rachel. Even so, Clement was fairly certain those folks were wondering if he was Rachel's new ranch hand, or maybe her new man. Getting a horse and getting back home felt even more pressing now.

Rachel directed him past the Barlow and Sanderson Company Stage Office, where two burly men were pulling the tarp cover off of a freight wagon. One of the men hollered at a youngster, his hands in his pockets leaning against the porch, "Go find Henry Lambert and tell him his table's here."

Pulling around to the right and then left up the other big

street, they passed a row of buildings. A barbershop. A blacksmith. A trading post. One had a long glass window with "Mockridge Mortuary" printed in fancy, gold-leaf lettering.

"I thought there was no mortuary here," Clement said.

"There isn't," Rachel said. "Vernon Mockridge died the day before he was to open for business. We used his hearse to carry his coffin to the cemetery. Mr. Carey keeps it out back of his livery. We still use it."

The Carey Hardware and Livery Stable had its name painted over the side of the adobe wall in black letters. The flat-roofed livery sat next to the hardware store. The sliding wooden door of the livery made a squeaky racket as a young man pushed it open. As they pulled past it, Clement saw it had a row of stalls on each side. At the far end was another open doorway where the black hearse sat just beyond it.

A couple of horses, a gray and a chestnut, were tied to a hitching rail out front of the hardware store. The front door was propped open and Clement could make out a man in a leather apron at the counter at the back helping a customer, somebody in a long dark coat.

"I'll go see Mr. Carey and get you some help with the coffin," Rachel said as she slipped her pistol into the buckboard boot and climbed down from the seat.

Clement decided the revolver he had shoved through his belt might get in his way when it came time to carry the coffin and left it in the boot as well. Going to the rear of the buckboard, he dropped the tailgate, took hold of the coffin and was pulling it off the bed a bit when he heard an unexpected but familiar voice.

"Well now, if it isn't the frog eater. I see you still don't carry a gun."

There in the doorway Clement saw the man in the long dark coat with the gun on his left hip, butt forward. The man who'd robbed him, the man whose nose he broke. He lowered the bandana, exposing that busted nose and a dark red and purple bruise.

Clement knew he was trying to goad him.

The man smirked and stepped out of the doorway. He held three boxes of bullets in his hand.

Clement felt anger welling up inside him but he needed to keep his head. His mind raced. Would he shoot me right here in the street? That gun of his is definitely loaded this time. I can't get to the revolvers in the boot. He's got my money somewhere. I need to find it. Lord, don't let anybody shoot him, at least until I can get that money back.

"I owe you," the man said and sniffed.

"I think you owe me something, too."

Rachel came out the door with the man in the leather apron, followed by a teenage assistant.

"Everything all right?" she asked. "What's—" She stopped, startled at seeing the man's face.

Clement wanted to protect her, pull her out of the way, but he stood fast, keeping his eyes on the man, who also kept his eyes on him.

"Things are fine," the man said. "Just having a little parley with the . . . grave digger here." He glanced at Rachel, looking her up and down. "That's a nice dress, ma'am."

The way Poth said it, and looking at Rachel, sizing her up like she was some common trollop, made Clement ball his fist. But this was not the time or the place to deal with him.

"We want no trouble here, mister," the man in the apron said.

"No trouble," the man said, looking back at Clement. "My business will keep me here awhile. We can finish this later, grave digger."

The man chuckled as he went to the chestnut horse at the

hitching rail, placed the boxes of bullets in a saddlebag, untied the horse and rode off toward the south end of town.

"Are you all right?" Rachel asked Clement, who nodded. "That's him, isn't it? The man who robbed you."

"That's him."

"Appears I was wrong about him being a Texan," she said. "There is something lower than a Texan. And lower than a damn Yankee."

Clement turned to the man in the apron. "Can you tell me anything about him? What he's doing here, where he's staying?"

"Name's Dixon Poth," the man in the apron said. "Said he's a new deputy."

Rachel shot Clement a worried look.

"He's staying at the hotel," the man in the apron continued and pointed across the street at the National Hotel.

"I'll be back shortly," Clement said and headed for the hotel.

"He's boarding his horses here, too," Clement heard the boy say and he hesitated. Horses . . . ?

"Is one of them a buckskin?" Clement asked.

The boy nodded.

"I'll be back," Clement said and started again for the hotel.

"Victor . . ." Rachel called to him, but he kept walking, making no reply. He was saying a prayer. Dear Lord, You know that I have devoted myself to Your service, but You also know me to be a weak man, a sinner. I fight temptation every day. You know how much I am tempted by Rachel. I need Your help to see me through that. Please. But I also beg for Your help, as I might have to break Your commandments. I'll probably have to tell more lies. And I'll have to steal, even though what I need to steal is the Archbishop's money that was stolen from me in the first place. I might also have to shoot that man because I may not have any choice. I humbly ask for Your help. And, I ask You to forgive me now for these and all my sins, in case I'm not able to later. Amen.

Entering the hotel lobby, Clement went to the front desk, where a bored-looking clerk sat. He wore a string tie and green sleeve garters and was making notes in a ledger book. Behind him were the mail slots for the twenty rooms in the hotel.

"I'm looking for a man," Clement said pleasantly. "I believe he's staying here."

"And who'd that be?"

"Dixon Poth."

That got the clerk's attention. He sat up straight and licked his lips. "Y-yes, sir," he said nervously and mumbled, "But I sure wish he wasn't."

"Why is that?"

"I'm sorry. I . . . I shouldn'ta said nothing. You . . . you ain't a friend of his, are you?"

"No," Clement said, shaking his head. "An acquaintance."

"Please don't tell him what I said." He was jittery, scratching the back of his neck like he had a rash.

"No, I won't."

The clerk mumbled something else.

"What?"

"I said that man scares the hell outta me," the clerk whispered, glancing at the front door.

"Please," Clement said gently. "Tell me what troubles you." Sitting in the confessional booth and listening to his parishioners confess their sins for the last ten years had taught him a few things about people.

The clerk leaned in closer to him, his voice low. "He come in last night to check in. Said Mr. Mills had arranged for his room. That was true enough. But wearing that mask on his face, I thought he was going to rob me sure."

"Go on."

"I asked him to sign the register. The look he give me, you'da thought I'd called him a dirty name. I swear I knew he was gonna to kill me on the spot."

"I understand. But you're still here."

"I guess. Be glad when he leaves, though." He blew out a breath.

"Did he say how long he's staying?"

"Nope."

Clement glanced at the mail slots and realized they were all empty. No keys sat in them. What were the odds that every room was taken and each occupant was out? Another thought struck him.

"How many guests do you have right now?"

"Just . . . just two."

"Do you have someplace that they can put their valuables?"

"Got a safe back in Mr. McCullough's office. He's the owner."

"Did my friend ask you to store anything in it?"

"No. Didn't ask, neither."

"Well, maybe I'll wait for him to come back."

"Suit yourself."

"Which room did you give him? Maybe I could wait there for him."

Clement saw the fear in the clerk's eyes when he said, "Oh, no."

"It's all right," Clement said. "I know him, like I told you."

"He told me I was not to tell anybody, not even Mr. Mills, what room is his, if he's in or nothing. Made me take all the keys outta here." He indicated the mail slots. "I told him the hotel's got rules. Said he didn't give a damn about no rules and nobody was to know when he or anybody else was in or out or nothing."

★ ★ ★ ★ ★

Just as Rachel had said, Allen Carey agreed to hold the coffin of her sister. And he did place it in an empty stall in the stable on top of two barrels with the assistance of his young helper, Jesse.

Carey also told her about a business deal he was considering regarding a couple of hundred head of horses and asked her if she'd consider going in on the venture with him. She said it sounded promising and that she'd give it serious thought, but her mind was distracted as she waited, getting more worried with each passing minute wondering what Victor was doing in the hotel. She hoped it wasn't something dangerous, or stupid. A couple of other customers came in and she decided she'd waited long enough. She was halfway across the street headed for the hotel when she saw Reverend McMains crossing toward her. He smiled and called her name.

"I'm glad I saw you," he said. "I almost didn't come down this way. I wanted to let you know I can perform your sister's funeral tomorrow, after Sunday services. Would that suit you?"

"That would be fine, Reverend. Thank you." She glanced at the hotel entrance. The only movement was a yellow dog sniffing at the porch stair, then loping on.

"And, are you absolutely sure that you don't want her buried near family?"

"I am."

"Fine, then," he said with a sigh. "I'll see to an appropriate spot. Oh, and how's Mr. Cheval? Feeling better?"

"I'd say he is. He helped me bring Hannah's coffin in. It's at Carey's Livery."

"I see. Will he be coming with you to the funeral?"

"I think so," she said, but she could tell something was on the Reverend's mind. "I get the feeling you have a question, Reverend."

"Perhaps this would be better discussed in private," he said.

Rachel didn't want to wait and she wanted to know what Victor was doing. She was very concerned about him, the way he ran off like he did. "No, this is fine," she said.

McMains nodded. He lowered his voice. "It's a matter of propriety, Rachel. This man living under your roof, it doesn't set well."

That riled her. She considered him a moment as she controlled her temper, then said evenly, "This is a man I nursed back to health. I found him near dead out on the prairie. I did the Christian thing. You of all people should see that."

"And I have. But there are those who feel differently."

"Like who?" Rachel asked, careful to keep the starch out of her voice.

"That's not the point, Rachel."

"You're right. The point is there is nothing improper or untoward going on in my house. You know me," she added firmly.

"I most certainly do."

"Then what is it?"

"I also know what's proper." He said it gently, and she took note of it. "And I know the way it looks. And I know you do, too."

Rachel hated this. She didn't want to admit that McMains was right. Not to him. Not to herself. In these few days, she had found herself drawn to Victor. To his smile, his laugh, even his shyness. That was odd, given stories she'd heard about Frenchmen. And he wasn't too hard to look at, either. No one would ever replace her husband, Ethan. But she could not deny it was a comfort having Victor around. He'd helped her run off those scoundrels who tried to burn down her barn. He helped with the chores. He talked to her. Listened to her. Made her smile. It had been such a long time . . .

"I can tell he's itching to move on," she said, though she

wasn't entirely certain about that. "Tomorrow, after the funeral. I'll see to it."

"Good," he said, nodded encouragingly and went on his way.

Though she was standing in the middle of the street, though several men on horseback rode right by her, though she heard little Sarah Travis and her mother, Martha, say good morning as they passed, it was a few moments before she realized it and got moving.

Inside the hotel, she saw the lobby was empty, except for Charlie Natwick, the desk clerk, who jerked his head in her direction when she entered. Walking to him, she saw he wore a worried expression.

"You all right, Charlie?" she asked.

"Yes ma'am," he said nervously. "I . . . I was afraid maybe you was somebody else coming in. But, yeah, I'm—everything's fine."

Rachel wasn't completely convinced but she needed to find Victor. "A man came in here, maybe fifteen minutes ago or so. Taller than me, dark hair. Has a French accent."

Charlie licked his lips then pressed them together tightly. "I, uh, think he . . . I'm not . . ."

She was about to ask him if he was sure nothing was wrong when Victor came out of the hallway where the rooms were located.

"There you are," she said, and glanced back at Charlie, who was looking strangely shamefaced. Next thing she knew, Victor had her arm, nodded at Charlie and was ushering her out of the hotel.

"What were you doing in there?" she asked once they were outside and headed back to Carey's.

"I went looking for my things," he said.

She stopped. "You went into that man's room? What if he'd come back and found you?"

"Well, if he'd come back, chances are we wouldn't be enjoying this walk right now."

She stared at him, and his sweet smile was not helping his case as far as she was concerned. A wagon was coming down the street and she grudgingly continued to walk. "That's not funny. That man's dangerous. And how did you figure out which room was his?"

"I asked the clerk."

"I've know Charlie Natwick for years. He wouldn't just up and tell a stranger which room a guest was staying in. What did you say to him?"

"I asked him which room Dixon Poth was staying in. He said he couldn't tell me."

Rachel waited a moment. "And?"

"I asked him if he was a gambling man." Victor shrugged. "He said he's played poker and tried his hand at faro a few times. I asked him for a deck of cards. He had one behind the counter. I said let's cut for high card. If he won, I would leave and not bother him anymore. But if I won, I wouldn't tell his boss what I knew."

"What? Are you saying Charlie is stealing or something?"

"Not at all."

"Well, what then?"

"I made no accusation," he said. "Perhaps his conscience was guilty. I have found that many people have something to hide. Sometimes, a little prodding is helpful. Even necessary."

"You sound like a lawyer."

"I'm not one of those."

"All right, he gave you the room number. Did you find your goods?"

"No. But since Poth is here, they must be here and I need them back."

The promise Rachel had made to McMains pulled her one

way, while her joy at Victor's decision to stay around pulled her another. She turned her face away so he would not see her smile, brief as it lasted.

"But," he said, "I want to see about that buckskin horse your friend Mr. Carey is holding."

Clement knew it wasn't right. It was his horse. And Allen Carey believed him. But he said that since Dixon Poth had brought the horse and saddle in claiming they belonged to him, and as Clement couldn't *prove* otherwise, like showing a bill of sale or a brand on the horse or a mark on the saddle, well, that didn't leave much room to haggle. There was no point in going to the sheriff. First, the robbery hadn't been committed in Colfax County so it was out of Chittenden's jurisdiction. But, more significantly, Poth was working for the sheriff, which meant he was working for the Ring. "Best we'd get is Ring justice and that means no justice," Rachel said. Stealing the horse was considered, but that was a hanging offense, if Clement was caught, and he didn't want to take that chance. He also didn't want to have to be watching every face he saw and worrying the rest of his life about it. Carey suggested Clement take the horse anyway, ride like hell out of the territory and never come back, but Clement said he wouldn't leave without his money. It quickly became apparent to all of them that in spite of the sourness this whole affair was leaving in their stomachs, the only thing to do was to pay Poth's price of fifty dollars to buy the buckskin. That included Clement's hackamore and saddle.

"I will pay you back, just as soon as I'm able," Clement said to Rachel. "As soon as I get the money Poth stole from me."

He wanted to wait in town in case Poth came back soon. "There's the chance he could lead me to where he's hiding my money."

Rachel said she had some things she could pick up at the

trading post along with a few other errands, but she insisted he arm himself.

With his revolver tucked inside his belt, Clement found a good spot at the corner of an adobe wall stretching up from Carey's store. It was tucked back away from the street and allowed Clement a clear view of the hotel. Carey gave him a couple of biscuits he'd brought with him that morning but didn't eat. "My wife made them. Here's some honey. It'll help."

The biscuits were hard and the honey did help. Over an hour passed and there was no sign of Poth. Clement thought back over his search of Poth's hotel room . . . *Opening the door, he saw the bed was unmade. That had been good. It meant he wouldn't have to be too careful about leaving things like he found them. He'd checked under the mattress and underneath the bed. Picking up the pillow he'd looked inside the pillowcase to see if Poth had stuffed the money there. He hadn't. A dirty shirt was tossed over a plain, wooden chair. A water basin painted with flowers and a pitcher, half full, sat on top of the chest of drawers. The top drawer contained a pair of flannel underwear, a couple of pairs of woolen socks and another bandana still marked with blood stains. The other two drawers were empty. A pair of dark trousers hung crookedly in the closet. He found nothing hidden down in the closet corners, hanging above from the wall or suspended overhead from the ceiling. Clement had felt around for loose boards in the walls and the floor. He'd checked behind the mirror hanging on the wall. There was no sign of his money. Merde.*

As Cimarron had no bank, it likely meant Poth either had the money on him, maybe in his saddlebags, or, God forbid, had hidden it somewhere in town or maybe even buried it. On a hunch, Clement took a quick walk around the hotel to see if there was any loose-packed dirt piled up anywhere or some kind of opening, anything that Poth might use to hide his money. There wasn't. Then it occurred to Clement that Poth worked for the sheriff and perhaps had stashed his money in the jailhouse. He might have thought it a safe enough place. It was worth checking. If the sheriff or another deputy was there, maybe he could "convince" them to help him, much like he had the hotel clerk.

As he'd seen when he and Rachel came into town earlier, there were still no horses hitched in front of the jail. That was fine. It was more likely then that no one was inside. Going through the gateway he saw nothing but coarse, hard-packed dirt around the jailhouse. He opened the door and stepped inside. His footsteps echoed dully on the stone floor.

"Hello! Anyone here?"

Nothing. He pulled the door closed. Knowing this would likely be his only chance he went to the cells first. Four cells. Each one had a hard, metal bunk set against the wall. No mattresses; just sorry-looking blankets for cover. He took a chance and quickly checked under each bunk. Nothing. Going back to the front, he stuck his head out the door and listened. It was quiet. He looked under the bunk near the door, checked around the cold stove, including the small pile of short firewood logs. He even lifted the lid on the black coffee pot. Nothing in it but half a pot of cold coffee. The gun rack was bolted securely to the wall. The rafters were open and bare. There wasn't a loose stone to be found, either. The sheriff's desk had three drawers. Opening the top one, Clement found a few "wanted" posters and other papers. The second held a whiskey bottle and a bag of coffee grounds. Inside the third drawer was a leather pouch. It wasn't his pouch and it felt far too light but he quickly undid the strap and, looking inside, discovered a few greenbacks and a couple of gold coins. This couldn't possibly be all that was left of his money! The front door opened. A nattily dressed man stood in the doorway. He held a bowler in his hand. His hair was combed and lacquered into place.

"Hold it right there, mister," he said, pulling a derringer from his coat pocket and placing the bowler back on his head. "Set down what you've got in your hands and get out from behind there."

Merde! Clement dropped the pouch and moved around in front of the desk.

"You armed? Open your coat and let me see," the man told him.

Clement pulled open his coat revealing the revolver stuck inside his belt.

"Pull that gun out real easy and put it on the desk."

Clement did as he was told. Keep your wits and don't say a word, he thought.

"Get your hands up and get in that first cell. Then we'll get some answers."

Clement turned and started toward the cell cautiously, glancing over his shoulder, keeping an eye on the man. The derringer in his hand he held steady as he followed close behind Clement.

"Hurry up," the man said. "You get in that cell, sit down and don't give me any trouble."

At the stove, Clement glanced back at the man, paused and frowned, looking up just above the man's head. The man stopped, wary, then raised his eyes to see what Clement was looking at as Clement grabbed the coffee pot and swung it hard, bashing it against the man's head. Coffee splashed out of the pot, the man went down, his bowler flew over the desk and his derringer clattered across the floor.

The man lay unconscious. He'd have a headache when he came to and coffee stains on his clothes, but he'd be all right otherwise, Clement felt certain.

Snatching his revolver from the desk, Clement went to the front door, cracked it open cautiously, peered out and saw no one. Listening, he heard no sounds, no footsteps, no horses coming.

He walked out as calmly as he could, closed the door behind him and went to the gateway, pulling it shut as well. Clement guessed the man must have walked over as no horse was tied to the hitching post. Taking a deep breath, he headed around the corner of the wall and into town. Folks were making their way on the streets but none paid him any mind. He quickened his pace, but not too much as to draw attention to himself. And he said a prayer of thanks to God and asked Him to get him out of town without further incident.

He saw Rachel outside the hardware store. She said she could tell from his face he'd had no luck. When he said they should go, she was surprised. He explained, saying he had to question his plan to wait Poth out. What he didn't tell her was that he'd begun to doubt getting his money back. God didn't seem to be offering much help.

With Paris tied behind the buckboard and sacks of grain and flour and sugar, and jars of molasses, honey and the like piled in the bed, Clement and Rachel, her revolver and hands tucked inside her coat, headed through town. Clement raised the collar of his coat and kept an eye out for the man in the bowler. What he didn't need was to be arrested. For all he knew, that man he knocked out could be someone important. An elected official, or the sheriff's relative. Clement needed to get far away from Cimarron, and quickly. It was hard to resist the temptation to snap the reins and make the horse team move faster.

As they turned onto the main street, an unexpected sight greeted them. A massive new billiard table, with fancy wood inlays and intricately carved and fluted legs, was being carried up the road by six men, one on each corner and one at each end. Though all six were puffing frosty blasts of breath, a couple of them appeared almost done in already. Another man with a walrus moustache and bandy legs was directing them. What drew Clement's added attention was that the man spoke with a heavy French accent.

"Don't drop it. *Mon Dieu!* Careful. You are carrying a precious cargo."

"Well now," Rachel said with a chuckle. "Looks like Henry Lambert finally got his billiard table. Let's stop. You'd like him."

With a furtive glance toward the jailhouse, Clement drew reins by the group.

Lambert saw Rachel and he ordered his movers to stop and take a rest but sternly admonished them not to sit on the table.

"*Madame* Scott," Lambert said looking up at her, "a pleasure to see you. What do you think?" He indicated the table.

"It'll be the prize in your saloon," she said happily, "and the envy of Mr. Schwenk."

"Ha," Lambert exclaimed. "*Monsieur* Schwenk is an upstart." He cocked his head at the building across from them on the corner. A large banner stretched across the front above the doorway read: "Schwenk's Hall." "It is not enough he is satisfied having one of two breweries in this county, he must have a tavern, too. So, he has beer, whiskey he calls 'Tangle Leg'," he rolled his eyes and grimaced, "and gaming tables. But he does not have one of these." He beamed at his new billiard table. "A Brunswick and Balke, all the way from Chicago. And who is your friend?"

Before she could answer, Clement introduced himself, saying, in French, "A traveler who is happy to hear the sound of his homeland." He glanced over at the jailhouse. No one around so far.

"Ahh," Lambert exclaimed and spread his arms and replied in French. "A fellow countryman! Welcome, *monsieur*! I am Henri Lambert."

"And I am Victor Cheval."

Clement bent down to shake Lambert's outstretched hand. Concerned as he was about the possibility of the man coming to in the jail, it also struck Clement that it was becoming easier for him to call himself by his legionnaire name. And that did not sit well with him, either.

Though enjoying their excited exchange, Rachel said to Lambert, "I don't know exactly what you two are saying and I don't want to interrupt, but we shouldn't keep you from your chore."

"No, no, it is a refreshing interruption," Lambert said, speaking again in English. "Tell me, *Monsieur* Cheval, will you be with us long?"

"It's difficult to say," Clement answered. He stiffened at seeing a rider nearing the jail but then the rider passed it by.

"Well, no matter," Lambert said. "I invite you to visit my establishment any time." He pointed up the street at a lone, whitewashed building. "Near the plaza. You cannot miss it. Lambert's Saloon. The best of everything. Lheraud Champagne. Kentucky bourbon. St. Louis beer. Though I wish I could make these cowboys leave their guns outside. At least twenty holes they have shot into my ceiling." He spread his hands in a helpless gesture. "*C'est la vie,* hmm?" He indicated the table. "Do you play, by chance?"

Clement shook his head. "I've never been lucky at billiards." And he wouldn't be lucky ever again if they didn't get moving, he thought.

"Ah, *oui.* For many years I did not consider myself fortunate, but that has changed, along with my fortune when I opened my saloon. No more digging for gold and silver. My customers, they bring them to me now. Perhaps the same may be said of you one day?"

"Perhaps," Clement said, briefly thinking of his parishioners and that in his years at Our Lady of Good Tidings church he could not recall ever seeing gold or silver in the collection plate.

Lambert glanced around furtively, as though checking to see

that no one he didn't want to hear what he was about to say was within earshot. "I am thinking of opening a hotel. An addition to my saloon."

Rachel was surprised.

"It would be *magnifique*. Two stories. Twenty rooms. A separate gambling parlor. A dining room."

"And what does your wife say about all that?" Rachel asked.

"Mary is already picking out beveled mirrors, velvet curtains and English china."

Rachel laughed, and Clement smiled, shooting another glance at the jail.

"Fresh opportunities will be coming once this land grant affair is settled," Lambert said, still keeping his voice low. "And I hope it is soon, as I know you do." He nodded sagely at Rachel. "Meanwhile, be careful."

Rachel thanked him. "And please, give my regards to Mary."

"Tres bien. She will be most pleased." He looked at Clement. "A pleasure to meet you, *monsieur.*"

"Merci," Clement said. *"Et vous."*

"Allez avec Dieu," Lambert said and stepped away from the buckboard.

Go with God. Clement wondered how many times he'd said that these last ten years.

He snapped the reins and the buckboard moved forward as Lambert motioned quickly with his hands at his workmen, saying, "Enough rest. *Vite! Vite!* You do not have all day!" It struck Clement that Lambert could have been speaking to him.

CHAPTER SIXTEEN

Sergeant Amos Tully, paper manifest in hand, was doing what he did best. Moving from freight wagon to freight wagon in front of storehouse number two, he shouted at his men. "Upshaw, Abadie, Slocum, my old grandma could move quicker than you three! She'd have that wagon loaded by now! The Lucero boys can't wait all day. Nolan, Kilbane, you make me ashamed to be Irish. Jaysus, I've seen molasses move faster!"

The Lucero brothers and their teamsters had arrived a couple of hours earlier with ten wagons to be loaded with blankets, boots, socks, uniform trousers and blouses, belts, canteens, buckets, lamps, cooking tins, barrels of coal oil and turpentine, as well as hammers, horseshoes, shoeing nails, grindstones, bottles of liniment, jugs of linseed oil and about a hundred other items that Fort Stanton and Fort Seldon needed. Tully had sent the Lucero brothers and their teamsters to the sutler's store until his men had the wagons ready.

"Upshaw!" Tully shouted as he studied his lists.

"Sergeant?" Upshaw called down from the nearest wagon.

"I'm going over to storehouse three. Some of these supplies we need got moved over there. Keep everybody moving."

"Yes, Sergeant."

Tully walked the few yards to the storehouse number three loading area, which sat directly behind storehouse number two, and was surprised to see Sergeant Nicholas Shumway, the Sergeant of the Guard. He carried a leather bag over his shoulder and a grim expression on his face.

"Trouble, Nic?" Tully asked.

Shumway kept his voice low. "I could lose my stripes for this but I owe you at least a chance."

"What . . . ?"

Shumway pulled him inside the fenced loading area. "The captain has ordered your arrest."

"Arrest?"

"Shut up and listen! It's something to do with whatever Howarth is telling the inspector general. He's been in with them for almost an hour. I don't know what he's saying, but you're in big trouble, my friend."

Tully was stunned. How much had Howarth told?

"Captain says he wants you in irons. The Lucero brothers, too."

Aw, Jaysus Christ Almighty! Howarth must be spilling everything: selling stolen government property, the misappropriation of the fund money, everything over the last three years. Every scheme. Lump it all together, Tully figured he was looking at life in prison.

"You saved my life back during the war," Shumway said. "I'm returning the favor. There's a bay horse saddled and ready right back of us in the mechanics' corral. Three white socks. Blacksmith just shoed him. You get caught with him, you stole him, understand? This, too." He reached inside the leather bag, pulled out an Army Colt revolver and holster and handed it to him. "Don't go back to your quarters. My boys are looking for you there. Don't let us see you. I'll be obliged to arrest you, and I wouldn't like that."

Shumway stuck out his hand. Tully shook it. "Thanks, Nic."

Nodding once, Shumway left.

Tully knew he had to move fast and he was scared but needed to keep his wits. Leaving the post he'd need a destination and a reason for the sentries. Get it straight in his head right now. He strapped on the holster and gun and walked quickly around to the mechanics' corral with its many stalls and sheds forming an enclosed square. Just inside was the saddled bay with three white socks, as Shumway had said. There was a blanket roll tied behind the saddle, too. A line of horses stood, waiting to be shod, on the other side of the corral. Tully could hear the clang of the blacksmith's hammer as he pounded a horseshoe into shape against his anvil. Peering back around the corner he saw the usual Saturday morning business of troopers policing the grounds, others airing bedding and still others trying to look busy so as not to get called as volunteers for some shitty detail.

Tully had no money, no civilian clothes, no food. What the hell was he going to do? First thing was to get away. Taking hold of the high pommel of the McClellen saddle, he stuck his boot into the stirrup and froze.

"I think I saw him come this way," he heard someone say.

Afraid to turn and look, Tully did anyway. Through the wide-open doorway, he saw several troopers pass by. They weren't armed so he figured they weren't looking for him. He wiped beads of sweat off his face and he saw it: the quartermaster's office. It sat directly across the grounds from the corral. Inside, under the floorboards by Howarth's desk, was three thousand five hundred dollars.

Please, Jaysus, whatever sins I committed, don't punish me now, Tully prayed as he walked his horse over to the quartermaster's office. He was careful to lead the horse by holding onto the underside of the bridle while he stayed on the outward side from the post so as to have a better chance of not being seen. All the way across the grounds he could hear the clanging of the blacksmith's hammer. He never felt so jittery in his life.

Thankfully, the two clerks at the counter were busy with bookkeeping, one calling off names and numbers from a list, the other making a mark in the book, and paid him no mind as he went back to Howarth's desk. As many times as he'd been in there before, why should they bother him? He lifted the floorboards, relieved to see the money still there. Glancing over the top of the desk, he saw the clerks still busy with their work. With sweaty hands, he shoved the greenbacks inside his blouse and walked back outside, careful to check for Shumway and the guard. No sign of them. Mounting his horse, he pulled down his hat, buttoned up his coat and trotted out of Fort Union.

A sentry patrol stopped him about two miles out.

"State your business, sergeant," the bored corporal asked.

Tully sat up straight. Keep it simple and quick. "Going to Mora. Got to talk to Valdes about his next grain and beef shipment for—"

The bored corporal waved him on. "Go ahead."

Tully kicked his stolen horse and rode away.

Chapter Seventeen

When Sheriff Chittenden and Evans came through the trees, they looked up the hillside and saw Floyd Kunkle outside his small cabin. He was hanging from a rope at one end of the front porch. His mouth hung open, his long beard twisted around under the rope. Drawing his revolver, Chittenden kicked his horse and bolted for the cabin, followed by Evans.

Reaching the front of the cabin, Chittenden saw his deputy, Isaiah Rinehart, sprawled on the wooden porch, face down. Quickly scanning the tree line, Chittenden saw no sign of anyone else. Rinehart's sorrel gelding and a saddled mule were tied to the porch rail.

"Cut him down," Chittenden told Evans and dismounted. He heard Rinehart moan. Grabbing his canteen hanging from his saddle pommel, Chittenden went to his deputy and rolled him over. He was relieved not to find him bleeding from a gunshot wound.

"Easy now," Chittenden said, helping Rinehart to a sitting position against the cabin wall. He gave him a sip of water. "Not so fast."

"I tried . . ." Rinehart groaned. "Somebody hit . . . hit me from behind."

Chittenden felt behind Rinehart's head. "You got a fair-sized lump back there, all right."

"Floyd's alive!" Evans shouted as he laid Floyd, gagging for air, on the porch and pulled the noose from around his neck.

"Give me that water."

Chittenden tossed Evans the canteen.

"Floyd ain't dead?" Rinehart said, sounding both surprised and pleased.

"No, he's breathing, for the time being anyway," Chittenden said. "What happened here?"

Rinehart ran his hand over his bristly, red hair and said about twenty armed men showed up at the cabin saying they wanted Floyd. "I told them I was taking him to Cimarron. Figured it wasn't safe for him around here. They said I wasn't taking him no place. That's when I pulled my pistol and told them boys any of you gets past me is welcome to him."

Chittenden grinned and nodded. "Good man. Then what?"

"They cussed me and went off a ways like they was discussing it. I kept watch on them from the doorway. After a while, they up and left. Floyd was on the bed inside, sobering up. I got him to his feet and was bringing him out to put him on his mule. Five or six of them miners was waiting for me. Said they was taking Floyd no matter what. I said come ahead and drew my pistol . . ."

"Go on," Chittenden said. "You're doing fine."

Rinehart rubbed his neck and closed his eyes. "It misfired."

Chittenden heard Evans spit, the juice hitting a floorboard with a wet plop. Glancing over at Evans, he saw him on his knee giving Floyd another swallow from his canteen and shaking his head disapprovingly.

"Never mind that now," Chittenden said. "You drew your pistol. Then what?"

"They come at me and I was trying to hold on to Floyd and one of them must've got in through a window because I felt something hit me from behind. I could swear I had those windows barred."

"Don't you worry about that," Chittenden told him. "You

did your job."

Rinehart reached back and winced as he felt the back of his head.

"You're going to be fine. That knot's a long way from your vitals," Chittenden said. "But you need to get a more reliable firearm."

"Yeah, I know. You been telling me since Kansas the .44 Walker is prone to misfire."

"You remember the men who came at you?"

Rinehart nodded. "Reckon so. Henderson. Taylor. All of them."

"Good, good. We'll deal with them later. Right now we got to get you and Floyd back to town." Chittenden looked over at Evans. "Can he ride?"

Evans nodded. "Think so." He helped Floyd sit up. "What do you say, Floyd?"

"It's my land," Floyd said, his voice cracking and hoarse. "I got a deed. All signed."

"I know all about that," Chittenden said. "But we got to get you out of here. Feel up to riding?"

Floyd held his head in one hand and gingerly prodded his neck with the other. "Where we going?"

"I'm taking you to Cimarron."

"What for?"

"Going to have to hold you. Partly for your own protection and partly—"

"My own protection?" he cut in. "What are you talking about?"

"On account of you clubbed Josh Teague with a big piece of wood. He might come looking for you to give you a taste of the same."

"I told you, he was on my land. Trespassing."

"I heard you. But there's going to be . . ." Chittenden suddenly didn't feel like explaining anymore. "We'll let Judge Longwell sort it out."

"Sort what out?"

"Get him on his feet," Chittenden told Evans, while he helped Rinehart over to his horse and helped him mount up.

"I don't need no damn judge or lawyer bastards," Floyd choked, holding on to Evans. "My deed. My land. All legal."

"Well, Teague's got a deed, too. I've seen it and it looks just as legal as yours. You should of let the judge handle this instead of getting drunk and going after Teague."

"Damn judge got voted out last month and that new one, Longwell? Sorry excuse for a sawbones if I ever seen one. He hasn't told me nothing about when he'll hear my case. I got tired of waiting's all."

"You got yourself some time to wait and cool off now."

Chittenden had a feeling Mills was likely behind this. Floyd's claim was one of the few actual land purchases made shortly after those English boys bought the Grant. Floyd had paid $2,550, a portion of which came from the gold he'd found and the rest from a small inheritance he'd received from a dead uncle in Ohio. But, sadly, even that transaction had become mired in legal quicksand on account of both Floyd and Teague claimed title, as each held a notarized deed from the Maxwell Land Grant Company. Chittenden decided he wouldn't be surprised to find out that Mills and one of the company lawyers had purposely pulled some legal shenanigans in order to generate extra fees for themselves. Hell, for that matter, Teague might as easily be in cahoots with both lawyers. He was an unpleasant little man rumored to have been a carpetbagger run out of Georgia for trying to swindle a couple of county magistrates and a brothel owner in a fraudulent land deal.

Chittenden and Evans helped Floyd get mounted on his mule.

"You should be glad we got here when we did," Chittenden

told Floyd. "Otherwise, you'd still be swinging from a rope, dead as Irish luck."

Evans made certain Floyd's feet were securely in the stirrups.

"I appreciate you coming to get me," Chittenden said to Evans who nodded, spit a brown stream of tobacco juice onto the ground and stepped back up on the porch.

As he mounted his horse, Chittenden glanced at Rinehart. "Glad you're still alive."

"Thought sure they were going to kill me," he said.

Evans let out a whoop.

Chittenden jerked his head at him. "Something on your mind?"

"You don't think we're stupid enough to kill one of you Ring law dogs, do you?" Evans said. "We did that, your friends down in Santa Fe would send them Yankee soldier boys up here and, shit Miss Agnes, we'd have a worse mess of things."

Chittenden knew he was probably right about that, but he wasn't about to tell him so.

"Let's go," Chittenden said, kicking his horse. Keeping Floyd and his mule between them, Chittenden and Rinehart rode down the hillside.

"No, we ain't stupid like you think," Chittenden heard Evans call after them. "Ain't going to lie and cheat and steal and try to scare you off like you Ringers do. It's our land, our claims. We're going to whip you! Fair and square and legal!"

Dixon Poth splashed across the Rayado River and up the gentle embankment. Pete Newcomb's ranch house lay across the grassy plain. Poth noted that Newcomb had himself a large house among a stand of aspens whose leaves were just starting to change color, green to yellow. It was a handsome place, except for the smell of sheep. Like damp hay and shit. Poth didn't much care for sheep. Cows, either. But he wasn't here about livestock. Then he saw them. A man was driving maybe twenty or thirty head of sheep into a pen near the barn.

Glancing around as he prodded his horse on, Poth didn't see any hands about. No activity around the house, either. That was fine by him. It would make his task easier. Mills was paying him to eliminate squatters claiming land, not the kitchen help. But if kitchen help—or anybody else, for that matter—got the urge to get in the way by sticking their nose into this business, well, that would be another affair and would require immediate action.

As he drew closer, Poth pulled down the bandana covering his face. He didn't want to make this man think he was a bandit come to rob him. No . . . no need to spook him. Or anybody else. Not yet anyway.

Poth saw the man turn and catch sight of his approach. Poth smiled as he watched this lanky man dressed in dungarees and a coat close the gate on the pen with the sheep now inside. The man in dungarees made no move toward the barn, the house or anywhere. Poth guessed he was armed. He likely had a pistol under that heavy coat.

"Hello," Poth offered as greeting as he trotted to a stop about ten feet from Newcomb. "I'm looking for Mr. Pete Newcomb."

"You found him," Newcomb said, placing his hands on his hips.

Poth could tell from the frown on Newcomb's face he was reacting to his broken nose and the purple bruise spread on either side of it. All because of that frog-eating grave digger. Poth would take care of him in good time, too.

"Nice place here," Poth said. He noticed the exposed brown brick at a couple of corners and around the doorway to the house. "Your adobe could use some patching."

"You come here looking for work?"

Poth shook his head and leaned forward in his saddle. "I was sent here to give you a warning."

"And who might you be?" Newcomb asked, cocking his head to one side.

"Sheriff's deputy." He kept the badge in the pocket of his coat, as he saw no need to wear the tin star. It wouldn't make any difference anyway. Not for this job.

"I already got my ejectment notice from Chittenden," Newcomb said. "And it don't mean shit. Neither does Chittenden's scare tactics. We got a legal right to be here and ain't—"

"I don't care," Poth cut him off, tired of the sheepherder's voice, and sat up straight.

He saw Newcomb narrow his eyes at him, like he was sizing him up. The sheepherder glanced at Poth's hands, which Poth kept on the horn of his saddle. Poth knew Newcomb was wondering what he was carrying under his coat. He thought of asking Newcomb if he'd like to guess. Then he saw Newcomb raise his chin at him.

"You don't scare me. I believe it'll take a helluva lot more than you to run me off my own land, Mister Deputy Sheriff," Newcomb said, adding a contemptuous tone to those last three words, pulling back his coat and revealing a Colt revolver.

This sheepherder was threatening him with a gun. That was all Poth needed. It was all he wanted. He'd told Mills and that self-important sheriff everything would be legal. The time had come. "Do you know your Scripture?"

"What?" Newcomb asked, genuinely puzzled.

"The cock has crowed three times." Poth reached his right hand around to the revolver on his left. "Time to go to the garden and weep."

The expression Poth saw on Newcomb's face was a look of realization Poth had seen before on so many other faces. It was a look that said Newcomb had waited too long and realized too late what was coming as he clumsily went for his gun.

Poth pulled his revolver, cocked it, aimed and fired. Frightened, the sheep in unison scattered around wildly to the rear of the pen and clustered there as the bullet entered Newcomb's mouth, shattered four teeth and exited out the back of his neck. Poth watched him fall backwards and hit the ground hard. Newcomb's boot twitched once in a death rattle and did not move again.

A scraping sound from the barn drew his attention. Still holding his revolver, Poth needed to make certain there was no one around to dispute his action.

"Come on out of there," he ordered, cocking the revolver.

No movement. Not a shadow. Not a sound. Nothing.

"Don't make me come in after you."

He tried to listen for anything that would tell him where someone was hiding inside. But those damn, dirty, rank-smelling sheep were bleating such that he couldn't discern anything helpful. And he wasn't about to blindly ride into that barn. Even some fool with a scattergun could get lucky. He holstered his revolver and was about to dismount when he heard a ruckus, drew his revolver and saw a gray cat pounce on a brown field mouse scurrying for his life as it tried to make a run across the entryway.

With a grunt, Poth turned his head, looking around for a sign of anyone. If there was someone lurking or hiding, they were cowardly and he would not worry about them. Not now, anyway. He took the list out of his pocket along with a pencil stub and drew a line through Newcomb's name at the top of the list.

Chapter Eighteen

Clement, thankful to have gotten out of Cimarron, spent much of the return trip considering his options. Maybe the thing to do was to go back to town tonight and follow Poth around, see where he went and if he talked to anybody. Following Poth would be less obvious in the dark. Then he could sneak up on him, knock him out, tie him up and make him tell him where he had the money. That was the legionnaire in him doing the thinking. That was something Dekker would have enjoyed. Clement smiled at the thought of his old friend. But was this something he could really do—kidnap Poth, force him to tell where he'd hidden his money? And if he were successful, he would have to leave right away. Run, like a thief in the night. Because Poth was relentless. A killer. Clement had seen it in the man's eyes. They were dead eyes. He knew Poth would search for him. No matter how long it took. If not to get the money back, Poth would hunt him for revenge. Looking over his shoulder the rest of his life was not a life. He was a priest. There were only two conclusions he saw: leave Cimarron and his money behind or steal his own money back. If only he could locate it, and the success of that felt less than slim anymore. Everything felt against him. Maybe God was trying to tell him so. And maybe it was time Clement listened.

Somewhere along the trip back, Clement noticed that Rachel was sitting closer to him on the buckboard seat. It had simply happened. She didn't seem to be aware of it. At least it appeared so to Clement. He'd detected no sidelong glances or coy looks. Though he'd spent nearly a decade as a priest, he hadn't forgotten how women, or some women nonetheless, made their intentions known by acting as though they had no intentions. He chose to make no mention of their new proximity. Besides, he had to admit, the warmth of her was comforting, and not only because the wind had picked up, making the air even more cold and bracing.

Rachel had been quiet for most of the journey. Clement thought she'd given him the time to mull his situation. And he'd appreciated her understanding. But she looked like she had something on her mind now and he asked her about it.

"I was thinking about supper," she said, rubbing her hands together against the cold. "I got the makings for a good stew but I wish I had a chicken to fry. Did I tell you Henry Lambert is probably the best cook in the county?"

"No, you didn't."

"He came over to this country and somehow got himself a job cooking for that damn Yankee general, U.S. Grant. Then that Yankee president, Lincoln, rest his poor soul, snatched him away to cook for him. I try not to hold any of that against Mr. Lambert, cooking and scrubbing for them. And his wife, she's a sweet woman. But I have to say, and it hurts me to do so, he can cook a chicken that makes your tongue do a dance."

Clement laughed.

"It's true," she went on. "My Ethan told me I made the best fried chicken he ever ate. But Mr. Lambert's chicken? He doesn't fry it, exactly. And he douses it with wine and adds mushrooms and the like. It sounds like some kind of fancy chicken stew, but I never tasted any better."

Clement smiled. Ah, *poulet au vin*. The last time he'd savored that had been back in Paris, a lifetime ago. "Some Frenchmen are gifted that way."

"We got all manner of folks in these parts. I could tell you stories."

"I'll listen," Clement said, happy to have his mind off of Poth and his money for a while.

"Mr. Carey, he was a school teacher. In Iowa, I believe he said. Joined the Yankee army and they put him in charge of stores. Oh, what do they call it? Quartermaster. Then he caught the measles. Nearly killed him. After he recovered and the Yankee army let him go, he packed up his family and brought them here for a new start. A good man, in spite of his being a Yankee. Never gouges on his prices."

Clement enjoyed her tales about the twin Crocker Brothers getting ready to open a mercantile store, the dream of a little Italian man whose name she couldn't pronounce to build an opera house in town, that she thought Mr. Schwenk and Mr. Lambert would eventually get along, and that Mary Lambert grows a wonderful garden and loves roses.

"All kinds of people here," she said. "Room for more that's got the ambition and not afraid of hard work."

Clement knew the sound of a woman's calculation in trying to arrange a man's life. It was no different spoken in French or Spanish. The idea was always the same; get a man to put down roots. He recalled laughing with friends in Paris about it, and that seemed like a hundred years ago. And there were women back in Penquero who couldn't help but meddle in the lives of others, playing matchmaker. Clement knew the best thing to do was to keep his eyes straight ahead and his mouth shut.

A moment later Rachel said, "But of all the people around here, one I don't much care for but truly puzzles me is this Melvin Mills."

Clement recalled she said he'd been elected to the territorial legislature.

"He's a damn Yankee, too. Come down from Michigan.

Didn't fight in the war. Rumor says he's a Quaker."

Clement looked at her, curious.

"I don't like trading in rumors, mind you," Rachel said. "The Bible tells us not to join hands to be a malicious witness. But I'll say this much; if he's a Quaker, he's like no Quaker I ever met, and Ethan and I knew a few back in Missouri. They're supposed to be peaceful, God-fearing folks. Mills is a Ring man, through and through. And money is the only thing they worship, far as I can tell. If they can't get money out of it, they aren't interested."

Clement had never known any Quakers, here, or in France. And certainly no "peaceful" man would join the legion. But this talk of money did make Clement curious.

"You said this Mills was the representative for the county, didn't you?"

"That's right. Lot of folks think he and the Ring stole the election. Word is they bought the Mexican vote."

"Where does that money come from?"

"Catron and Elkins, I would say. Crooked lawyers, the whole bunch. Mills, Catron, all of them."

"So anything the Ring wants or needs to purchase here, they would send the money to Mills?"

"Makes sense."

"Does the Ring pay the sheriff and his deputies?"

"The Ring owns them. Got the sheriff elected."

It occurred to Clement that if Catron sent the money to Mills, and Mills pays the sheriff and deputies, then Mills must have someplace he keeps all that money. Someplace safe. Might Poth have left his money with Mills? "Where does Mills live?"

"In town," she said. "Adobe house just a little ways up from the jail. Hold on. Are you thinking of doing something foolish?"

"Not at all," he said, catching a glimpse of her watching him, and probably wondering what he was thinking. And what he was thinking was how to get into Mills's house without getting caught.

"Now what's this about?" Rachel asked as they came around a rutted bend.

Clement saw the two men on horseback up ahead, as well. They faced each other. From their horses and clothing, neither appeared to be Poth. Clement asked, "Do you know them?"

"Sure do. That's my neighbor Bill Low on the right." Her voice lowered. "The other one belongs to Sheriff Chittenden. Cruz Vega."

"Do you think he was one of the ones who tried to burn down your barn?"

"Either him or his friend, Cardenas. One was a Mex, that's certain."

Clement wasn't about to make any accusation without proof. He saw both men turn in their direction. Low was an older man with a white moustache, a floppy hat and a faded kerchief around his neck army-style. Vega had curly, black hair with a bandana tied around his head. Clement wondered if he was part Indian. His face was full and round and he appeared stocky, but it may have been the thick red coat he had on that made him seem so. Vega's horse moved and Clement squinted his eyes against a flash of sunlight and realized Vega had silver on his saddle, something Clement knew many Mexicans liked, if they could afford it. Or steal, as some would do. Neither man appeared concerned at the sight of the approaching wagon. And Rachel made no attempt to move away from Clement on the buckboard seat. But as they got closer, he saw the insolent stare Vega was giving her, as well as her icy response.

Clement took an instant dislike to Vega. It wasn't proper for a priest to do so, he knew. We're all God's children, he had sermonized from the pulpit. But he couldn't help not liking the man. It was as immediate as that.

"Afternoon, Rachel," Low said, as Clement pulled the wagon to a stop.

"Hello, Mr. Low," Rachel said, ignoring Vega. "This is Victor Cheval."

"Mr. Cheval," Low said, nodding at Clement. "I've heard some about you."

"It was good, I hope," Clement said and noticed Vega giving him a quizzical look.

"Wasn't bad," Low said. "Clay Allison came by my place not too long ago . . ."

Clement heard Rachel utter a disapproving sound.

". . . said Rachel's been nursing a lost French fellow back to health."

"That is true," Clement said.

"I'm Deputy Sheriff Cruz Vega." He nodded at Clement. "You look familiar to me, *señor.* Perhaps we have met someplace before?"

Merde! Out the corner of his eye, Clement saw Rachel turn her face toward him as he stared at Vega, anxiously trying to place him. If the deputy did know him from somewhere and blurted it out, that would be very bad. No. It would be worse. *Catastrophique!* Clement was no more prepared to have to admit being a priest to Rachel than to have to deny it to this deputy. "I don't think so," Clement said. He wanted to snap those reins and get going.

"I have a memory for faces."

Clement shrugged and shook his head. "I don't believe we've met."

"Well, I need to get a move on," Low said.

Clement felt relieved. They would all go on their way now. Then Vega spoke to Low.

"I will be there tonight," Vega said.

"Something going on tonight?" Rachel asked.

"Oh, a . . ." Low said, looking a little sheepish, Clement thought. "Varmints been tearing up my winter corn. Could be Indians. Deputy Vega said he'd come by the next two, three nights. Run them off for me."

"Better be careful he doesn't set fire to your cornfield," Rachel said.

God help us. Clement didn't expect Rachel to make an accusation, but it was out now. He kept his eyes on Vega, not knowing what he might do next. Vega stared at Rachel. Low didn't move, taken by surprise, his eyes darting back and forth from Vega to Rachel.

Vega spoke. "That is an unfair thing to say, *señora.*"

"Unfair? What's unfair is a couple of men tried to set fire to my barn last night. One of them was a Mex. Might've been you." There was a fine flaming color in her face and an insolent tone in her voice.

"There are many of my *compadres* in this county," Vega said, the insolence in his voice matching hers, "but I don't know the business of all of them. And to know where they are all the time, well, that is *imposible.* But if you have an accusation to make, and maybe the proof to go with it, I would be happy to escort you to the town and you can tell the sheriff."

Was he serious, or was it a bluff? Clement thought. Cockiness was sometimes known to mask a jellied spine. Regardless, Clement felt the tension in the air. Seemed like he was practically breathing it in. "Maybe we should all be on our way," he said.

Rachel blinked twice. But she said nothing, which Clement took as a good sign that she wouldn't press the issue. Especially considering the go-to-hell look she had fixed on Vega.

"You may be right, *señor,*" Vega said.

Clement was about to snap the reins when Vega spoke again.

"But I still think I've seen you somewhere. Have you ever

been in Colorado? Trinidad, perhaps?"

Clement made himself smile. "No."

Rachel mumbled something under her breath. All Clement heard was "reckoning one day." He wanted to tell her to be quiet.

"Do you wish to say something, *señora*?" Vega asked.

She drew her lips in, crossed her arms and shook her head. Clement was glad she wasn't reaching inside her coat for her revolver.

Vega waited, keeping his eyes on her. To Clement it was like Vega was hoping, wishing she would say something. Then he saw the deputy shift his eyes back to him. "Maybe it was in *Tejas* our paths crossed." Vega tapped a finger against his lips. "Ah, I know. San Antonio. *¿Verdad?*"

"You must have me confused with—"

"Wait!" Vega said, wagging his finger. "It was Santa Fe. During the celebration for the new archbishop."

No, no, no, Clement thought. Don't let on. Don't look at Rachel. He kept his eyes on Vega. "No," he said. "You have me confused with someone else."

"No, I'm sure of it. I remember you. But you look, different." He made a motion with his hand. "Something is different."

"I wasn't there," Clement said evenly, his mouth a tight smile. "We should get going now." He nodded at Vega. *"Con permiso."*

A wide condescending smile spread across Vega's face. *"Como no."* He waved his arm, like some grand gesture inviting them to pass.

Clement snapped the reins, relieved and glad to be going, getting Rachel as far away from Vega as possible, as quickly as he could. Thank You, Lord, for our deliverance.

As they passed, out the corner of his eye, Clement saw Vega watching him, trying to remember where he'd seen him. That worried Clement. But the brazen deputy's insolence rankled him. His impudent manner. Everything about that man rankled him. Rachel had goaded him, no question about that. But the more he thought about it, the more Vega's response was clearly a threat. Happy to escort you to town, he'd said. But it was the way he'd said it. Daring her. Provoking her. Come to think of it, maybe the Mexican had been trying to prod him to see which of them was the big he-bull. Clement's animus for Vega only intensified. Love your neighbor, Jesus told us. He didn't say anything about having to like him.

"Your face will come to me, *señor,*" he heard Vega say. "I know I have seen you."

Clement paid Vega no mind. Rachel was still angry—her arms crossed, her jaw set.

A few moments later, Clement glanced back. Vega and Low parted company. Vega headed off toward town and Low went north into the woods. Good. Vega wasn't following them.

They rode in silence for a ways and Clement couldn't help wondering what Rachel had been thinking accusing Vega that way. Like it or not, the man represented the law. And that badge gave him rights and powers, deserved or not. That little incident could have gone much worse, for all of them. And had Vega seen him before in Santa Fe? The investiture of the archbishop had been such a crowded affair. Had Clement spoken to the man at some point? The last thing he needed was somebody recognizing him and telling every soul in sight that he was a priest. He didn't even want to think about the questions, the shame and the consequences if Vega had called him out. How could he explain that now, especially to Rachel?

"I want to tell you something," Rachel said. "I have a temper and I didn't mean to let it . . . I hate what's happening around here and I know you were trying to protect me. Thank you."

Clement nodded. She could be headstrong, that was a fact. And that fiery color in her cheeks when she was going eye to eye with Vega had been something to see.

Rachel shifted on the seat, frowning. Clement asked her what was bothering her.

She said she couldn't understand why Bill Low would ask the Mexican to watch his field. "He's had that field for longer than I've been here and he's always been the one to run off anything sniffing around."

"He must have his reasons."

"Mr. Low started his place here over twenty years ago. He was a friend of Mr. Maxwell's. Helped him build his first home down on the Rayado. He isn't afraid of anything on two legs or four. Something doesn't make sense."

Chapter Nineteen

"Put Floyd in a cell," Chittenden told Rinehart as the three men rode up to the jail. "I'll get Doc Longwell. He should take a look at him. And check that lump on the back of your head, too."

"I'm all right," Rinehart said. "Just need some coffee is all."

"Got any whiskey to put in that coffee?" Floyd asked.

"No whiskey for you," Chittenden said, looping the reins of his horse around the hitching rail and heading for Longwell's house.

Halfway there, he remembered court was in session this morning and made a detour to the adobe courthouse. As he went through the doorway, he saw Judge Longwell at his table putting some papers into his valise. When Longwell looked up, Chittenden could tell he was displeased.

"You're a little late, Sheriff," Longwell growled.

"What do you mean?"

"I mean I had no deputy here for my court session."

"I told Vega four days ago it was his turn."

"Well, he wasn't here, and Mills made a point that it wasn't the proper way to conduct the proceedings."

Mills can go to hell, Chittenden thought.

"I sent him out to find you or a deputy. He didn't like it, either. Took his sweet time getting back, too. But I wasn't about to dismiss court. Lucky for all of us no one got unruly," Longwell continued and opened his blue coat revealing a revolver.

"Good thing I had this in case. But you better have a talk with your deputy."

"As soon as I see the little chili picker," Chittenden said. "But right now I need you to come to the jail."

"Somebody bleeding to death in there?"

Chittenden told Longwell about Floyd clobbering Teague and the subsequent attempted hanging.

"I need to go to my place and check on Deputy Wilcox first," Longwell said.

"How's he doing?" Chittenden asked.

"Got a fever and chills."

"But he'll be all right, won't he?"

"We'll see. I wrapped him in a couple of good wool blankets, trying to break that fever. Don't want it getting any worse. Floyd Kunkle's probably got a hell of a neck burn at the very least, but you say he's breathing, so chances are he'll make it through."

"And take a look at Rinehart, too. Somebody clubbed him during the fracas."

"I'll do that," Longwell said. He closed his valise and they headed out the door. "Now, as to Floyd Kunkle's legal matters, sounds like you're going to have to hold him here for awhile until we can sort out this mess. My predecessor in this job left me such a backlog of cases it'll be better than a week before I can hear his case for assaulting Teague. He better have counsel. Maybe Jim Hazlett." Longwell scratched his heavy sideburns. "Well, I'll discuss it with Floyd when I see him at the jail."

The mention of legal matters reminded Chittenden of the deed situation.

As they walked toward Longwell's house, Chittenden said, "This whole business with Floyd and Teague started on account of both of them hold a signed deed for the same piece of land."

Longwell chuckled. "You mean to tell me in all this time you didn't know?"

"Know what?"

Sitting on his chestnut mare, Dixon Poth thought about shooting the meek little German man who was standing in his doorway looking up at him. Leo Hensel was worth more to him dead than alive. But Hensel was unarmed. Hensel also said it wasn't right that Poth was threatening him. Reverend McMains was taking the grant case to Washington and a court was going to decide the matter. And besides, Hensel had children to care for. He was a widower; his wife passed away two years ago. Hensel claimed he had no money. Poth didn't care. Taking a corner of the bandana draped around his neck, he wiped his crooked, swollen nose. He was getting tired of listening to this schnitzel-eater whine when two small, blond-haired children came out of the house and peered out from behind his legs. A boy and a girl. Poth guessed them to be around eight or nine years of age.

The little girl looked frightened. The boy stared up at him. Poth heard the girl say something in German and Hensel shushed her. She was probably saying something about his ugly busted nose, Poth felt certain, and decided to have a little fun. He opened his mouth and screamed at them like some banshee.

Eyes wide in terror, the children screamed, and buried their faces in their father's pant legs.

Poth laughed. He didn't know which was funnier, those little brats hiding or their father nearly jumping out of his skin.

Hensel hurried his kids back inside the house and closed the door. Turning back to Poth, he looked as scared now as they had.

"Don't hurt them," Hensel said, his voice shaky.

Still laughing, Poth said, "As long as you don't give me a reason."

He wasn't the mad-dog killer some had claimed. At least, he didn't believe it to be true. It was a fact he'd killed women and children during the late war. They'd given aid to the enemy and an example had to be made to discourage others from like actions. Poth always prided himself on having a clear reason to achieve his aims. It was no different then than it was today.

"Now you listen to me," Poth said, his voice deadly now, his right hand resting on the butt of the revolver on his left side. "You understand that I will come back here tomorrow."

"Yes, I do," Hensel said, and sniffed. "But how am I supposed to get all our belongings packed up, and where do we go then?"

"I don't care, as long you're not here. But if you don't leave, you will hear the cock crow."

Hensel looked like he was about to burst into tears. "This isn't . . . this isn't right. I bring my family to this country. All the way from Prussia. I become citizen. This—"

Poth pulled his revolver, aimed it at Hensel and cocked it in one swift motion. The German trembled, his mouth shut tight. Poth let a few moments pass, decided his point was made, holstered his gun and left.

Of all the business needing tending to that intruded on Chittenden's mind as he rode to Rachel Scott's place, the one that ate him the most was still the stranger out there with her. But he couldn't ignore what he'd been told about Melvin Mills. That dandified pipsqueak was also a thieving son-of-a-bitch. Judge Longwell had confirmed the whole messy business of the dual deeds. Mills was behind it, all right. He'd convinced one of the Maxwell Land Grant and Railroad Company attorneys to join in his scheme. And Teague was playing along, having been promised a tidy sum for his help in this scam.

Chittenden understood it was one thing to get squatters to

leave. He could even stomach the midnight "encouragement" his deputies visited on them. These were squatters, after all. But Floyd owned his land. He paid for it. And Mills was trying to line his own pockets by playing Floyd against Teague in this despicable legal game he'd concocted.

And that wasn't Mills's only scam. Longwell tipped him that Mills and a handful of other lawyers in cahoots with him in Cimarron and Elizabethtown were making fictitious indictments against folks all over the county—claims of trespass, insufficient payment, breach of contract and the like. The charges were nothing so egregious as to warrant arrest and jail time but serious enough to require the accused to appear at the courthouse in Cimarron. "Once there," Longwell had told him, "Mills or one of his cohorts would inform them, with a big smile, mind you, that he'd gotten the charges dismissed. The grateful folks would then be presented with a bill for services of ten or twenty dollars, which they'd pay, with thanks."

"You think maybe we should put a stop to this?" Chittenden suggested.

Longwell chortled. "The way Melvin Mills operates, he'd have two more schemes going before noon. Besides, he gives me a percentage to look the other way. But I'll talk to him and see that he starts slipping you a few dollars, too. It's only fair."

"No need."

"It's no trouble. He should've been including you all along anyway."

No, Chittenden did not like this. These were petty little games Mills was playing with folks. And he didn't approve of Longwell allowing it, but knew Longwell went along and did what he was told by Mills, who took his orders from that high and mighty Catron sitting down there in Santa Fe. No, by damn, Chittenden didn't like it, or that thieving, oily-haired little bastard Mills. But he didn't want to think about this anymore now. He wasn't far from Rachel's place and needed to ready himself to deal with that stranger there. And, just as importantly, to fix in his mind what he was going to say to her.

Chapter Twenty

Helping Rachel fill several pails with water from the creek, Clement hated the decision he'd made, but he knew it was the right thing, the best thing and the only thing now. Much as he wanted to get his money back from Poth, he couldn't take the chance Vega, or someone else, might recognize him. All of this had to be a message from God.

Yet, looking at Rachel, Clement felt more confounded. She was a desirable woman. Spirited and formidable, too, as she'd proven on several occasions. She'd nursed him back to health, helped him when he most needed it. And what had he done in response? Lied to her. Of course he'd justified it as necessary to hide his true identity. But he'd told the lie so many times, and to so many people! The deception was laying heavy on his soul. He'd devoted his life to the Almighty. And there was his parish to consider. His responsibilities were there, the needs of his parishioners. And the archbishop. But Rachel was stirring needs and desires in him he could not, he must not, succumb to.

She turned to him, after filling her pails. Brushing a few loose strands of hair away from her face with her forearm.

He had to go. He needed to go. Say it, he told himself. Tell her now.

"I hope you'll come with me to town tomorrow," she said, a little nervously. "After services we'll be burying Hannah. I'd appreciate it if you'd be there with me."

"Of course," Clement said. "And, Rachel, after the funeral—"

"I know what you're going to say," she cut in as she picked up her pails and started back to her cabin. "But let's not worry ourselves about that now."

Taking his water pails he caught up with her. He wanted to look at her, to see her face, but he forced himself not to, afraid he would lose his nerve and tell her he wouldn't leave if he saw her upset. It occurred to him it might be best if he slept in the barn tonight, too.

A big man on horseback appeared from behind the cabin. Clement saw the tin star pinned to his coat. Clement guessed he was the sheriff.

"Good Lord," he heard Rachel mutter. "What's he want?"

The big man dismounted as Clement and Rachel returned to the cabin and set down their water pails by the door. Clement saw the man give him a quick, surly once-over, then turn his attention to Rachel.

"Afternoon, Rachel," the big man said, holding the bridle reins in his hand. He waited a moment then added, "Aren't you going to introduce me to your friend here?"

"He's just that, Sheriff," she said evenly. "My friend."

He kept his eyes on her, sniffed, then narrowed his gaze to Clement. "What's your name, mister?"

"Victor Cheval." How many more times would he have to tell this lie, Clement wondered.

"Now you know who he is," Rachel said. "What do you want? Can't be an ejectment notice. You already served me one of those. Or maybe you came to apologize."

He frowned. "Apologize? For what?"

"Two of your boys tried to set fire to my barn last night. You going to do anything about it?"

"My boys?"

"Your deputies." She practically spit the word out.

"That's a serious accusation, Rachel. I'll make sure to look into it. But it wasn't any of my deputies, I assure you."

"One was white. One was Mex."

"A lot of both in this county."

"So I've been told," she said brusquely.

Chittenden grunted. "What makes you so certain they were deputies?"

Clement saw the expression on her face go from disgusted to bemused. She breathed a big sigh and said, "I'm not going to argue with you about it, Sheriff. You aren't going to do anything anyway. You came out here to say something. Say it and get."

The Sheriff shifted his shoulders, shot a look at Clement and licked his lips. "I want . . ." He glanced at Clement again and back at her. "I'd like to talk to you. Alone."

"Anything you want to say to me you can say right here and now."

"I'll take the water inside," Clement said.

"You don't need to go, Victor," she said, keeping her eyes fixed on the sheriff. "Matter of fact, I'd rather you stayed."

Clement could tell the big sheriff was wishing this were going differently as he nervously slapped the reins against the palm of his hand.

"I, uh . . ." the sheriff began. "What I have to say would be better said alone."

Rachel set her jaw. Clement felt very awkward standing there. He thought the sheriff might just get back up on his horse and ride away, but he did not.

"Sheriff Chittenden," Rachel said, "I have chores to tend to."

He took a step toward her and she did not back away. Chittenden narrowed his eyes at Clement again and tried to keep his voice low. Clement dropped his head down, trying not to listen, but he couldn't help hearing what he said.

"I could make things a lot different for you, Rachel. Better for you. I'd like to do that. If you'll let me."

It sounded almost like a proposal of marriage. Clement waited. It was so quiet he heard the wings of a hawk flap gently overhead. Rachel said nothing. Her mouth was a thin line. Chittenden had not taken his eyes from her. Finally, Rachel spoke.

"I told you no once before. Anything else you want to know, Sheriff?"

Chittenden had the look of man going from defeated to embarrassed to angry. Clement almost felt sorry for him.

"I guess I know all I need to know," Chittenden said bitterly and mounted his horse. Without another word, he reined the horse in the direction of Cimarron and rode away.

Clement watched him go. Rachel stood there, shaking her head in angry disbelief, then looked at him. It was like she was searching for the right words to say. "I'm sorry you had to . . . Oh, the gall of that man!" She impatiently reached for her water pails. "I got chores to get on with."

Clement wanted to comfort her. As a priest, he had learned to offer solace with the word of God. But no words came to him. He felt the urge to go to her, to hold her in his arms, to reassure her that everything would be all right. He took a step toward her. She was straightening up, water pails in hand, and facing away from him, starting for the cabin door. He was about to say her name when they heard Chittenden call out and saw him wheel his horse around and come trotting back to them. Setting down her pails, Rachel was none too pleased at Chittenden's return.

"There is something else I want to know," he announced, reining in before them. This time he didn't dismount. He looked squarely at Clement. "How long you been around here, mister? In this county."

"A few days," Clement said. "Not a week yet."

"He got waylaid by your new deputy," Rachel said tersely.

Chittenden appeared surprised for a moment then said, "I

am speaking to Cheval here, Mrs. Scott," all the while keeping his eyes on Clement.

Rachel let out a gruff sigh.

"Now," Chittenden said to Clement, "are you claiming that Dixon Poth attacked and robbed you?"

"That's right," Clement said.

"You the one busted his nose?" Chittenden asked.

Clement nodded. He saw a faint smile cross Chittenden's face.

"And where'd this happen?" Chittenden's smile disappeared.

Rachel said, "San Miguel County. I was coming back from Texas and—"

Not looking at her, Chittenden cut her off sharply saying, "I'm asking him."

"It probably was San Miguel," Clement said. "I haven't been in this county before."

"Well, San Miguel's out of my jurisdiction," the sheriff said.

"The man's a thief," Rachel said, the color rising in her face. "He stole this man's horse and money. Left him for dead. We found his horse at Carey's. Had to buy it back."

Chittenden still had not looked at Rachel. "How much money do you claim he stole?"

"About fourteen hundred dollars."

Chittenden sat back in his saddle. "Can you prove it?"

"I wish I could," Clement replied. He meant it.

"Where'd you win all this money?"

He didn't want to tell him Fort Union. What if the sheriff were to make inquiries? What if he found out he was really a priest? Committing himself could prove dangerous. "Different places," he lied.

"So, you're a gambler, then?" Chittenden asked.

"I just got lucky at cards. I'm a . . . nothing. A drifter."

"I call that shiftless. A saddle bum."

Rachel put her hands on her hips.

"You claim you've never been in this county before," Chittenden said.

"That's right."

"Never stepped foot here."

What was he after? Clement wondered. "No," he answered.

"I see. Then tell me something," Chittenden said. "Where were you about the middle of last month?"

Clement certainly couldn't tell him he was tending his parish, but this had caught him off guard. "I don't remember."

"Well, try."

Clement couldn't think of anything to say.

"You meet up with anybody? Get into one of your lucky card games?" Chittenden persisted. "Stay any place where they'd remember you? Some whorehouse, maybe?"

He's trying to goad me, Clement thought, or embarrass me in front of Rachel. "No," he said, simply.

"What are you doing, Sheriff?" Rachel demanded.

"I want to know where you've been, mister. Can anybody vouch for your whereabouts?"

Only the people who know I'm a priest, Clement thought, as he shook his head.

"Hold on here," Rachel said, her anger rising. "You aren't saying you think this man had something to do with Reverend Tolby's killing?"

"It's a murder that is so far unsolved. I'm still looking into it. Your 'friend' here's got no alibi."

"You listen to me, Sheriff," Rachel said. "He doesn't need one. You got no proof to accuse him, either. And now, you can get the hell off my land. Take your dirty accusations with you and don't come back. You aren't welcome here, or wanted."

Now they were glaring at each other. Clement prayed the sheriff didn't say anything else and hoped he wouldn't step down off his horse. If he did either one, Clement knew there'd be hell to pay. Rachel was liable to wallop Chittenden with one of those water pails. It felt like an eternity passed before the sheriff spoke.

"We'll see." He pulled his horse around and rode off for the second time.

Clement and Rachel watched until he disappeared into the trees.

When Rachel turned to Clement, he saw the uneasy look on her face.

"I know you didn't kill the reverend," she said. "But I wouldn't put it past these Ring bastards to invent evidence. Pardon my unchristian language. As much as I hate to say it, you need to get out of this county, and fast."

Clement went up to her. "I said I'd see you to your sister's funeral tomorrow."

Picking up two water pails, he walked through the cabin doorway and heard her whisper, "Stubborn man."

All the way back to Cimarron, Chittenden cursed his bad luck. Everything was a mess. What the hell had he been thinking with that idiotic proposal to Rachel? Saying it out there in the open like that. Letting her push him into it. Damn! And right in front of that man, that Victor Cheval. Helping her fetch water. If that's what she wants, she was welcome to him! Don't know what she sees in him, anyway. And her getting tetchy the way she did. Hell's bells, of course he knew Cheval hadn't killed Tolby. He was only trying to scare him off. But that Frenchy didn't look scared and what's more he didn't look like he would get scared. And it sure as hell didn't appear like he was in any hurry to be leaving, either. Damn it! On top of that, Chittenden figured he'd made himself look like ten kinds of a damn fool. He'd let Rachel run him off. That was a hard fact. He was swimming in a shit stew all right. One that he'd helped concoct, too: the disastrous business with Rachel, that little bastard Mills giving him orders, that damn Poth, this Reverend Tolby blunder, this whole miserable affair of the Maxwell Land Grant. God damn it!

When he rode up to the jailhouse, Chittenden saw Floyd's mule still hitched out front, along with Rinehart's sorrel and the painted horse Vega rode, and that damn gaudy, silver, Mex saddle.

Going inside, he found Rinehart and Vega playing cards at his desk.

"Where the hell you been, Vega?" Chittenden demanded. "And both of you get away from my desk. This ain't some saloon."

Vega got up slowly while Rinehart moved around over by the stove. Going to his desk, Chittenden caught sight of Floyd asleep on the bunk back in the first cell.

"I'm waiting for an answer, Vega."

Vega shrugged. "*Aqui.* Here. All afternoon."

"No. Where were you this morning when you were supposed to be in Judge Longwell's courtroom?"

"Not me," Vega said, resting his thumbs on top of his gun belt. "You told Cardenas to go."

"No. I told you."

Glancing at Rinehart then Chittenden, Vega said, "No, you say to me to take ejectment notices to the squatters on North Ponil Creek. That is what I did."

"Two days. That's all it should've taken. You had plenty of time to be back here for courtroom duty."

Vega shrugged. "It took me longer."

Chittenden didn't care for this Mex's lippy tone. "That so," the sheriff said. "You hand them all out?"

"Sí," Vega said.

"So I go out and check your saddlebag, I won't find any undelivered notices in it. That what you're saying?"

Vega curled his lips tight. *"Esto es mierda,"* he said.

"You're damn right this is shit," Chittenden said loudly. "Your excuse is shit, too."

"Hey," Floyd called out from his cell. "What's all that hollering about?"

"Shut your damn mouth, Floyd!" Chittenden shouted, keeping his attention on the Mexican. "Anything else you got to say, Vega?"

"I no answer to you!"

"Get the hell out of here! You're fired. Get out! See Mills for your pay!"

"¡Hijo de puta!" Vega shouted, snatching his badge off his shirt and throwing it on the floor.

Chittenden made a move toward him, but stopped himself as the Mexican scurried past him, snatching his red coat off the rack, and ran out the door.

"Get the hell out of this county you God damn chili picker!" Chittenden shouted and slammed the door shut. He heard Vega cursing him in Mex talk outside, calling him everything but a white man, but paid it no mind.

"You listen here," Chittenden said, turning to Rinehart. "No more ejectment notices until I say otherwise."

"No more?" Rinehart asked, surprised.

"Not a one. And no more midnight visits, either." He went to the stove and picked up the coffee pot to pour himself a cup. Examining the big dent on one side he said, "What happened to this pot?"

"Found it like that on the floor when I brought Floyd in."

Chittenden recalled Longwell telling him about sending Mills out to bring him to the courthouse. He probably threw a tantrum when he couldn't find him. Damn jackass! "Haven't you got something you should be doing?" he barked at Rinehart.

Rinehart gave him a sullen look, snatched up his hat and left.

Still wearing his coat, Chittenden sat down heavily behind his desk. No coffee ready. Dented pot. "Damn it all!" he swore. Everything was going to hell. And God damn it, it was all Mills's fault. Hiring useless Mexicans. Special talents, my ass. Bullshit! Mills had vouched for Vega. Cardenas, too. Bunch of ignorant, back-shooting chili stealers, as far as he was concerned. And that low-down son-of-a-bitch Poth pulling a gun on him right here, his own office! Not one of them worth a tinker's damn in a real stand-up fight. No, this whole business won't do, not anymore! If Mills wants to run things, he can damn well go ahead and try. Let's see how he likes that!

Chapter Twenty-One

Amos Tully cupped his cold hands over his mouth and blew to try to warm them up as he reconnoitered the sod hut. He heard no sound, saw no chimney smoke. Just the same, he was careful in his approach. After ground tethering his horse, he hit the wooded door twice with the flat of his hand. "Anybody home?" No answer.

Glancing about the surrounding clearing, he saw no one coming and opened the door. No one was asleep inside. Or dead, for that matter, though it reeked of some foul odor. Some embers still glowed in the fireplace. The bed was unmade. A plate on the table had leftover food still on it. He saw no rifle or pistol. Perhaps they'd gone hunting. At any rate, someone lived here and they'd be back, sooner or later.

Tully worked fast. A chest sat over in a corner. Opening it, he found a couple of blankets, a broken clock and, thank you Jaysus, a pair of corduroy trousers. Holding them up to his waist, he could tell they were a little bigger than he was, but he didn't care. Better too big than too small. He needed to shuck this blue uniform. He put on the trousers and pulled his belt tight at the waist to hold them up. His army boots would be fine. Underneath the blankets he found an old plaid shirt and a buckskin coat. He slipped it on and surprisingly it fit pretty well. Maybe the man who lived here had inherited it. Or stolen it from somebody.

He found some hardtack by the fireplace, but not much else

in the way of food. But there was a covered bowl he opened and inside was a small cloth bag containing six dollars in coins and a few greenbacks, which he slipped into his pocket. He also found a plaid shirt rolled into a ball in a corner. It smelled ripe, but he didn't care. He stuck his uniform in the chest and covered it with the blankets.

Outside, Tully mounted his horse. He knew patrols were out looking for him. Deserters had to be found. Tully was hoping they'd guess he'd head south for old Mexico. That's why he was heading north. He figured to get to Cimarron tomorrow and then on to Colorado. Or maybe turn west to California.

Arriving back in Cimarron just before evening, Dixon Poth went straight to Mills's house. Once inside his office, Poth told Mills about shooting Newcomb.

"Excellent," Mills said.

"I wish I'd shot that whiney German, Hensel," Poth said, "but I'll go back there tomorrow, see if he's packed up his snot-nosed kids."

"Any others?" Mills asked gleefully.

Poth said he'd gone looking for two other names on Mills's list. "The Dewhurst place was already deserted. From the looks of things, he pulled out pretty recently."

"I heard a rumor he'd run already."

"The other one was Gries."

"Tell me you shot him," Mills said. "Man's a real agitator."

Poth had, he said, along with Gries's wife, a skinny, cantankerous woman. She was sitting on a crate in front of her cabin plucking a dead chicken and claimed her man had gone to Santa Fe on business and cussed a blue streak at Poth. When Poth wheeled his horse around to leave, a rifle bullet buzzed past his head. Poth drew his revolver and spun in time to see Gries in the cabin window fire again. Poth fired, hitting Gries, who fell backwards. Gries's wife screamed and pulled a pistol she had hidden behind the crate and fired wildly. Poth fired and killed her instantly, hitting her in the chest. He heard moans and swearing from inside the cabin. Dismounting, he went in, saw Gries sprawled on the floor, his rifle just out of his reach. "I made him suffer," Poth said, and showed Mills the nick in the curled front brim of his hat Gries's bullet had made. "I wore this hat through the war. Never a mark, until today."

After Mills paid him two hundred and fifty dollars for Newcomb, Gries and his wife, Poth rode over to the livery stable at Carey's Hardware to put his horse up for the night. Considering Carey's demeanor, it seemed to Poth that the merchant was holding a grudge against him for his words with the grave digger earlier that day. Poth didn't care. And when Carey told Poth he'd sold the buckskin horse and tack for him, Poth took the fifty dollars and headed across the street for the hotel, not even offering Carey a fee for the sale. Poth figured he was under no obligation since no discussion was made regarding a fee.

Entering the lobby, he saw the desk clerk with the green garter sleeves sweeping the floor. The clerk looked in his direction and the blood drained from his face. Still a scared mouse, Poth chuckled to himself. The clerk stopped his sweeping, stepped behind the desk and fidgeted with worry. Instinctively, Poth knew he was hiding something. And there was a good chance it was something he needed to know.

When Poth got to the desk, the scared clerk was looking everywhere but at him.

"You look like you got something on your mind," Poth said.

"N-no, I . . . I don't," the clerk stuttered nervously.

"Look at me," Poth said grimly.

The clerk blinked and tried to keep from shaking.

"There's something on your mind. You look like you're afraid to tell me. You should be afraid not to tell me."

The clerk's mouth moved but no sound came out.

"I'm not asking you again," Poth said, pulling his revolver and shoving it up under the clerk's nose.

Eyes squeezed shut, the clerk stuttered, "I-I—"

Poth cocked the revolver.

"Don't, don't shoot me. Please. It . . . it was a Frenchy. Said he knew you."

Poth chuckled. "That's a fact. You know where he is now?"

The clerk barely shook his head.

"Was anybody with him?"

"N-no. But a local woman came in asking for him and he come out and th-they left together."

"Blue dress. Red hair. Good-looking?"

"Yes."

"Tell me her name."

The clerk bit his lip trying to form the words. "Rachel S-scott."

"Where does she live? And don't lie to me. Or you will hear the cock crow three times."

Rachel felt pulled in a dozen different directions. She did not want Victor to leave. In spite of the words she'd had with Reverend McMains in town earlier and though she had told Victor she didn't wish to talk about his going tomorrow, she dreaded the thought of his departure. Victor had mentioned something about it being best if he slept out in the barn tonight and she couldn't remember now what she'd said to him. Sheriff Chittenden's ridiculous proposal and accusation had left her so angry that she'd hardly spoken three words to Victor in as many hours. Of course, she also knew she was using Chittenden as a foolish excuse because she was afraid to talk to Victor, afraid she would burst into tears or worse. It was like she was a youngster again suffering from a silly schoolgirl infatuation.

And then as they were finishing up supper, though neither of them had been particularly hungry, Rachel had an idea.

"I was talking to Mr. Carey earlier," she said. "He made me a proposition. Said there's a man he knows down south with a herd of horses he wants to sell. Maybe two hundred head. He asked me if I'd like to go into business with him. I could run the herd here on my land. Folks need horses. You know that well enough. He said we would split the profits on the sales. The thing is, if I did go into business with him, I could use some help with those horses."

"That is a tempting offer," he said, pushing the brown beans around on his plate with his spoon. "But I can't stay. I have things I need to do."

From some men, that would have sounded like a hollow excuse to leave, not a reason. But she believed Victor. She didn't want to accuse him of hiding something from her. It wasn't any of her business anyway. Besides that, she didn't believe he was hiding anything. She also knew that men did take strange ideas into their heads at times. Some felt compelled to roam, to give the bear his due. And some weren't the settling down kind. They wanted, even needed, the solitary life. That was a plain fact. She just wished Victor wasn't set on leaving.

"You needn't sleep out in the barn tonight," she said.

"I think it's best," he said. "I'm better now, thanks to you. It wouldn't look right."

"Maybe not, but it's cold out there. I can sleep in my rocking chair. You should take the bed. Get a good night's sleep since you're moving on tomorrow." Those last words nearly caught in her throat.

"I'll be fine. An extra blanket or two is all I need. There's plenty of hay. Believe me, I've slept harder places."

"But it's silly for you to sleep in the barn," she said. "I want you . . . to stay." That almost didn't come out right. She did want him, but not to throw herself at him like some callous harlot. "I insist."

She was scared. There was a big empty hole in her gut. She did not want Victor to go. Not tonight. Not tomorrow. Time was the enemy for it did not stop. Time, and other people's opinions.

"Let me help you clean up these dishes," he said as he picked them up and took them to the basin she used to wash them off in.

Rachel had always strived to live her life by God's teachings, to find salvation. But to hell with what Reverend McMains had said about how having Victor in her house looked, and to hell with what any of the rest of the busybodies hereabouts thought. Victor was a decent man. They could have a good life here together. Of that she felt certain. No man had stirred her as Victor had. Not even Ethan, good man and provider that he was. Reverend McMains spoke often during services about God's judgment, that we are all accountable before God for our choices. "Temptation lurks all around and we are corrupted by sin," he'd said. "But God's divine grace is also within our reach if we have the courage to accept it." It seemed to her that God had put Victor in her path for a reason. She'd had one good marriage. Why not another? To her recollection, there was nothing in the Bible that said a woman could not ask a man to marry. And even if there was, at this moment, she didn't care.

"Victor, I want to—"

The sound of a horse galloping up outside distracted her. Victor went to the door and opened it. In the light cast from inside the cabin, they saw Reverend McMains slide weakly from his horse and drop to the ground.

"Good Lord!" Rachel cried.

She and Victor rushed outside and helped him into the cabin. McMains's breathing was shallow and he coughed from the cold air. Victor set him in the rocking chair by the fireplace while Rachel got the bottle of Collier's and a cup. She poured two fingers and held it out to him.

"Take a sip, Reverend," she said. "Catch your breath."

He waved the glass away. "I-I tried to . . . to stop it."

"Stop what?" Victor asked.

"I told you," McMains said as Rachel rubbed his cold bare hands.

"What are you talking about?" she asked.

"I found the man, the man who shot Reverend Tolby. They have him. At Bill Low's place. I tried to stop them. They're . . . they're going to kill him."

"Who?" Rachel asked.

"Deputy Vega. Bill Low got him to come out there. Said . . . said he needed help with something. We . . . I could use that drink now."

Rachel put the cup in his hand and he took it all in one gulp.

"Go on," Rachel said.

McMains shook his head. "We were waiting for them, Bill and Vega. Bill built a campfire. We rode down on them. Vega tried to run. We tied his hands. I told him we knew he'd been hired to carry the mail to Elizabethtown. Just for that day. We knew he was there on the road waiting for Reverend Tolby."

He held up his cup and Rachel poured him another drink. This time he took a sip.

"Did he admit it?" Rachel asked.

"No. Swore he wasn't there. That's when Clay—"

"Clay Allison?" Rachel said, a concerned edge in her voice.

McMains nodded. "He got tired of waiting, started to pistol-whip him, threw a noose around his neck and said he'd hang him if he told another lie."

"What were you thinking getting Clay involved?"

"I thought . . ." he said dejectedly. "I told him to stop. He told me if I couldn't stomach it to get out. Please, come help me stop this. I don't know what else to do."

Rachel despised Vega, but left in the hands of Allison, she knew justice would not be served. She looked at Victor. "Blood on our hands makes us no better than the Ring."

"Maybe there's still time," Victor said, pulling on his coat and hat. "I'll go saddle my horse."

"I'm so sorry," McMains said after Victor left. "I tried to do right. You do believe me? Tell me you believe me."

"Of course I believe you," Rachel said.

"I didn't mean for this to happen." He took another sip of whiskey. "I just wanted him to admit what he'd done. Confess. God forgive me." He set the cup on the table and buried his face in his hands.

Victor came back a few minutes later, an unlit torch in his hand. While he helped McMains out the door and onto his horse, Rachel went to the fireplace and lit the torch.

"Follow the creek until you come to the telegraph poles and follow them to Low's," Rachel said, handing Victor the torch, and they rode away into the dark night. She watched for a few moments and told herself Victor would be all right. To be safe, she asked God to keep him safe. Going back inside, she busied herself clearing the rest of the table and noticed the shotgun standing by the door. She wished she'd thought to give it to him. If Victor faced Clay Allison, that shotgun would help to do a lot of convincing. A terrible thought struck her. She jerked her head at the chest of drawers. Both of her revolvers lay on top, right where they had put them on their return from town. Victor had rushed out unarmed!

She heard the sound of a horse approaching. Thank you, Lord! She took the shotgun by the barrels, so as to hand it to him easily, certain Victor had realized what he'd forgotten and come back. Opening the door, she said, "Thank the Lord. You might need—" Dixon Poth stood there, pointing his revolver at her.

"An unexpected greeting," he said.

She didn't move, too startled at seeing him.

He indicated the shotgun. "Hand it here. Slow. And back up."

Rachel wanted to club him with it but did as he instructed.

Poth opened the breach, shucked the shells, threw them and the shotgun into the dark and shut the door.

Rachel kept her eyes fixed on him. Don't give him a reason to look at the chest of drawers. She had to find a way to get to the revolvers there.

"Where's the grave digger?"

"He'll be right back."

"I doubt that. I watched him ride off with your Reverend McMains. And without a gun, I'd say." He smiled. "I'm guessing they'll be gone a while. Sit down." He pointed at a chair and holstered his revolver. "I got a message for the grave digger. You're going to give it to him."

"Go to hell."

When he chuckled, Rachel thought his blue eyes looked dead.

"You speak right up," he said. "I like that. But right now you're going to listen. You tell the grave digger he's never getting his money. I know he searched my hotel room. Tell him if he keeps looking, he should prepare himself for the consequences." He smiled again. "And I know he's going to keep looking."

"No, he's not. He's leaving tomorrow."

"Is he now? I say you're lying."

He was standing between her and the dresser. That meant he didn't see the revolvers. If he'd leave, she could get to them and shoot him herself. She didn't care if she ventilated him in the front or the back. All she cared about was protecting Victor.

"Those beans smell good," he said. "How about you fix me some."

Grudgingly she stood, took a plate from the shelf.

"And don't get any bright ideas," Poth warned her.

She ladled out beans from the bubbling kettle onto a plate and held it out to him.

"Set it down and get me a spoon. I don't eat with my fingers."

And she shoved the plate of hot beans into his face.

Poth yelled in pain and tried clutching at her. She wanted to grab his revolver, but he got hold of her dress and she instinctively spun loose, tearing her dress, and raced for the chest of drawers. Grasping a revolver, she turned, but Poth braced her from behind with a forearm across her throat, his face dripping beans.

"Bitch!" He twisted the revolver out of her hand and threw it across the cabin. Pulling her arm roughly behind her, he bent her over onto the bed. Seeing the second revolver on the dresser, he tossed it away.

"I would send you to the garden to weep but you've got my message to deliver." He yanked up her skirts. "So I'm going to teach you some manners. And you're going to be nice."

Rachel struggled and felt him twist her arm up tighter.

"I told you be nice."

She screamed.

"Nobody can hear you."

CHAPTER TWENTY-TWO

Clement and McMains followed the creek and then the telegraph poles as Rachel said. The only words McMains had spoken to him were, "We must hurry." Clement pulled his coat collar closer around his neck against the cold. The torch fire helped some. He knew Rachel had been right in her reasoning about helping Vega. Killing him would do Rachel and the rest of the squatters no good. God forgive him, Clement didn't want to help that mouthy Mexican either, but he also dreaded the prospect of Vega truly knowing him and blurting out his name. Especially in front of Allison and McMains. Please God, Clement prayed, don't let that happen.

Coming through a rocky outcropping, Clement saw a corner of the cornfield lit up by the torches many of the men there held. The line of telegraph poles ran past it. There were twenty-four men by Clement's count. Most were on horseback in a rough three-quarter circle around the tree. In the torchlight, Clement could see blasts of frosty air shooting from the nostrils of the horses and shorter, sharper breaths from the men. Allison stood in front of Vega. Two other men, one in a dark hat, the other heavyset, held the Mexican, his hands still tied behind his back. His face was a bloody mess. He was on his feet with the noose still around his neck. Another three men held the rope they had stretched over a telegraph pole.

"They've taken them off," McMains said, sounding surprised.

"What?" Clement asked.

"We had our faces covered, to scare Vega. They've all taken off their masks."

Clement knew that meant these men weren't concerned that Vega could identify them because they'd decided Vega would not see the sunrise.

Allison drew his arm back and hit Vega in the face. "Haul him up," he shouted, his cold, gray breath hanging briefly in the air like a foul curse.

The men on the rope took hold and pulled. Vega's legs kicked wildly, his eyes squeezed shut. The rope drew tight up under his chin. Thin vapors of breath stuttered out of his mouth. An ugly gurgling sound carried across the cold night air.

The words flew out of Clement's mouth. "Let him down!" Kicking Paris hard, Clement charged the group, McMains close behind him.

Several of the mounted men drew their revolvers and aimed at them.

"Who the hell . . . ?" one of them said.

"Get out of here, Frenchman!" Allison shouted. "This is none of your affair! And take the gutless reverend with you."

"No!" Clement knew he was outnumbered, just like in that Mexican village so long ago. Reaching into his coat for his revolver, he suddenly realized he'd left it behind in the cabin. Damn!

"You must stop this, Clay Allison," McMains pleaded.

Clement saw Vega's right eye was swollen shut, his lips split and bloody.

Allison motioned to the men on the rope. "Let him down. Let's see if he's ready to talk."

Vega hit the ground, his legs buckling, and went facedown into the dirt.

"This man is going to confess," Allison said.

"Not this way," Clement said.

Allison pulled his revolver and pointed it at Clement. "You don't give me orders, understand? Now get!"

Vega rolled over on his back, choking and gasping for air. The two men got him to his feet and propped him up between them.

Clement pulled the collar of his coat up to try to cover his face, worried in case Vega might recognize him. He hated himself for his cowardice.

"Last warning, Frenchman. This is not your concern," Allison said, cocking his gun.

"All you're going to do is kill him," Clement said.

"He's right, Clay," McMains said. "We'll have nothing."

"No," Allison said, lowering his revolver but keeping it in his hand. "We'll have answers."

"You'll have a dead man," Clement said. "Let him loose."

"Hey, hey, he's trying to say something, I think," Dark Hat said.

"Let's hear it," Allison said and the heavyset man loosened the noose around Vega's raw neck.

Vega coughed and spit. "Card-es," he said, his voice croaking.

"What? Get him some water," Allison said.

Someone threw a canteen down at Vega's feet. Dark Hat picked it up and put the lip to Vega's mouth. He started to drink but coughed, spitting water.

"That's enough. What are you saying?" Allison asked.

"Cardenas," Vega said hoarsely. "It was Cardenas. He killed the man. He shot, not me."

"That's a pretty one," Allison said. "You and your Mex friend did the deed."

"No. I no shoot him."

"You got your answer," Clement said. "Let him go." He saw Vega look up at him, his sweat-streaked and swelling face twitching.

"*¡Dios mio, padre!*" Vega said, voice straining, good eye begging. "*¡Por favor!* Help me!"

Oh, God, he does know me, Clement thought fearfully. He glanced around to see if anyone was looking at him queerly. No one was. They just started laughing, led by Allison.

"He's gone loco," someone said.

"This ignorant Mex bastard wants a priest." Allison laughed and brought his face close to Vega's. "Say your prayers, assassin. Your Maker's waiting." He motioned to the men on the rope. They pulled, raising Vega off the ground.

"No!" Clement shouted. He couldn't allow this travesty, no matter the consequences.

Allison aimed his revolver at Vega, twisting and kicking for life, and shot him twice in the chest.

The crack of the gunfire echoed sharply in Clement's ears.

"Tie him off, boys," Allison said. "Leave him as a warning. Now we'll go get Cardenas. See what he has to say."

"I'm taking Vega's horse and saddle," someone announced. "I know a place I can get money for both over in Texas. No questions asked."

Jeers and laughter erupted. Clement felt helpless and ashamed. Vega's body hung there, swaying gently, the rope creaking against the wooden pole.

McMains raised his head, a dull look in his eyes, his voice breaking. "Since the fall in the garden, man's free will has been his greatest burden. God forgive us."

Allison mounted his horse and eyed Clement. "Get out of here, Frenchman. Take the 'Reverend' with you."

"I'll take him," Clement heard a voice behind him say. Twisting around, he recognized Bill Low, a torch in his hand. He must've been here the whole time and Clement didn't realize it.

"My house isn't far," Low continued, his eyes on Clement. "I get the feeling from the look on your face you think I'm some kind of Judas."

Clement didn't think he wore any kind of expression.

"Vega was no friend. He only came here on account of I offered to pay him. What he got he deserved." He pulled his horse around by McMains. "You shouldn't have come here, Mr. Cheval. None of your business." He patted McMains's leg. "Come on, Reverend."

His head hanging, McMains followed Low.

"Get going!" Allison barked at Clement.

Everything was upside down, Clement thought as he made his way back to Rachel's. He had acted cowardly and shamefully out of fear of being exposed as a liar and a man had lost his life. How would he atone? He felt so helpless. His feelings for Rachel had only complicated things and left him vulnerable. He should have done more, could have done more to try to save Vega. But even if he'd had a revolver, what could he have done to change things? Would he have shot Allison? If he had, he'd probably be lying back in that cornfield dead. There were no *juaristas* to come to his rescue here. Colfax County was a deadly place. What was done was done and nothing could change it. He prayed for his soul. And Vega's.

After putting Paris in the corral, Clement walked up to Rachel's cabin. Light shown through the crack of one of the window shutters. She had waited up for him.

Entering, Clement found her sitting on the bed, wrapped in a blanket. Her eyes were red and puffy. She'd been crying. He saw no sign of trouble. Dishes were washed and put away. The table wiped clean. The shotgun stood by the front door and the revolvers still on top of the chest of drawers.

"What's wrong, Rachel?" he asked, going to her. He also saw that she'd changed her clothes.

"That man came here," she said, her voice quivering slightly. "After you left."

"What man?" Clement asked, alarmed.

"Poth," she said.

"Did he hurt you?"

She shook her head. "Scared me is all."

"You look more than scared, Rachel."

"No, I'm fine," she said.

He didn't push it. "What did he want?"

"He wants you to come looking for him. That man is crazy evil."

He saw the fear in her eyes.

"Promise me, Victor," she said. "You won't go looking for him. Say it."

Now was not the time to argue. "I promise."

That seemed to calm her. "Good," she said. "Just stay with me. Please."

It may not have been the priestly thing to do, but he knew it was the compassionate thing. He sat next to her on the bed and placed his arm around her shoulder. She leaned against him, holding her blanket close. A minute passed. He felt her tremble. Lifting his hand, he gently touched her hair. Her trembling stopped. He let his fingers stroke her hair once. Twice.

So much had happened this night, so much to sort out. Vega. McMains. Rachel. Especially his feelings. About Rachel. About himself. About his choices.

Rachel had fallen asleep. Clement held her gently. He held her through the night.

CHAPTER TWENTY-THREE

It was just past seven in the morning and Melvin Mills was galled at being summoned to Longwell's house. *Summoned!* Like he was house help. He had business affairs to tend to in Colorado and needed to finish packing and preparing papers. It was imperative that he catch the northbound ten o'clock stage. He expected to be away about ten days. A man in Trinidad named Burdett wanted to sell his property, about a thousand acres. It was on grant land and Mills would act as the agent for the sale. And that meant a sizable commission. His vexation increased, however, as he walked across town bundled in his coat against the cold and passed the Barlow and Sanderson Company Stage Line office. Sanderson was putting out a sign saying that the ten o'clock stage was delayed. When Mills asked how long a delay, Sanderson said it would be at least an hour, maybe longer. Mills shook his head in disgust. Reaching Longwell's house he went up the steps and opened the front door. He saw Chittenden standing in the hallway by Longwell's examination room.

"What is so damn important that I have to come here right now?" he demanded as he headed down the hallway. "I have to catch the Taos stage and—" Mills stopped abruptly inside the doorway. On the examination table lay Vega's body, stripped to the waist. His face was purple and swollen and bruised. Both lips were split open. Red, raw rope burns surrounded his neck. Two bullet holes perforated his chest.

Mills felt like he was going to retch. Quickly reaching into his pocket, he pulled out a handkerchief and covered his mouth. He saw Chittenden smirk. How he hated that man now.

Mills took a couple of deep breaths. "How did this happen?" he asked through the handkerchief.

"Don't know exactly yet," Chittenden said. "Deputy Rinehart heard some talk over at Lambert's late last night. He rode out to Bill Low's place early this morning. Found Vega hanging from a telegraph pole by Low's cornfield, cut him down and brought him here."

"Do you know who did this?" Mills asked.

"From what Rinehart says he heard, rumor is that Clay Allison was involved."

"Have you questioned him?"

"Not yet. I only—"

"Well, when are you?" Mills demanded, raising his voice.

"As quick as I get around to it," Chittenden snapped.

"All right, calm down," Longwell said, his voice low. "I still have Zeke Wilcox in the room across the way. Sleeping, I hope. Let's continue this in the front parlor."

Mills glared at Chittenden and followed Longwell down the hall, wiping his mouth and stuffing the handkerchief back in his pocket.

"How is Wilcox, by the way?" Mills asked.

"His fever broke this morning, so that's good. But he still needs rest."

Once in the parlor, Mills said haughtily, "Now then, Sheriff, why don't you tell me what you do know."

"I'd say it's a pretty sure bet Vega was killed in retaliation for Tolby. Tolby was shot twice. So was Vega."

"But how would anyone know that Vega was involved?"

"Vega probably opened his mouth."

"Where's Cardenas?" Mills asked impatiently.

"I sent him up to Willow Springs," Chittenden said. "Told him to stay there until I sent word."

"Can you trust him?"

"You hired him. You tell me."

Mills held his temper. He'd had about enough of Sheriff Chittenden. Perhaps he would go see Catron as soon as he returned from Colorado. Chittenden needed to be replaced. Catron would want reasons, details. Mills would start right now.

"You ask me," Longwell said, "that Reverend McMains had something to do with this."

"No doubt," Mills said. "Sheriff, how do you propose to deal with this?"

"Ask questions, of course. What the hell do you think?"

"Well, I think that it's obvious you haven't been doing enough to drive these squatters out."

"I've been doing my job."

"Not well enough. A deputy has been murdered."

"You mean one of your hired killers. Not worth a damn!"

"I have given you deputies to enforce the law," Mills said. "Do the job you are being paid to do. If you no longer feel you can handle the job, perhaps it's time you moved on. It would be best, you know."

Chittenden's face flushed red. Mills saw his jaw working. He hoped the sheriff would quit on the spot. But he didn't. He walked past Mills without another word and out the door.

"You think that's such a smart thing to do?" Longwell asked, shutting the door. "Goading him like that?"

Mills huffed. "I'm no longer convinced we can depend on Sheriff Chittenden."

"But—"

"But what? Mr. Catron wants results. Sheriff Chittenden gives us arguments and excuses."

"Catron won't like it if this whole county goes up like a Roman candle."

"What we need is someone who understands how to take orders."

"You don't mean Poth, do you?"

"I'm thinking about it. He's wasted no time going after the names on the list."

"List?"

"Didn't I tell you? I gave him a list with twenty names on it. Allison, Newcomb, Dewhurst, Cass, Gries, Whitman. The real troublemakers. Poth's already gotten rid of Newcomb and says Dewhurst has cleared out. Once they're all gone, I doubt the rest of these squatters will put up much of a fight."

"What do you mean Poth's 'gotten rid' of Newcomb?"

"Don't worry. Poth is no mad dog. He has a way of getting his point across. Be assured of that."

"We thought Vega and Cardenas could handle Tolby and look what's happened."

"You worry too much," Mills said, waving his hand. "Besides, it's not like we're butchering cattle. May I remind you, these are squatters with no rights to this land."

"But Dewhurst and Cass and Whitman have families. I expect a lot of other names on your list do, too."

"Like I said, Poth has a way of making a point." Mills chuckled. "You know, I even put Hensel on the list."

"Hensel? What for? He's nothing."

"It's a nice piece of land he's on. I want it."

"You son-of-a-bitch," Longwell chortled. "Wait, you didn't put McMains on the list, did you?"

Mills shook his head. "We can't afford another dead preacher. Too much coincidence. Besides, once these squatters start leaving when Poth finishes his work, McMains won't have much of a congregation to stir up."

"You know what I think?"

"What?"

"I think that if Mr. Catron were to decide to retire from our little Ring, you could take his place."

Mills liked the sound of that.

Chittenden was so angry, he didn't even feel the icy air biting at his face as he marched up the street toward Lambert's Saloon. Some of Lambert's strong coffee was what he needed. That and breakfast. It would help him clear his head. Damn it—he'd let Mills get the upper hand, allowed the little bastard to rile him. Be more careful. That's what Chittenden needed to do. Then it dawned on him that it was Sunday morning. Lambert didn't open up until around noon.

Balling his fists and shoving them into his coat pockets, Chittenden turned to head for the jail when he saw Francisco Griego riding down the street. A stony expression was etched on the Mexican's face. He wore a sombrero, a coat and boots. Chittenden knew he also carried a Colt revolver, the same one he'd used to shoot two soldiers inside Lambert's one night last May. They'd accused him of cheating at cards. Revolvers were pulled. Griego was the one left standing. No one else was in the bar at the time, Lambert having gone in the back to retrieve a new keg of beer. Griego pleaded self-defense. Mills had defended him and won an acquittal. Griego had been very grateful. Later, Mills had made sure to remind him of that appreciation when he asked him to deliver the Mexican votes which Griego gladly did, getting Mills, Longwell and Chittenden elected. Chittenden had a grudging respect for Griego, but he was still a Mexican.

"Is it true what I hear about Vega?" Griego called out as he approached Chittenden. "Is my *amigo* dead?"

"He is," Chittenden said.

"Do you know who did it?"

"No, I don't," Chittenden said. "But I'll find out."

"I know. That *hijo de puta,* Clay Allison."

"Somebody tell you that?"

"No one has to tell me," the Mexican said, slapped the reins against his horse and rode away.

Shit! Chittenden thought. Griego was out for blood. If he stirred up the Mexicans in the county it would get even worse. And Rinehart was the only deputy left in town. A fuse was lit and burning at both ends. And at that moment Chittenden made up his mind. He might not keep his job much longer, but he'd do everything he could to frustrate and hinder that lying, swindling, oily-haired Mills at every opportunity.

Chapter Twenty-Four

"I made a promise to see you to town," Clement said to Rachel. "I said I'd help you bury your sister."

They were leaving Rachel's place in the buckboard. He noticed a squeaking sound but then it stopped. Rachel sat beside him on the same blanket she'd put on the seat yesterday. It was about half past ten. Clement had placed his saddle and hackamore in the bed and tied Paris to the back. He'd depart Cimarron after the funeral. That was a decision he'd wrestled with off and on during the night while he held Rachel as she slept.

"I'll be fine," Rachel said. "Poth isn't after me. But you need to go. There's still time. Go now."

Clement heard the worry in her voice. She was a strong woman. Yet also fragile.

"I made you a promise."

She closed her eyes a moment and gave him a brief smile. Lord, he would miss that smile. She sunk deeper into her coat as a cold breeze wafted by. Clement adjusted his coat collar closer around his neck, and kept a sharp eye on the road and trees in case Poth decided to show himself. Truth be told, he was hoping to confront him. He had his revolver in his belt. Rachel kept hers inside a pocket in her coat. In her hands she cradled the shotgun. She'd insisted on bringing it.

A hawk cried and swooped overhead. Its brief shadow crossed the trail and made Rachel stiffen, her thumb immediately tensed over the hammers. Clement told her everything was all right.

They traveled in silence for the first few miles. It took that long before it seemed Rachel managed to relax some. Clement, though, pondered and weighed and considered things he'd started thinking about last night. Like leaving the priesthood. He'd devoted his life to God for over ten years. But he'd fallen in love with Rachel. At least, he was pretty certain he had, unexpected as it was. And those feelings, once started, couldn't be stopped. He didn't know when they'd begun. Maybe it was the moment he set eyes on her that first night, when she came in wearing that buckskin coat and skirt, her green eyes catching the firelight. But his lies, his deceptions and all this business over his money had jumbled everything up. And that terrible disquiet he still felt over his hesitation and guilt about Vega. Somehow he would have to atone for all of it. The ride back to Penquero would give him time to sort it all out. He hoped.

Clement guessed they were halfway to town when they saw a wagon up ahead. Pieces of furniture—a chest of drawers, a brass bed frame, a wooden table, four or five chairs, boxes, and crates—were crammed into the bed. A young, blond-haired boy peered over the rear of the rig.

"Pa!" the boy shouted.

The driver jerked his head around, a fearful expression on his face. A little girl sat next to him. All three were bundled against the cold.

"Leo Hensel," Rachel said, concerned. "Looks like everything they own is in that wagon."

Hensel pulled back on the reins. When Clement and Rachel came up along side, the little boy had climbed up to where his father and sister sat. Clement saw the little girl had her arms around Hensel, her eyes full of fear. But when Rachel said hello to her, calling her Eva, she relaxed somewhat. Rachel asked him what he was doing.

"I'm getting out," he said.

"But why?" Rachel asked, sadly.

"On account of I was threatened and I don't need this no more. I've had enough. I got to protect my *kinder.*"

"Who threatened you?" she asked.

"I don't know his name but he had a busted nose, all right."

Clement saw the alarm on Rachel's face. That bastard Poth.

"What did he say?" Clement asked.

"He was like a crazy man. He screamed at us and laughed and told me I had better be gone before he come back today. He said something strange then. Sound like a threat to me."

"What was it?" Clement asked, certain he knew the answer.

"He said I would hear the cock crow." Hensel shook his head and put his arm around his little girl, who had buried her face in his coat.

Damn that man, Clement thought.

"I'm so sorry," Rachel said. "Where will you go?"

"Maybe some work in Santa Fe," Hensel said. "I don't know. I have to protect the *kinder.*"

"I wish you luck," Rachel said.

Hensel thanked her, wiped his eyes and snapped his reins.

"That damn Ring," Rachel said.

Clement smelled the scent of burning pine as they approached Cimarron. Thread-like columns of gray smoke drifted lazily up from the chimneys of homes and some businesses. Rachel seemed less tense the closer they got to town. Glancing over at the cemetery, Clement noticed there was a large, fresh mound of dirt piled at the far side. That had to be the spot McMains had picked out for Rachel's sister's burial. The plan was to attend the service, then go to Carey's livery, where McMains, Rachel and Clement would follow the hearse to the cemetery to bury Hannah.

Clement pulled his floppy hat down closer over his face as they neared the jail. The memory of smashing the coffee pot against that man's head in there yesterday was still fresh. Whoever that was he'd confronted might still be about.

A man rode up to the jail, dismounted and tethered his sorrel gelding by another horse that looked a lot like the sheriff's and went inside. The man did have a shiny star pinned to his coat.

Shortly after they'd passed the jail, Rachel spoke. "You remember I was telling you about the head Ring man around here, Melvin Mills?" She jerked her chin forward, indicating a man wearing a bowler and carrying a carpetbag and valise leaving a small, adobe house just ahead, his legs moving quickly up the street. "That's him."

Merde! I assaulted an elected representative of the territory, Clement thought miserably. But Mills might also be the one he believed could well be holding the money Poth stole from him.

"Is that his house?" he asked.

She nodded.

A stagecoach waited in front of Barlow and Sanderson's. A man came out wearing a heavy fur coat and hat, glanced up and down the street, saw Mills and hollered at him. "You the one taking this stage?"

Clement saw Mills's head bob.

"Get aboard. I'm leaving," the man said.

Clement breathed easier seeing Mills board the stage. The driver climbed into the seat, took the reins in hand, called out to the horses and the stage rolled up the street.

"Do you know where that stage is going?" Clement asked.

"That's the Taos stage. Running late today. After Taos it goes on to Trinidad and Denver."

So Mills won't be back today, Clement thought. This could be his only opportunity to see about getting the archbishop's money.

Rachel directed Clement to the courthouse near the north end of town. It was an adobe with a pitched roof. A few wagons and buggies were out front along with a dozen or so horses tied to a rail. Clement guessed about thirty people were milling outside, men conversing, women with babies in arms, restless teenagers, young children chasing each other. Rachel had told him that Reverend Tolby had arranged for its use for services until a proper church could be built. Only half the funds had been collected thus far.

Drawing rein at the courthouse, Clement couldn't help hearing the name Vega. Nearly everyone was talking about his hanging. "Vega murdered Tolby and deserved what he got." "Someone said that other Mexican did it." "I still say the Ring is responsible." "I heard Reverend McMains was there." "Who told you that?" "This whole county is going to hell." "Festus Reade, you watch what you're saying—it's Sunday."

Clement pushed away his concerns about Vega. He was anxious to get to Mills's house. He'd slip away during the service. God must have had a reason for letting him see Mills leave on that stage.

Movement across an open area to the right caught Clement's eye. It was Henry Lambert standing outside his saloon, waving them over. "Rachel! Victor!" he called out. "Please come!"

"He never fails," Rachel said, sounding almost happy. She left the shotgun and her revolver in the boot as they climbed down off the wagon and started across the open field toward Lambert's. Clement kept his revolver. Something told him it would be a good idea.

"What doesn't he fail?" Clement asked.

"Oh, Reverend McMains preaches the circuit. He's here almost every other Sunday for services. When he is, Mr. Lambert brings us hot coffee in the winter and cold lemonade in the summer."

"How long has he been doing that?" Clement asked with a chuckle.

"Ever since that priest was transferred. Mr. Lambert's a Catholic so he's got nowhere to go hereabouts. Says this makes him feel like he's doing some good."

Clement asked God to bless Henri Lambert. He also thanked God for helping Rachel to push this calamity with Poth away, even if only for this short time in town.

At the open doorway, Lambert greeted them and handed Rachel a large tray of cups and glasses.

"Can you manage all right?" he asked her.

"Of course," she said and headed back to the courthouse.

"And Victor, if you would, help me with the pots, *oui*?"

"À votre service," Clement said and followed him inside. Across the saloon on the bar sat two large steaming pots, a folded bar towel under each of them.

Lambert pointed at the ceiling. "See the holes?"

Glancing up at the pressed tin ceiling that had been painted white, Clement did see a number of small black holes.

"Gunshots," Lambert said, wearily shaking his head. "Twenty-six so far. These cowboys get drunk and think it's funny to shoot into my ceiling. *Ces cowboys n'ont aucun respect.*"

Clement saw four card players at a table near the window.

"Do you need anything, gentlemen?" Lambert asked them.

Three of the men shook their heads.

"These pots are hot," Lambert said. "Use one hand to carry and the other to hold the towel underneath. I will take one if you would get the other."

Clement nodded. *"Oui."*

As each of them lifted a pot, Lambert said to Clement, "I wanted to mention to you that I could use some help, if you were inclined. That expansion I plan, for the hotel, it will keep me very busy. I will need someone I can trust. You have an honest face, I believe."

That was the second job offer he'd had in as many days. First from Rachel yesterday and now Lambert.

"That's—" Clement said, pot in his hands and caught a reflection in the bar mirror. There was Poth sitting alone at a table tucked in the corner back near the entrance. Poth dropped a half-eaten piece of toast on the plate before him and grinned.

"Well, Lambert's got a new waitress," Poth said. "Did you get tired of digging graves?"

Clement set down the pot and slowly turned, knowing his revolver was under his coat.

The card players stopped and watched, afraid to move.

"I want no trouble here," Lambert said.

"You got no trouble," Poth said, his eyes fixed on Clement.

"Good," Lambert said and motioned to Clement. "We have to go."

"But the new waitress isn't going anywhere," Poth said. "We got a score to settle, you and me."

From what Clement could tell, whatever words Lambert wanted to say caught in his throat.

"Your lady friend," Poth said. "She gave you my message, didn't she?"

Clement nodded.

"She's real nice. Real nice."

The taunt in his tone and that mocking smile told Clement that Poth had attacked and raped Rachel.

"You armed this time?" Poth asked.

"I am."

Poth's chair scraped across the floor as he pushed it back and stood up. He wore his long coat. Using his left hand, he pulled back the left side of the coat, revealing his revolver, butt forward, on his left hip. Slowly, he moved his right hand across his belly into position to draw. "Let's get to it."

Clement remembered full well the promise he'd made to Rachel, and at this moment, he didn't care. Poth was a man—no, something evil—that needed killing. Clement knew that even thinking it, he was in danger of putting everything he believed, everything he'd devoted his life to, his life as a priest, his very soul, in jeopardy. But he didn't care about that, either. The sight of this man, grotesque in his arrogance and depravity and evil, compelled Clement to face him, to gun him down. He wouldn't be breaking the Lord's Fifth Commandment because this wouldn't be a murder out of lust or greed. This would be a justified killing. Maybe it was God's handiwork that he hadn't left his revolver behind in the wagon.

Clement reached his hand around to unbutton his coat.

"Not in my establishment!" Lambert said, finding his voice, the pot still in his hands.

A voice came through the open front doorway. "Henry! I'm in the mood for a mess of fried eggs and a steak." It was Sheriff Chittenden.

Clement and Poth kept their eyes locked on each other.

"What in the hell?" Chittenden said.

"This is none of your affair, Sheriff," Poth said.

"The hell it isn't," Chittenden said, drawing his revolver. "Don't anybody move. And I mean anybody."

"I told them, no gunfights in here," Lambert said.

"All right, Henry," Chittenden said, "set down your pot and tell me what happened."

Poth spoke up, jutting his chin at Clement. "That one called me a dirty thief."

"He did no such thing," Lambert said.

"I say he did."

Clement kept his mouth shut. He noted that Chittenden had his revolver pointed at Poth this whole time.

"Henry," Chittenden said, "who started this fracas?"

Lambert pointed at Poth. "He did."

Clement saw the sinister look Poth shot at Lambert.

"You boys," Chittenden said to the card players, his eyes never leaving Poth. "That how you saw it?"

"I . . . ah . . . we . . . well . . ." a couple of them stammered.

"Good enough for me," Chittenden said. "I'm running you in Poth, for disturbing the peace."

"You forget I'm a deputy," Poth said.

"That's right," Chittenden said. "You're fired. Now take that gun out, good and slow using just your thumb and forefinger, or I will be forced to shoot you."

The card players inched their way toward the door and quickly bolted out.

Clement couldn't help but grin at Poth's predicament. Whether it was the grin or the dilemma Clement couldn't say, but one or both must have triggered something in Poth, for he lowered his head, like a bull preparing to charge, his eyes rolling up yet still fixed on him. If that was what Rachel had seen last night, Clement understood what she meant by crazy evil.

"Don't test me, Poth," Chittenden said in deadly earnest and cocked his revolver.

Clement watched as Poth pulled out his revolver.

"Drop it."

Poth let go, the revolver thudding against the wooden floor.

"This isn't over, grave digger," Poth said, his mouth tight, his eyes still crazy evil.

"Shut your mouth," Chittenden ordered. "Raise your hands. Henry, pick up his gun and hand it to me."

Lambert nodded and cautiously did as he was told.

"And what's he owe you for his food?" Chittenden asked.

"Oh, uh, a dollar and a half."

"Whatever's in your pockets, take it out, put it on the table. And this Dragoon of mine has an easy trigger," Chittenden warned him.

Poth pulled a wad of folded money from his shirt pocket.

"Count out two dollars," Chittenden said. "That extra's a gratuity for Henry. All right with you, Henry?"

Lambert nodded.

Poth slapped the bills on the table.

"Now, set the rest of that money on the table, put your hands up, turn around and face the wall," Chittenden said. As Poth turned, Chittenden took the remaining money from the table. "About two hundred and fifty dollars here." He shoved the money in his coat. "I'll hold on to this for you for the time being."

"That's my money," Poth said. "I earned it, same as you."

"You won't need it in jail. Step away from the table and get going. And you, Cheval, I advise you to pick your fights real careful in the future."

Hands up shoulder high, Poth went out the door with Chittenden right behind.

Clement realized his coat was open and his hand had been poised over the handle of his revolver, ready to draw this whole time. He looked at Lambert, who had nearly stopped breathing.

"God is watching over us today," Clement said.

"Mon Dieu!" Lambert said. "What if he had killed you?"

Clement shrugged. "I suppose you'd have to get these pots to the courthouse by yourself."

Lambert stared at him a moment and started to laugh. Clement joined him and they picked up the pots and headed for the courthouse, where Rachel and just about everyone else was watching Chittenden march Poth, hands raised, down to the jail.

"What happened?" Rachel asked, touching Clement's arm. Everyone wanted to know as they followed Clement and Lambert inside the courthouse.

"He got arrested for disturbing the peace," Clement said, setting his pot down on a table next to the tray of cups and glasses.

"The deputy and Victor, they almost had a gunfight," Lambert said and the churchgoers peppered him with questions as he filled cups and glasses with coffee.

Rachel gave Clement a frightened look.

"It's all right now," he said gently. "Your sheriff doesn't like Poth. Something tells me he won't be around much longer."

Rachel's eyes welled up, a quivering smile crossed her face and she lowered her head as if in silent prayer.

Clement thanked God for her relief. He also thanked God for his own good fortune, and it struck him that God had protected him. There had to be a reason. Poth was in jail. Mills had left town. The archbishop's money might well be in Mills's house. That money had been the reason for everything, *everything* that had happened. More than ever Clement wanted to place that money in the archbishop's hands. There wouldn't be another chance. Lamy's parting words came back to him. Providence will not abandon you.

McMains entered, a black book in his hand. He appeared haggard, his eyes red from lack of sleep. He saw Clement and quickly turned away, like a man hiding a terrible shame.

"Forgive my lateness," McMains said.

"Did you hear, Reverend?" someone asked. "The sheriff arrested one of his deputies."

"And there was nearly a gunfight, right over in Lambert's," someone else said and pointed at Clement. "Between the deputy and this man."

"This is the Lord's day," McMains said and held up his book. "The Bible says to keep it holy. Let us do so."

"There's something I need to do," Clement whispered to Rachel. "It's important. I'll be back." He didn't give her a chance to say anything and left the courthouse. She'll be safe there, he told himself. McMains's opening words followed Clement outside and he wondered if McMains was addressing him or himself.

"Pride is a terrible sin. Pride goeth before destruction, and a haughty spirit before a fall. Pride cost Adam and Eve their place in Paradise. A man's pride shall bring him low."

Chapter Twenty-Five

Clement noted there were few people on the streets and even fewer businesses open. Only the National Hotel, Lambert's, Carey's Hardware and Livery, Schwenk's, and the barbershop by his count. It was Sunday, and it was cold. He made his way down past the front of Mills's house, then around the side, trying not to draw attention. One or two of the windows looked like he might be able to slide up and crawl through, but a door would be easier. At the back door, he glanced around to see if anyone was watching. Grasping the knob, he turned it and was surprised but pleased to find it unlocked. He quickly slipped inside, shutting the door gently behind him.

The quiet of the house was almost eerie as he carefully made his way past a small kitchen area and continued down the hallway. Nearing the first door on the left, his footfall on the floor made the wood moan, the sound seeming to fill the house. Clement grimaced.

He looked in that first room and saw a desk with a lamp on it and chairs. Mills's office, Clement guessed. The curtains over the window were drawn. That was good. Enough light came through them so he didn't need to light the lamp. He slid open each drawer. Papers, a few pens and a bottle of whiskey were all that he found. Looking under the desk, he thought he might find a safe. No luck. There was a closet. He opened it and saw the strongbox inside, with L-shaped braces of pig iron forming a resting place for it attached to the wall. There were two padlocks, one on the box and one securing the iron cage. Clement took hold of a couple of the braces with both hands and gave the cage a good jerk. Whoever had affixed it to the wall had not done a bad job, but Clement needed into that box.

Opening the back door a crack, he checked for any prying eyes. Nothing. Stepping out, he pulled the door closed quietly behind him. A cold wind came up. Shoving his hands in his coat pockets, Clement crossed an open area to the next street over and headed up to Cary's Hardware and Livery. No one was in the hardware store but the livery door was open. Inside, he found Jesse mucking out stalls with a pitchfork. He asked him if Carey was around and the wooden door at the other end of the livery slid open, pushed by Carey, revealing the black hearse outside and the corral beyond. He thought he recognized Poth's chestnut horse with a few others in the corral.

"Say, Jess," Carey called out, "set down that pitchfork and help me get this coffin loaded. Oh, Mr. Cheval. What can we do for you?"

"I have a favor to ask."

"If I can help."

"Could I borrow a sledgehammer for just a few minutes? A five-pound would do it."

Inside the jail, Deputy Rinehart unlocked Floyd Kunkle's cell. "Come on out, Floyd," Rinehart told him, pulling open the cell door.

"About time," Floyd said. "Pretty damn tired sitting in that cage."

"But you're to remain in town until your court date."

"What do you mean?" Floyd asked, scratching his beard as he stepped out of the cell.

"You go back to your cabin you're liable to get another necktie party. We can't watch your place day and night."

"Where am I supposed to stay? And how do I pay for it? Tell me that, Mr. Deputy."

"Come out here and I'll tell you," Chittenden hollered from the front of the jail.

Rinehart closed Floyd's cell door and glanced over his shoulder at the cell opposite where Poth sat locked inside. Poth was watching him, a cold, flinty look on his face. Rinehart felt real uneasy. It was like he could see Poth calculating how he might kill him and escape.

"You got good credit at Schwenk's," Rinehart heard Chittenden telling Floyd as he came in and hung the iron key ring on a hook sticking out of the stone wall by Chittenden's desk. The sheriff was at the stove about to pour a cup of coffee.

"And how do you know that, Sheriff?" Floyd asked indignantly.

"It's my business to know," Chittenden said, setting the pot down, steaming cup in hand.

"You think I'm made of money?"

"I don't know and I don't care, but you're not going back to E-town, not for a while. It's for your own good. Tell you what, though, you can sleep here in the jail."

"Well, ain't that dandy. And when am I supposed to go to court?"

"Whenever Judge Longwell says so. Deputy, will you see Floyd out?"

"Longwell," Floyd said disgustedly as Rinehart opened the front door and escorted him outside. "And what if that son-of-a-bitch Teague comes looking for me here? Or worse, moves into my place?"

"Sheriff says he's going to E-town shortly and tell Teague to stay away from here and your cabin," Rinehart said, taking him through the gateway and out past the stone wall. In spite of the cold, Rinehart was in no hurry to go back inside where Poth would be watching him with that look of his. Even with Chittenden there, Rinehart still felt scared.

"A lot of good that'll do," Floyd groused.

"You stay sober while you're here, Floyd," Rinehart said as they reached the end of the wall and pointed Floyd in the direction of Schwenk's. "Go get something to eat and stop your bellyaching. Nobody likes hearing it, especially me."

Floyd mumbled complaints as he headed up the street, but Rinehart paid him no mind. He was certain he'd just caught sight of somebody slipping through the back door of Mills's house.

Clement laid his coat over the cage to hopefully soften the sound and then swung the sledgehammer over his shoulder, bringing it down hard on the pig-iron cage. The braces rattled and the two top bolts holding it into the wall popped out a couple of inches. Clement swung again. The hammer struck and the whole cage dislodged from the wall sending it and the strongbox crashing to the floor. Reaching into the cage, he pulled out the strong box, which was mostly wood with iron brackets to reinforce it, set it on the floor and struck the padlock with the hammer. The hasp on the box popped loose and the broken lock hit the floor.

Clement threw open the lid, praying his money was inside. Lamy's leather pouch lay right on top of some papers. He opened the pouch. It looked like all the money was still there. Behind him, out in the hallway, the floor moaned. As he turned, he heard the distinct double click of a revolver cocking and saw a man with a badge pinned to his coat.

The jailhouse door swung open and Chittenden frowned at seeing Judge Longwell enter excitedly, bundled in his fancy, gray coat. Behind him was that Cheval fellow and behind him, Rinehart, with two revolvers at Cheval's back.

"Sheriff," Longwell said, "this man was found in Mr. Mills's house. He broke in and destroyed property. I was going by taking my daily constitutional when I saw your deputy here haul him out."

"Had this on him," Rinehart said, holding up the second revolver.

Longwell slapped a leather pouch down in front of Chittenden. "And he caught him red-handed with this. A little over fourteen hundred dollars, by my count."

Chittenden reached for the pouch and saw Poth suddenly leap up and grab the bars of his cell, looking his way.

"That money in a leather pouch?" Poth called out.

"What's he locked up for?" Longwell asked, surprised.

"Disturbing the peace, for one," Chittenden said.

"That money's mine!" Poth yelled. "Belongs to me. I gave it to Mills to hold."

"Maybe, maybe not," Chittenden said.

"What are you—" Longwell began but Chittenden held up his hand. He opened the pouch and took a quick look at the greenbacks inside, then up at Cheval standing in front of his desk. The Frenchman appeared pensive.

"You told me you had around fourteen hundred dollars stolen from you, is that right?" Chittenden asked Cheval.

Longwell looked dumbfounded. "You know this miscreant?"

Chittenden paid him no mind. He kept his eyes on Cheval, who nodded.

"And you said you broke the nose of the man who stole it?"

"I did," Cheval said.

"Poth's nose was broken when I first saw him the other day," Chittenden said to Longwell. "Look at him. You agree his nose is busted?"

Longwell glanced back at Poth, then at Chittenden. "That's

not evidence. It's supposition. Circumstantial at best."

"We need to get to the bottom of this, then," Chittenden said.

"You do that, but no bail for this man," the judge said, pointing his finger at Cheval. "He broke into the representative's home, destroyed property and attempted to steal that money. Those are pure facts."

Chittenden got up, took the metal key ring from the hook on the wall and motioned to Rinehart. "Put Cheval here in a cell."

Rinehart set Cheval's revolver on the desk, took the key ring and poked Cheval with the end of his gun. "You heard him. Get."

While Rinehart locked Cheval in the cell across from Poth, Chittenden put Cheval's gun in his bottom desk drawer where he already had Poth's revolver and then stood close to Longwell, his voice low. "We might be missing an opportunity here, Judge."

"How so?" Longwell whispered.

"If this money does belong to that man, he's not going anywhere. He'll stay around to get it back."

"That doesn't justify his breaking into Mills's house."

"You're right. But I'm thinking about us."

Longwell scowled at him.

"My point is, you let him sit in a cell and all we got is a prisoner. But if you grant him bail, we can split it between us."

"Well . . ."

"Set the bail high, say two hundred and fifty dollars. If Cheval can't pay it, he stays here in jail. If he can pay it, he's still here and we got free money. As for the breaking-in charge, set a court date and fine him for the damages. I have a suspicion that fourteen hundred is his anyway. Whatever damages you order him to pay, he can pay it out of that."

Longwell rubbed his finger over his lips and chuckled. "Fine.

Bail is set at two hundred and fifty dollars."

"I'll see to it," Chittenden said.

Longwell left and Chittenden told Rinehart to go find Rachel Scott. "I know she came in for Sunday services. Tell her we got her friend here."

Rinehart went out and Chittenden sat down. He was pretty pleased with himself.

"What are you up to?" Poth demanded.

Chittenden ignored Poth and glanced over at Cheval, who sat on the metal cot in his cell, leaning forward, elbows on his legs, hands clasped. It was like he was praying.

Don't you worry there, Mr. Frenchman, Chittenden thought and opened his top desk drawer. Inside was the wad of greenbacks he'd taken earlier from Poth. As far as Chittenden was concerned, the Frenchman's bail was paid, courtesy of Dixon Poth. The sheriff smiled. He was starting to make things right here in Colfax County.

The service had ended and Rachel was concerned that Victor hadn't returned. McMains said they should go to Carey's livery, as Carey would be waiting with the hearse. "Perhaps Mr. Cheval is already there," McMains said.

Rachel nodded, tied Paris to the back of her wagon, climbed up into the seat and followed McMains on his horse.

At the livery, Carey and Jesse were indeed waiting in black frock coats to drive the hearse to the cemetery. The horse team wore black plumes fixed atop their bridles. Rachel asked Carey if he'd seen Victor.

"About a half an hour ago," Carey said. "Asked me if he could borrow a sledgehammer."

"A sledgehammer?"

"Mrs. Scott!"

Rachel turned and saw Deputy Rinehart approaching from

the other end of the livery.

"Sheriff sent me to find you," he said. "Needs you to come to the jail."

"What for?" she asked, worried it had something to do with Victor.

"Little problem of attempted theft with your French friend," Rinehart said.

Rachel didn't care for the smirk on Rinehart's face.

"What about your sister's funeral?" McMains asked.

"I'm sorry," she said. "I have to go."

"But—"

"Please, just bury her," Rachel said as she went with Rinehart. "She'll be happier I'm not there anyway."

Clement jumped up from the cot in his cell and watched through the iron bars as Rachel came into the jail, followed by Rinehart. He saw the concern etched on her face.

"She can't help you," he heard Poth say quietly from across the way. "You're still a dead man."

Rinehart came over and added a couple of short logs to the stove and stood with his back to it warming himself, standing there purposely, like he wanted to be in Clement's way. Clement moved from side to side to keep his eyes on Rachel and Chittenden, who had come around to the front of his desk to face her.

"Your friend in there broke into Melvin Mills's house," Clement heard Chittenden say to Rachel. "He was caught stealing this." Chittenden picked up the leather pouch from his desk. "A lot of money in here."

"It's mine!" Poth shouted.

Clement saw Rachel jump at the sound of Poth's voice.

"Shut your mouth!" Chittenden hollered.

"I left that money with Mills! Ask him!"

"And I told you he left on the stage. Not another word."

Poth turned and kicked his cell door.

"Deputy," Chittenden said to Rinehart, "you take out that Colt Walker of yours, and point it at Poth there. If he makes another sound, shoot him."

Clement caught the uneasy look on Rinehart's face as he pulled out his gun and moved over by Poth's cell. Disgusted, Poth paced his cell, casting dark glances from Chittenden to Rinehart.

Chittenden leaned in closer to Rachel. Clement couldn't hear what he was saying. He did see Rachel nod her head a couple of times. Then Chittenden went around his desk, opened a bottom drawer, took out Clement's revolver, grabbed the key ring from the hook and walked to Clement's cell.

"Your bail is paid," Chittenden said, unlocking the cell door.

A disbelieving look crossed Rinehart's face.

Clement stepped out and Chittenden handed him his gun and pointed at the front door. He followed Rachel out and heard Poth shout, "He gets bail?"

As they hurried toward town, Clement asked her, "How did you get me out? What did he say?"

"He told me your bail was posted."

"How?"

"I don't know. But he did tell me he doesn't like you, but he hates Mills."

"I don't understand."

"I don't either, but he gave me this." She reached inside her coat and handed him the pouch.

He opened it and saw all the money was there. "My God."

"The sheriff said you need to go right now, and he told me to tell you not to come back to Colfax County. He'll have to arrest you if you do."

Things were happening so fast, Clement hardly noticed the

slump-shouldered, weary-looking man wearing a buckskin coat and riding a sorrel with three white socks coming toward them, headed into town, just like them.

At first Amos Tully paid the couple rounding the stone wall no mind. He was tired and hungry and hoped to get something decent to eat in town. He hadn't been here before but had been told by some of the soldiers sent here on patrols that good food could be had at Lambert's. And he heard the man in the floppy hat saying something about a funeral. Must be that one he passed about a quarter mile out. Two men, a boy and a hearse. But this man here, he spoke with a French accent that sounded familiar to Tully. Damn familiar. And the man held a brown leather pouch in his hand. That pouch looked real familiar, too. Tully decided to wait on food and see where these two went. They were in a big hurry.

Rinehart didn't know what it was, but something had been worked out between the sheriff and Mrs. Scott. All of a sudden his prisoner had walked out free as you please? They concocted something, sure as he was standing there. He wanted to ask Chittenden about it but the way the sheriff had been acting of late, like no more midnight visits on these squatters, Rinehart figured he'd get some answer that made no sense. None at all.

Chittenden asked him for a cup of coffee. While he was pouring it, the bartender from Schwenk's came running in, panicky.

"You got to come, Sheriff," the bartender said. "Floyd Kunkle is drunk. He busted our bar mirror and he's threatening Mr. Schwenk with a chair leg."

Rinehart knew Chittenden was about to tell him to take care of it when Poth hollered, "I need to use the facilities. My bowels feel like they're about to bust!"

Getting up from his chair, Chittenden said to Rinehart, "You see to Poth, and put the cuffs on him before you take him outside," and left with the antsy bartender.

"Damn it," Rinehart mumbled. Dealing with a drunk was easily preferable to being left alone with Poth. And having to take him outside the wall to the outhouse made him feel even more skittish.

"Come on," Poth said urgently, "I have to go."

"You heard the sheriff," Rinehart said, going to the desk and pulling out a pair of handcuffs. He tossed them through the bars. "Put them on. And don't get any ideas or I'll make you sorry you were born, I swear."

Poth swore an oath as he hurriedly cuffed himself. "Now open up."

Rinehart pulled out his Colt Walker revolver and unlocked the cell door. Poth took an unsteady step and doubled over. "Oh, God," he moaned.

"Come on out," Rinehart said.

Poth took another step and clutched his stomach again. "I'm not going to make it."

"Shit," Rinehart said, stepped inside the cell, went to Poth's side and using his free hand, took Poth's arm to help him up.

"You better not be—" was as far as Rinehart got as he felt himself jammed hard against the cell door frame. Two hands grabbed his head and there was a sharp thud as his face slammed into the iron bars. Feebly, he tried to bring his gun up but his face hit the bars again and he slumped down to the floor.

A boot kicked him in the ribs and all the air went out of his lungs. His gun was no longer in his hand as he gasped for air. Somebody was digging in his trouser pocket for something. All he had in there was the key to the cuffs and a few coins. The clang of the cell door rang in his ears and he thought he heard a voice that sounded far away and it was saying, ". . . you sorry you were born, you silly son-of-a-bitch? I ought to send you to the garden to weep."

Poth stuck Rinehart's Walker into the front of his trousers, quickly slipped on his coat, and got his holster and revolver out of Chittenden's desk. As much as he wanted to shoot Rinehart, he didn't want to take the chance of drawing attention from any nosey passers-by hearing a shot. At the moment, it was much more vital that the frog-eating bastard not get away with that money. Poth needed to get to the livery and get his horse. Then he'd track down that bastard. He owed that frog eater. Plenty. And then he'd come back and take care of that damn Chittenden.

Outside Carey's Livery, Clement dropped the rear gate of Rachel's wagon, climbed in and picked up his saddle from behind the boot. He hated the thought of leaving, but there was no time to think about that right now.

Rachel threw the horse blanket over Paris's back. "You have to hurry, Victor." The worry and urgency in her voice were clear.

Clement guessed she was holding back her feelings, hustling him along like she was trying to outrun the pain her emotions were stirring up. His insides were churning much the same.

Jumping down from the wagon, he picked up the saddle and heaved it up onto Paris. Taking the pouch from his inside coat pocket, he placed it in the saddlebag, then changed his mind and slipped it back into his coat pocket. It seemed safer to keep it in reach.

"This hackamore of yours has seen its last days," Rachel said, showing it to him.

Rubbing the hemp between his fingers, Clement had to admit it was fairly well frayed in places. But it was Rachel's face he was studying. He wanted to remember every contour, every strand of hair, the way the light caught her eyes. If he kissed her, he was afraid he'd never leave. And if he didn't kiss her . . .

She looked up at him. He took her gently by her shoulders, leaned in and kissed her on the mouth. Her lips were as soft as velvet and warm like a summer breeze. It lasted only a brief, magical moment.

"That shouldn't have happened," he said.

"I'm glad it did," she said, her eyes moist. She wiped them and turned away. "I'll get you that bridle."

Yes, he'd be back as soon as he got things in order. Clement placed the stirrup over the horn and cinched up the saddle on Paris. He glanced up and down the street. A few folks crossed here and there. Across the way a man in a buckskin coat was tethering his horse in front of the National Hotel.

What was keeping Rachel? He went into the livery and called her name. Nothing. He saw several bridles hanging from pegs about halfway down on the right side where there was an opening between the stalls. Jesse had left his pitchfork propped against a stall post there.

"Rachel?" He started down the breezeway and stopped at seeing her appear out of a shadow by that opening. Poth held her in front of him, fear white around her eyes. His left hand covered her mouth and both her hands gripped his arm. In his right hand he held his revolver, pointed at Clement.

"Give me my money, grave digger," Poth said.

Clement stopped himself from reaching for the gun in his belt. "Let her go."

"Well," Clement heard a voice with an Irish brogue say from behind him. "This is a predicament, ain't it now?"

Clement glanced back and saw the man in the buckskin coat. *Merde.* It was Tully, the sergeant who couldn't stop betting. He had his gun drawn and aimed in his direction. Tully was about twenty feet away from him, and Poth another fifteen or so.

"Get out of here, mister," Poth warned him.

"Not likely," Tully said. "Not until I get what's mine."

"I got no patience for any games," Poth said. "Get out or I'll have to send you to the garden to weep."

Tully grinned. "I'll be going just as soon as he gives me the money he cheated me out of."

Clement had been accused of cheating once before. And that was by a fool, too. He'd also faced much worse odds than these in Mexico. But the difference was that at Camerone he only had his life to lose. Now there was Rachel. Poth was evil enough to just shoot her. Clement knew he had to kill Poth. But he had no good plan. Only hope. God, please guide my aim. His eyes on Poth, Clement drew his revolver and Poth let out a pained yell. Rachel had pulled his arm down and sunk her teeth into the top of his hand. Poth yanked his hand from her mouth. She twisted away as he took quick aim at Clement and fired.

Clement felt the bullet nick his left arm through his coat, like a hot iron searing his flesh.

Behind him he heard another gunshot and a bullet struck the stall post near his head. Clement spun around, extended his arm and fired at Tully, who clutched his belly and fell to his knees, his revolver still gripped in his hand.

Clement wheeled to face Poth, whose bleeding left hand hung at his side and in his other hand his gun, aimed at Clement's head. Poth cocked the hammer. The double click sounded so loud to Clement. And Poth's eyes blinked, startled. A sickening gurgle sputtered from his slack mouth. His long coat hung open. Blood trails appeared, running down the front of his shirt. The gun dropped from his hand. He staggered forward a step and fell to his hands and knees, the pitchfork stuck in his back. Rachel stood behind him, tears on her cheeks. Poth slumped forward, his face sliding into the dirt and horse shit.

Relief broke across Clement's face. He started toward Rachel and heard another shot fired. Rachel's face registered shock. Clement's eyes went wide. The fire in his back raced through his body buckling his knees. Rachel screamed "No!" Clement was on the ground, looking up at the rafters. Then he saw Rachel and she took his revolver from his hand and moved away toward Tully. He heard two shots explode. Get up, get up, Clement told himself. The ground felt so cold. His legs. They wouldn't move. Oh, God, not now. Not now . . .

Rachel's face appeared above him. He lifted his hand to brush away her tears. His hand felt so heavy, his fingers numb. She clasped his hand and held it to her cheek. Please, God, give me time, he prayed. He heard people shouting, drawing close. "Get the sheriff!" "Go find the doc!" "There's been a killing!"

"Rachel," he said, "I-I need you to do something."

"Tell me," she said.

He felt her hand touch his forehead. "The money. Take it to Penquero. Give it to the archbishop."

"I—"

"It belongs to him," Clement cut in. He couldn't feel his legs. His lungs burned with every breath.

"But—"

"Tell him it's from Father Grantaire. He . . . he won it, at cards." His eyes started to flutter. Her face shifted, blurred. He concentrated and she became clear again. So lovely.

"I don't understand," she said, trying to keep her voice steady. "Who's Father Grantaire?"

His lips curled into a half smile. "Someone I once knew."

Confusion clouded her eyes.

His last words, Clement thought, what were Lamy's last words? He gasped for air.

"Where's the doctor?" Rachel cried out.

"Please," Clement said faintly.

She leaned in close.

"Tell the archbishop, Providence will not abandon us. He needs to know. Ask . . . ask him to . . . to pray for me. Tell him, I'm sorry for all my sins." He squeezed her hand. "But I'm not sorry I fell in love wi-with you, Rachel."

He felt her trembling kiss on his lips. So sweet . . .

Epilogue

Sheriff Orson K. Chittenden

His attempts to undermine Melvin Mills and the Santa Fe Ring proved in vain. As anarchy spread and murders became more commonplace in Colfax County, Governor Samuel B. Axtell was forced to send troops from Fort Union to quell the violence. For a short time, Cimarron and much of the county was quiet and the troops departed. But by January, brawls, shootings and more mayhem forced Chittenden to wire Governor Axtell: "It is impossible for me to enforce the civil law." The governor wrote back, "Will accept your resignation." Chittenden served as sheriff of Colfax County for only four months.

Manuel Cardenas

Though ordered by Chittenden to Willow Springs near Raton Pass, Cardenas had decided to spend some time in Elizabeth-town instead. Following the killing of Cruz Vega, vigilantes discovered him in E-town and, based upon Vega's "confession," Cardenas was charged with the murder of Reverend Tolby. He insisted that Vega had done the actual killing and stated that he and Vega had been hired by Melvin Mills and Judge Robert Longwell to kill Tolby. Within hours he recanted his story. A few days later, a hearing was held in Cimarron. It lasted late into the night. As Deputy Rinehart was escorting him back to the jail, a single shot rang out, striking Cardenas in the head, killing him instantly. No arrest was ever made, but there was much speculation that the Santa Fe Ring had hired the unknown assailant.

Melvin Mills

After completing his business in Colorado, Mills ignored warnings not to return to Cimarron due to the inflamed passions generated by Cardenas's confession. Immediately upon his arrival in town, he was seized by a mob with a rope and dragged to the nearest cottonwood tree. In an attempt to stop the lynching, Henry Lambert offered a free drink to everyone present. All parties adjourned to Lambert's Saloon. One drink led to another and the matter of Mills was postponed until the following day. A hearing was held before a justice of the peace. Mills testified in his own defense. His case was dismissed for lack of evidence.

In a letter he wrote to a friend in 1924, Mills stated that he knew of "no reason why any man even with evil intention should have coveted the life of Mr. Tolby." He added that Tolby's murder "was an unfortunate fatality that has blocked my career in life . . . and I have found it difficult to rise above it."

Judge Robert Longwell

Within minutes of the word of Cardenas's confession reaching Cimarron, Longwell fled for the protection of Fort Union. He never returned to Cimarron, and, according to some reports, enjoyed a thriving medical practice in Santa Fe.

Thomas Benton Catron

By 1894, Catron, the leader of the Santa Fe Ring, was estimated to have interests in over seventy land grants and personally owned nearly two million acres. He was a driving force for New Mexico statehood and was elected United States Senator for the 47th state in 1912. When he died in 1921, the *Santa Fe New Mexican* wrote in part: "Mr. Catron was a powerful leader of his time; blunt, outspoken, uncompromising, at times he ruled with a rod of iron in the days of his greatest political ascendancy. He was frankly a 'practical politician'; the appellation 'boss' complimented instead of offending him, political power was meat and drink to him . . ."

Clay Allison

Continued to raise hell in Colfax County. He and friends confronted Francisco Griego and a few Mexican mourners at the Cimarron cemetery where Griego had brought the body of Cruz Vega for burial. Allison told Griego "the greaser who murdered Reverend Tolby would not be buried in the same cemetery as the Reverend." Griego was forced to bury Vega half a mile away. That evening, Griego threatened Allison in Lambert's Saloon. Both men pulled their revolvers and Allison ventilated him with two bullets. A few days later, Allison went back to Lambert's, stripped naked and did a "war dance" over the spot where Griego died. Allison was charged with murder, but the court ruled the shooting a justifiable homicide.

A few years later, Allison married and moved to Pope's Wells in southwest Texas with his wife and two daughters. In July of 1887, he was driving a freight wagon to his ranch when a jolt sent a grain sack sliding off the bed. Trying to catch it, Allison fell from the wagon and a wheel rolled over his head, killing him instantly.

Reverend O. P. McMains

Charged with the murder of Cruz Vega, McMains was found "guilty in the fifth." However, a new trial was ordered as the verdict did not state the crime he'd been found guilty of committing. The new trial was set, but the case was thrown out for lack of evidence.

McMains spent the rest of his life fighting against the owners of the Maxwell Land Grant Company. The land rights of the grant were eventually settled in favor of the owners, forcing most of the squatters to either give up or give in by early 1900. McMains died of consumption the year before, in the spring.

Deputy Isaiah Rinehart

Was appointed Sheriff by the Santa Fe Ring upon Chittenden's resignation and finished out his term. During Rinehart's tenure, Davy Crockett, who claimed to be the grandnephew of the famous defender of the Alamo, found the town of Cimarron to his liking and soon became a town bully. In one instance, he forced Rinehart at gunpoint to drink until he became incapacitated. Another time, he purchased a new suit and had the bill sent to Rinehart. Crockett's brazen behavior finally became too much and Rinehart, along with a two-man posse, went after him. Accounts differ as to what transpired next. One states that Rinehart and his men confronted Crockett at a barn in town, ordered him to put up his hands and Crockett dared them to fire, which they did. Crockett's horse bolted and Crockett was later found outside of town, dead. Another version is that Rinehart and his posse ambushed Crockett and shot him in the back.

Deputy Zeke Wilcox

Recovered from the loss of his arm and left Colfax County before year's end. It was rumored that he prospered for a short time as a whiskey peddler in Los Angeles but died there in the smallpox outbreak of 1877.

Floyd Kunkle

On Christmas Eve, Kunkle and Teague, in a drunken brawl, killed each other in front of Kunkle's house. Teague stabbed Kunkle with a large knife. Kunkle grabbed Teague by his hair, pulled a revolver he carried hidden on him and shot Teague through the heart. Teague was buried in the Elizabethtown cemetery. Kunkle was laid to rest in the Cimarron cemetery. He requested his plot be in view of Schwenk's Saloon.

Sergeant Red Howarth

Was found guilty by a general court martial of misappropriation of funds, unauthorized sale of government property and conduct prejudicial to the good order of military discipline. He was sentenced "to forfeit all pay and allowances that are now or may become due him, to have his head shaved, to walk a ring daily for six hours for one month twelve feet in diameter, then placed under charge of the Guard at hard labor, with ball and chain attached to his leg until an opportunity affords for him to be transported with ball and chain to Fort Leavenworth and there be drummed out of the service."

Colonel Charles Dupin

Following the French withdrawal from Mexico in 1867, Dupin returned to France. He died the next year, possibly from poisoning.

Rachel Scott

After burying Victor Cheval the next day, Rachel went to Penquero to find Archbishop Lamy. She told him that Victor had asked her to come see him and handed him the pouch with the money. "He said Father Clement Grantaire had won it playing cards." At the mention of Father Grantaire, she saw Lamy's stern visage soften and he asked her how this Victor Cheval had come to be in possession of the pouch. She told him the story of having found him unconscious on the prairie and his dogged search for the money. "What did *Monsieur* Cheval look like?" Lamy asked. "A handsome man," she replied. "And he had an old scar on his forehead. He told me to ask you to pray for him and to say he was sorry for his sins." Lamy said he would come to Cimarron shortly and would like to see Victor's grave.

When he got to Cimarron, Rachel joined him at the cemetery. As he placed his long purple stole around his neck in preparation for the funeral service, he asked Rachel about the inscription on Victor's grave. She said, "Didn't I tell you? They were his words to you. I thought he would like them on his headstone." It read:

Victor Cheval
Beloved
"Providence will not abandon us"

Lamy performed the service and blessed Victor's grave with holy water. Afterward, Lamy asked about the grave near Victor's with the name Ethan Scott. "Your husband?" She told him, "Yes. He was a good man, too. When my time comes, I'll be buried between them."

Archbishop Jean-Baptiste Lamy

Continued to make numerous journeys across the archdiocese of Santa Fe seeking loans and taking donations for the next eleven years in an effort to see his cathedral completed. On March 7, 1886, more than a decade and a half after European architects and masons and New Mexican laborers began construction, Lamy blessed the cathedral, though it still wasn't finished. Some plans, such as tall wooden spires atop the two bell towers, would be abandoned completely.

Shortly before he died on February 14, 1888, Lamy was asked if he regretted not seeing his cathedral completed. "There can be no regrets when so many have given so much," he said. Then he added that he hoped to be in heaven with the Lord soon, and when he arrived that his friend, Father Clement Grantaire, would have a grand story to tell him.

AUTHOR'S NOTE

This is a work of historical fiction.

The battle at Camerone is considered the greatest battle in the history of the French Foreign Legion, their defining moment. Many consider it the Legion's Alamo. While I have taken some license in recreating the battle, I believe I have stayed true to the spirit and bravery of the participants. Among the best sources I found during my research on the French Foreign Legion and the battle at Camerone were: *The History of the French Foreign Legion: From 1831 to Present Day* by David Jordan (The Lyons Press, 2005); *The French Foreign Legion* by Douglas Porch (Skyhorse Publishing, 2010); and *Camerone: The French Foreign Legion's Greatest Battle* by James W. Ryan (Praeger, 1996). It is important to note that Captain Jean Danjou, Lieutenant Clement Maudet, Lieutenant Napoleon Vilain, Sergeant Vincent Morzycki, Legionnaires Bertolomo, Burgiser, Catteau, Constantin, Groux, Kurz, Maine, van Opstal and Wenzel all fought in the battle. Colonel Pierre Jeanningros and Colonel Charles Dupin played their roles before and after the battle.

The Colfax County War lasted for nearly thirty years. Some say it has never ended. In researching it, I discovered there are facts, opinions and conjectures. Newspaper accounts at the time reflected political leanings. There is no disagreement that Lucian Maxwell's sale of his land grant precipitated the Colfax County War, but there is disagreement about the reason for the murder of Reverend Franklin J. Tolby. We shall likely never know the true story. The Colfax County War has generated a number of books, some reliable, others not. Sources I consulted were: *Desert Lawmen: The High Sheriffs of New Mexico and Arizona 1846-1912* by Larry D. Ball (University of New Mexico Press 2011); *Frank Springer and New Mexico: From the Colfax County War to the Emergence of Modern Santa Fe* by David L. Caffey (Texas A&M University Press, 2006); *The Morleys:Young Upstarts on the Southwest Frontier* by Norman Cleaveland with George Fitzpatrick (Calvin Horn Publisher, Inc., 1971); *The Maxwell Land Grant* by Jim Berry Pearson (University of Oklahoma Press, 1961); and *O. P. McMains and the Maxwell Land Grant Conflict* by Morris F. Taylor (University of Arizona Press, 1979). Once again, it is important to note that Robert Clay Allison, Manuel Cardenas, Allen Carey, Thomas B. Catron, Sheriff Orson K. Chittenden, Francisco Griego, Henry Lambert, Archbishop Jean-Baptiste Lamy, Robert Longwell, William Low, Reverend Oscar P. McMains, Melvin Mills, Isaiah Rinehart and Cruz Vega are not inventions but their words are mine.

For a look at the life of Archbishop Lamy and the priests who followed him, I recommend *Lamy's Legion* by Nancy Hanks (HRM Books, 2000) and *Lamy of Santa Fe* by Paul Horgan (Farrar, Straus, Giroux, 1975). For background on the territory of New Mexico I consulted *The Fabulous Frontier* by William H. Keleher (University of New Mexico, 1962) and *The Far Southwest 1846-1912: A Territorial History* by Howard R. Lamar (W. W. Norton and Company, 1970).

My grateful thanks to the following for their invaluable assistance: In Santa Fe, New Mexico: Monsignor Jerome Martinez y Alire, former rector at the Cathedral Basilica of St. Francis of Assisi, who first told me the tale that set me on the path of this story; Marina Ochoa, Director, Archdiocese of Santa Fe Museum and Archives; Bernadette Lucero, Assistant to the

Director, Archdiocese of Santa Fe Museum and Archives; Patricia Hewitt, Senior Cataloguer, Fray Angelico Chavez History Library; and Daniel Kosharek, Photo Archivist, Palace of the Governors, Photo Archives. In Cimarron, New Mexico: Candee Rindee, Executive Secretary, Cimarron Chamber of Commerce; Sonja Vincent, former Executive Secretary, Cimarron Chamber of Commerce; and Gene Lamm, author. And at the Fort Union National Monument, thank you to Ron Harvey, Historian.

Thomas D. Clagett
Santa Fe, New Mexico

ABOUT THE AUTHOR

Thomas D. Clagett graduated from the University of Southern California with a degree in journalism, and then spent nearly twenty years working as an assistant film editor. His credits include *The Two Jakes,* Jack Nicholson's sequel to *Chinatown,* and the MTM TV series *St. Elsewhere.*

He is the author of *William Friedkin: Films of Aberration, Obsession and Reality,* about the Academy Award–winning director of *The French Connection* and *The Exorcist. Classic Images* called it "the definitive work on the subject."

Clagett has contributed to several New Mexico publications. He is a member of the Western Writers of America.

Booklist praised his first novel, *The Pursuit of Murieta,* as a "well told, disquieting story."

West of Penance is his second novel.

A native Californian, Clagett lives with his wife, Marilyn, and their cat, Cody, in Santa Fe, New Mexico. His website is www.thomasdclagett.com.